THE OFFICIAL

unORDINARY

COLORING BOOK

T0390618

Walter Foster

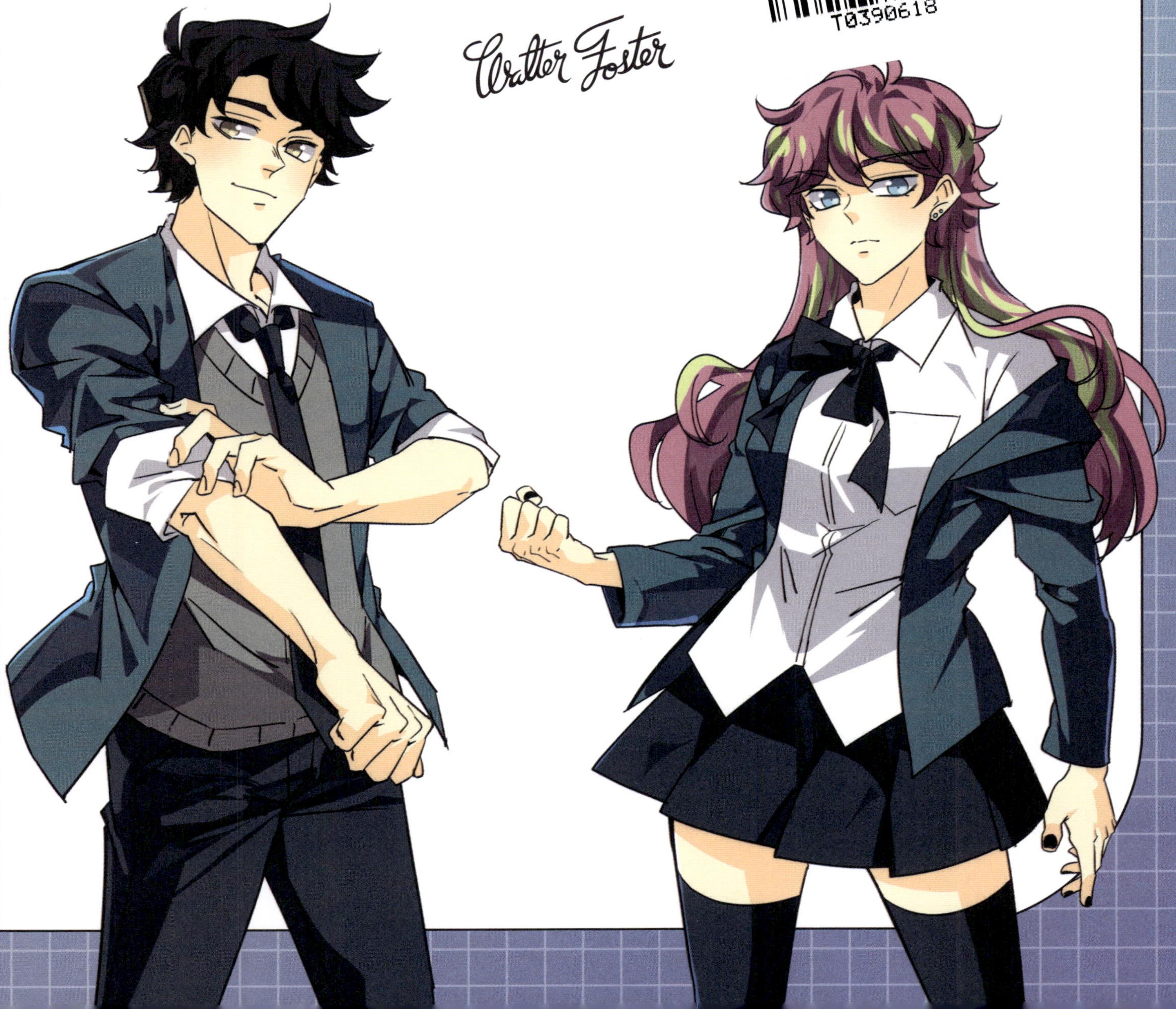

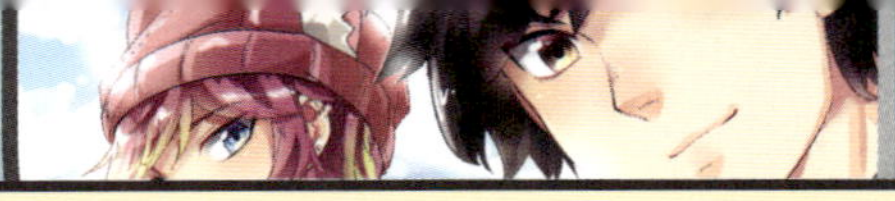
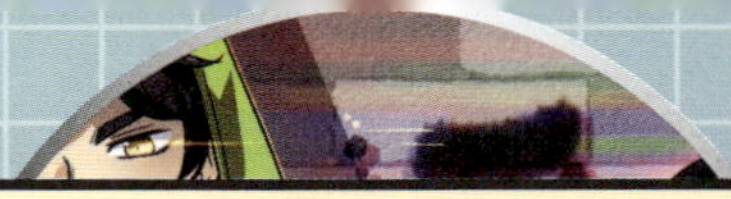
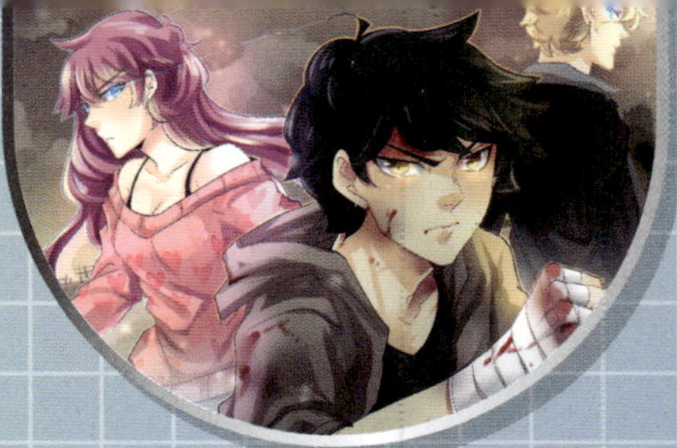

INTRODUCTION

Develop your superpower coloring skills while learning about the heroes and antiheroes of the hit WEBTOON Originals series unOrdinary.

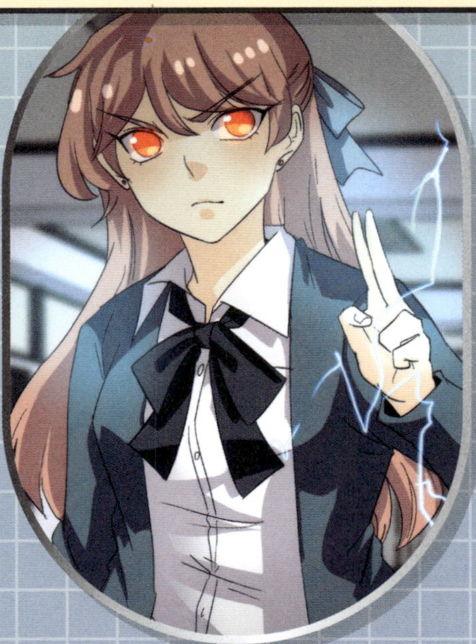
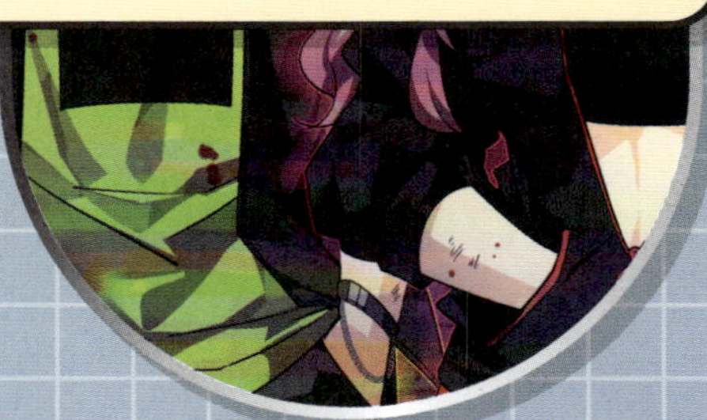
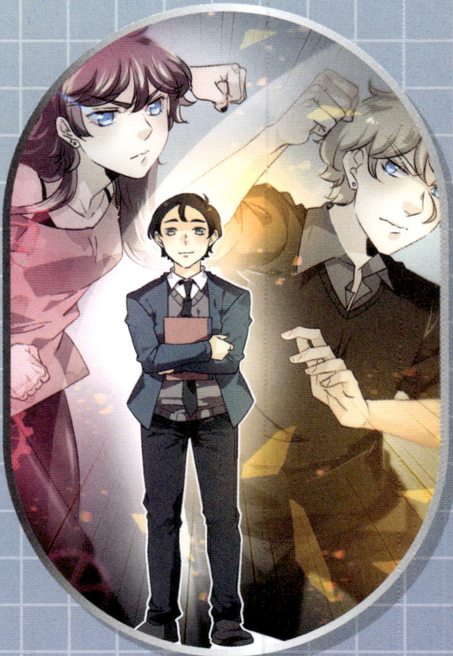
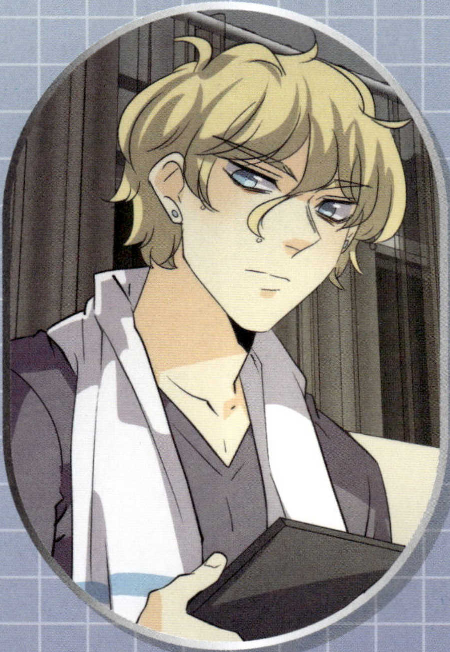
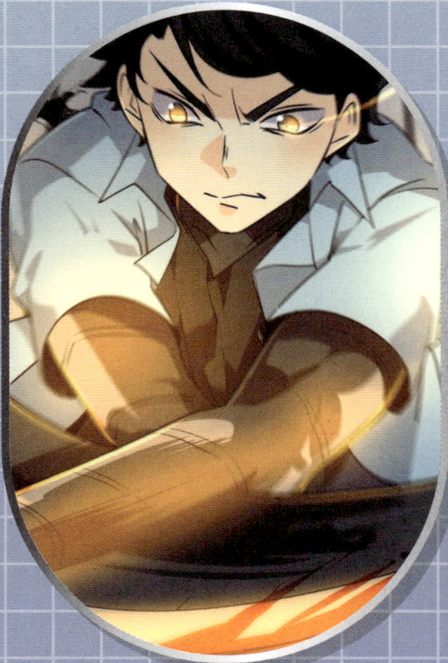
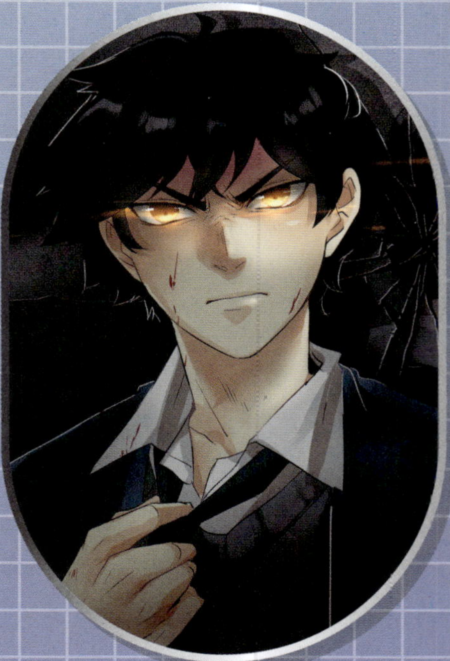
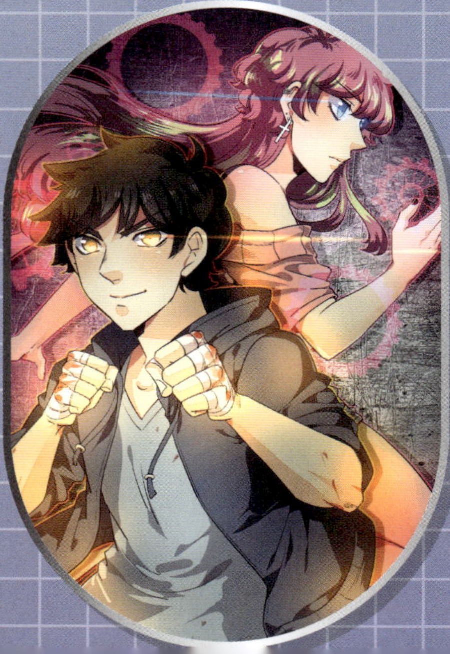
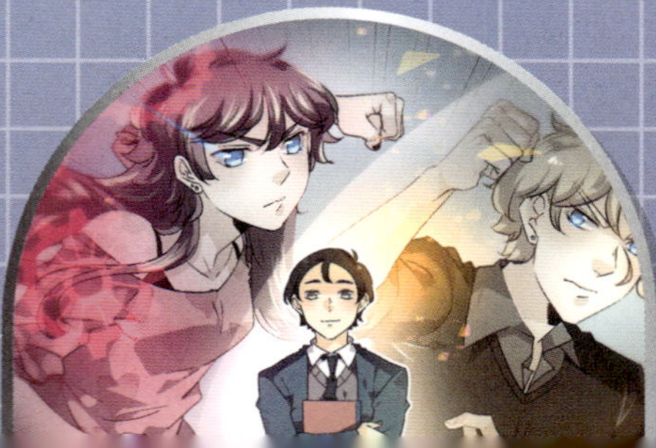
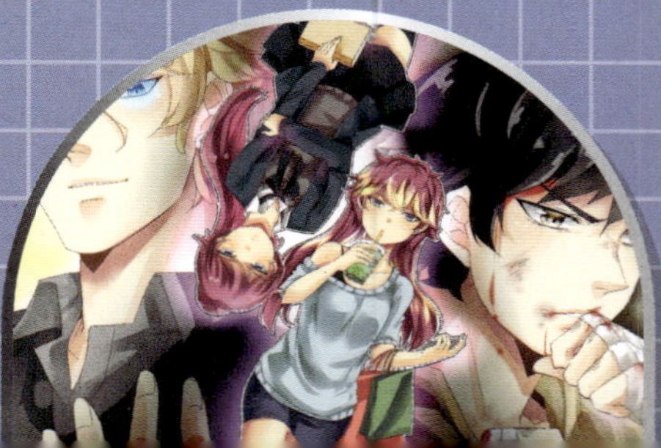

What Is unOrdinary?

Nobody paid much attention to John—a normal teenager at a high school where the social elite happen to possess unthinkable powers and abilities. But John's got a secret past that threatens to bring down the school's whole social order and more. Fulfilling his destiny won't be easy though because there are battles, frenemies, and deadly conspiracies around every corner.

Check out the latest episode of the hit WEBTOON series.

SYNOPSIS

Welcome to Wellston Private High School—an [un]ordinary educational institution with an extra[un]ordinary student body where every student possesses a superpower—except for John.

Seraphina, the popular Ace of Wellston, has the power to manipulate time, while Wellston's King, Arlo, can form a barrier of protection around himself. Isen, Blyke, and Remi each have their own special powers too. But John is the subject of merciless bullying because he's a "weakling" who lacks a superpower. As a friendship between John and Seraphina grows, Seraphina discovers that the powerless are worthy and the true measure of strength is how you protect others. When John and Seraphina uncover a movement that threatens the status quo, they form an alliance to restore order to their world. But is John really who he appears to be? Or will his bullies discover they've been toying with a force the world has yet to see unleashed?

Note from the Creator

UnOrdinary combines a superpower world and a high school story illustrated in an anime and manga style. The series includes small bits of a variety of genres, and the themes cover mental health, self-discovery, self-forgiveness, and some philosophy and current events. I hope you enjoy coloring these memorable scenes taken from the halls of Wellston Private High School and beyond!

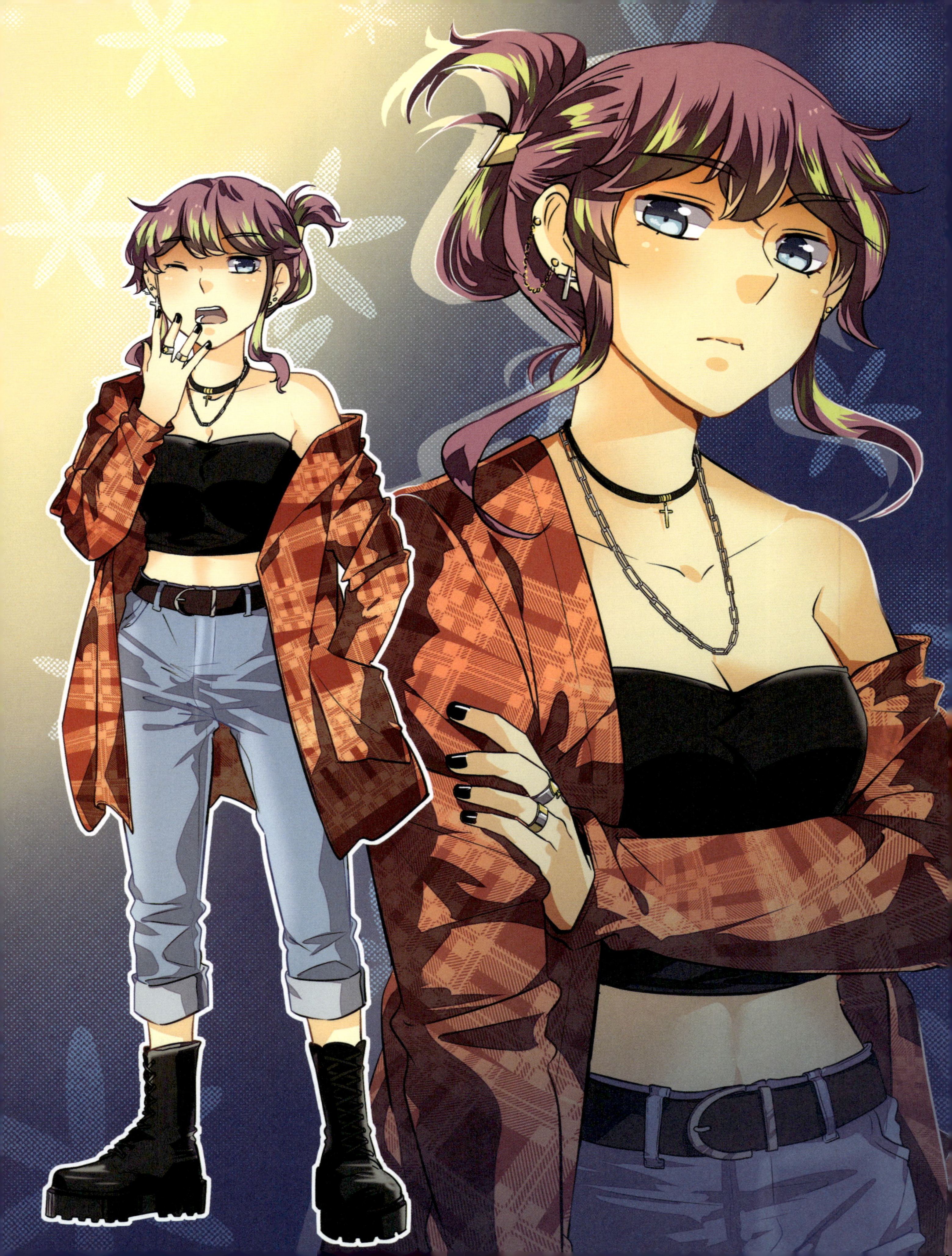

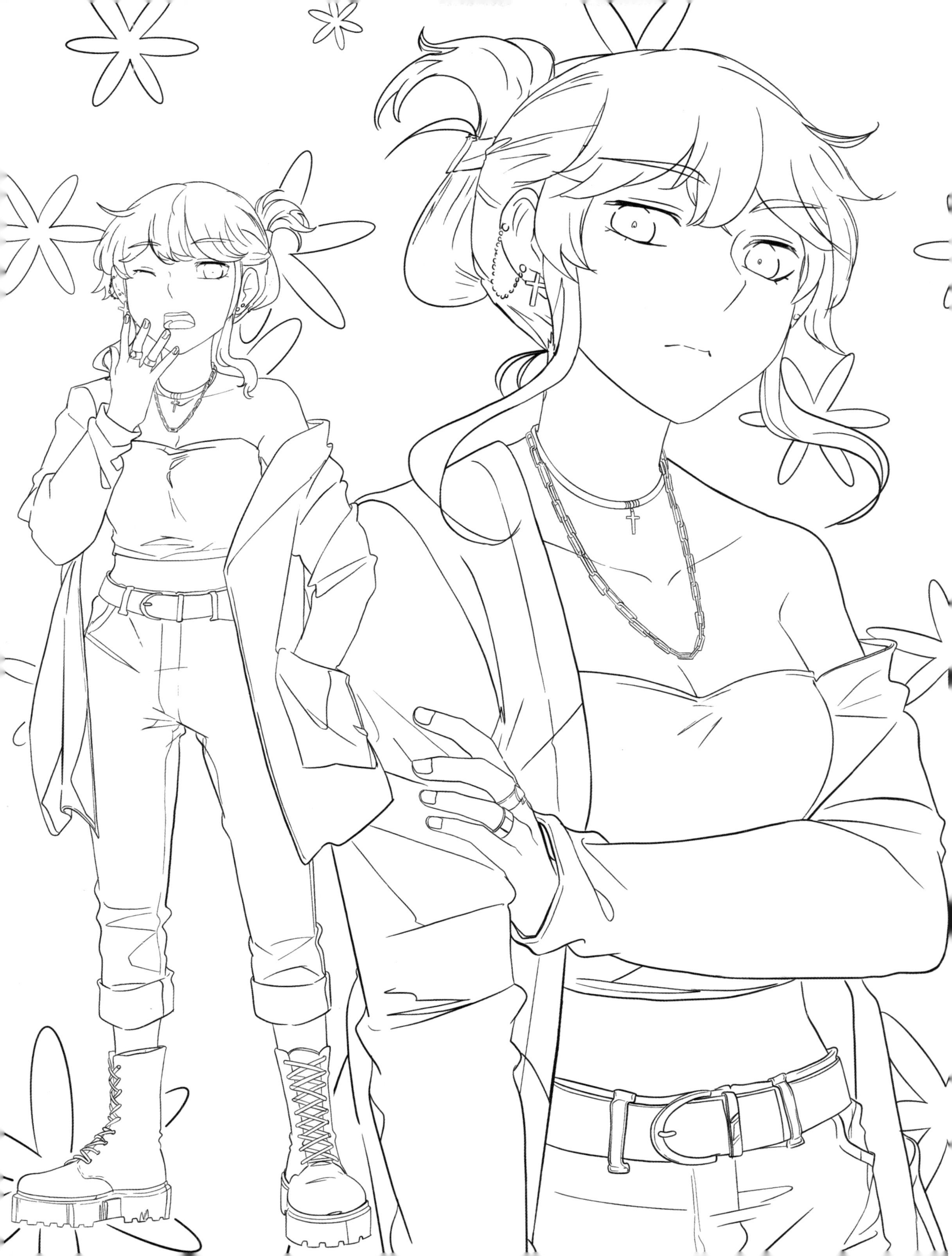

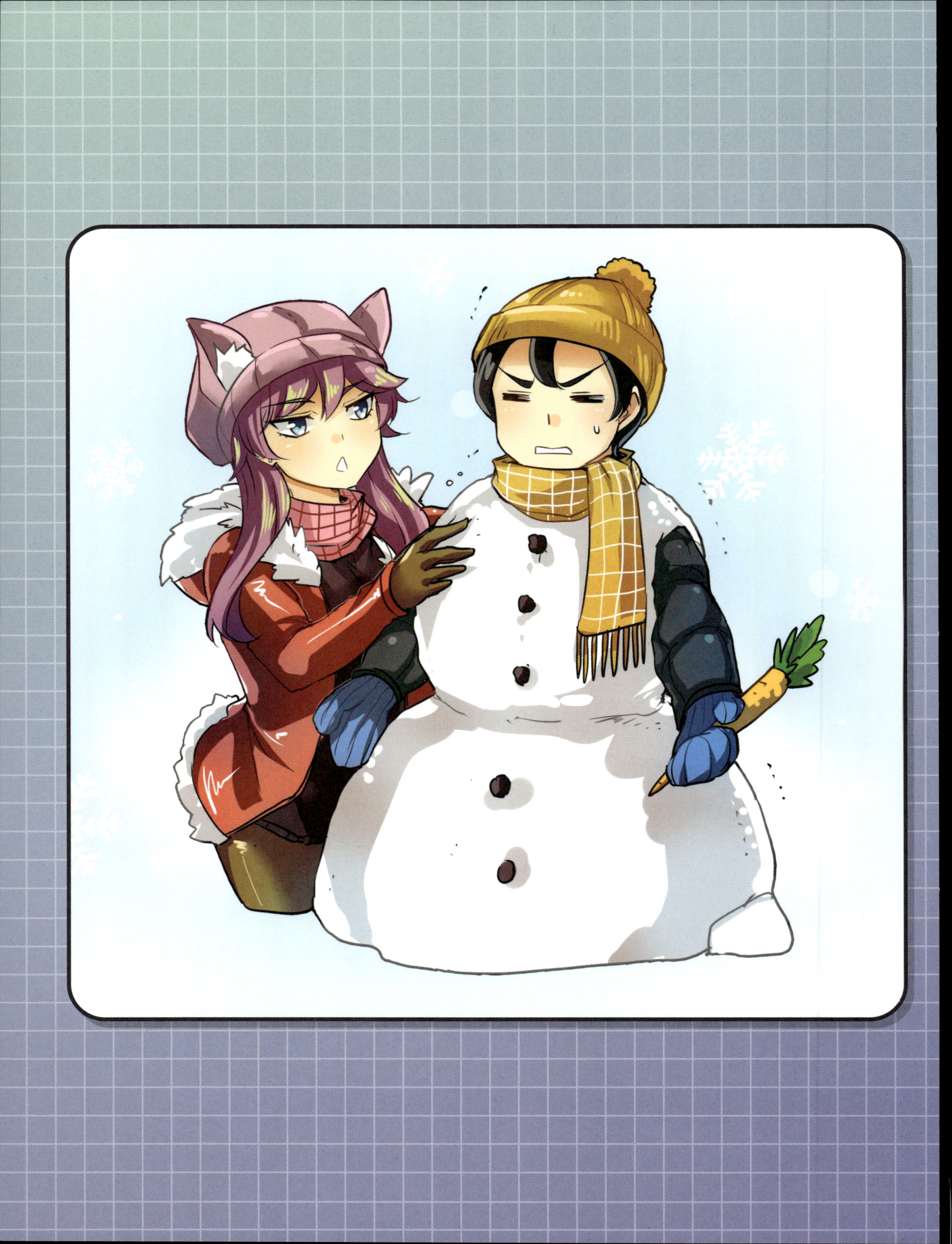

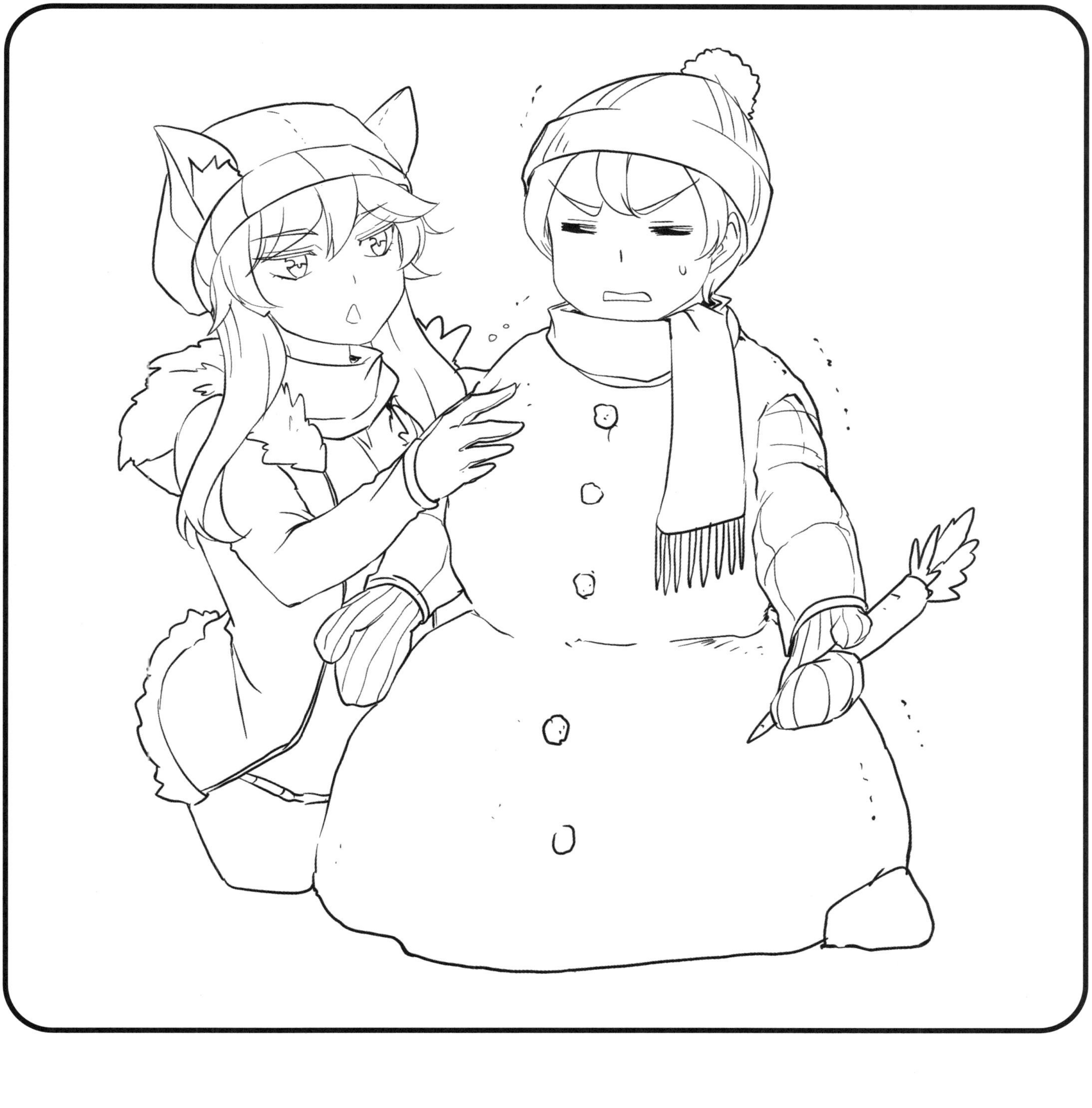

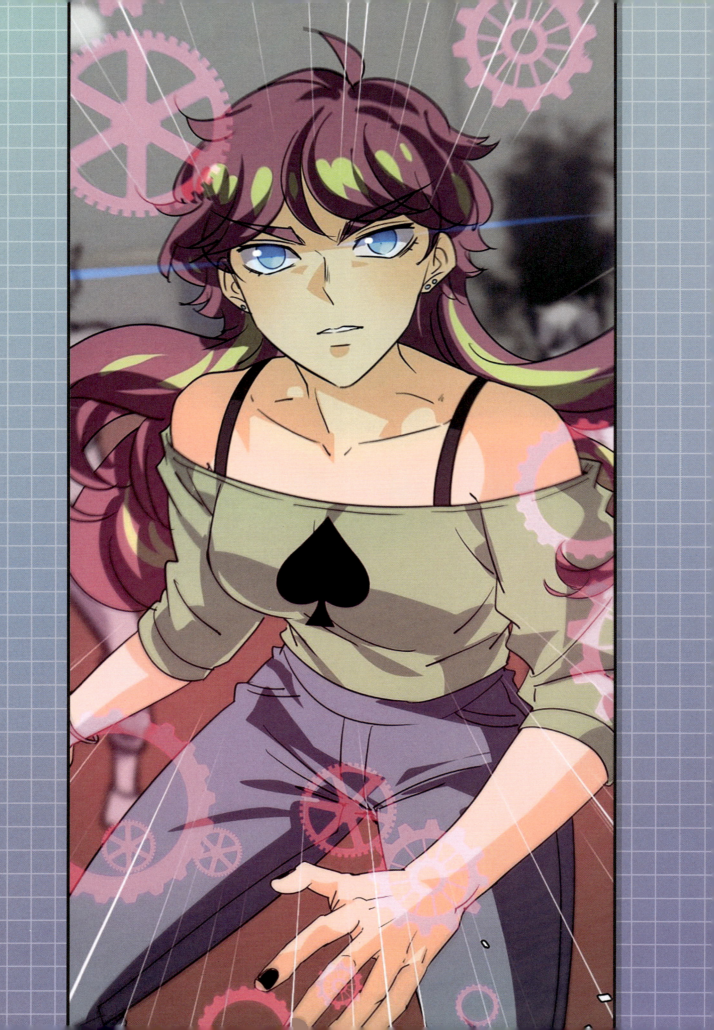

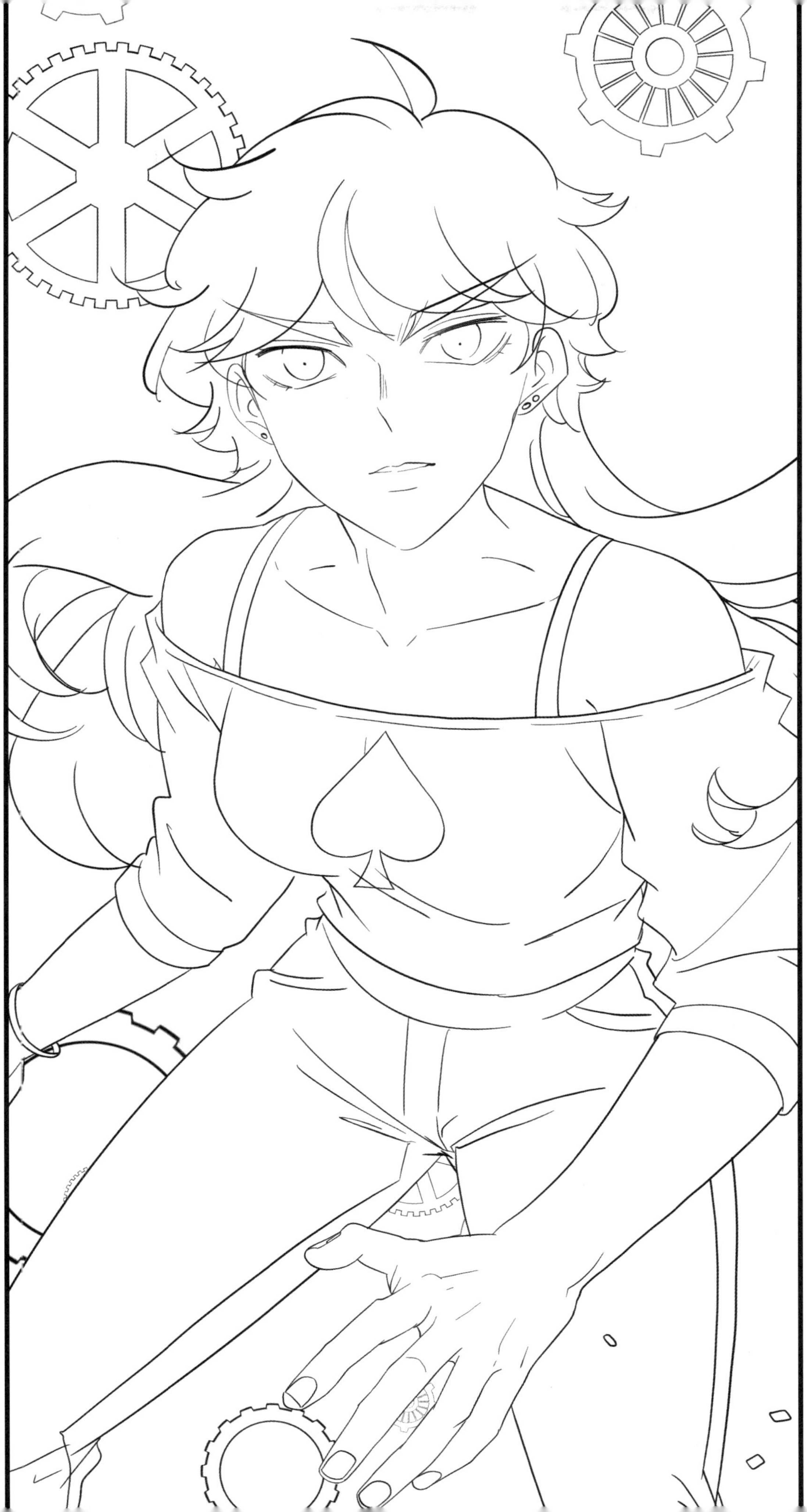

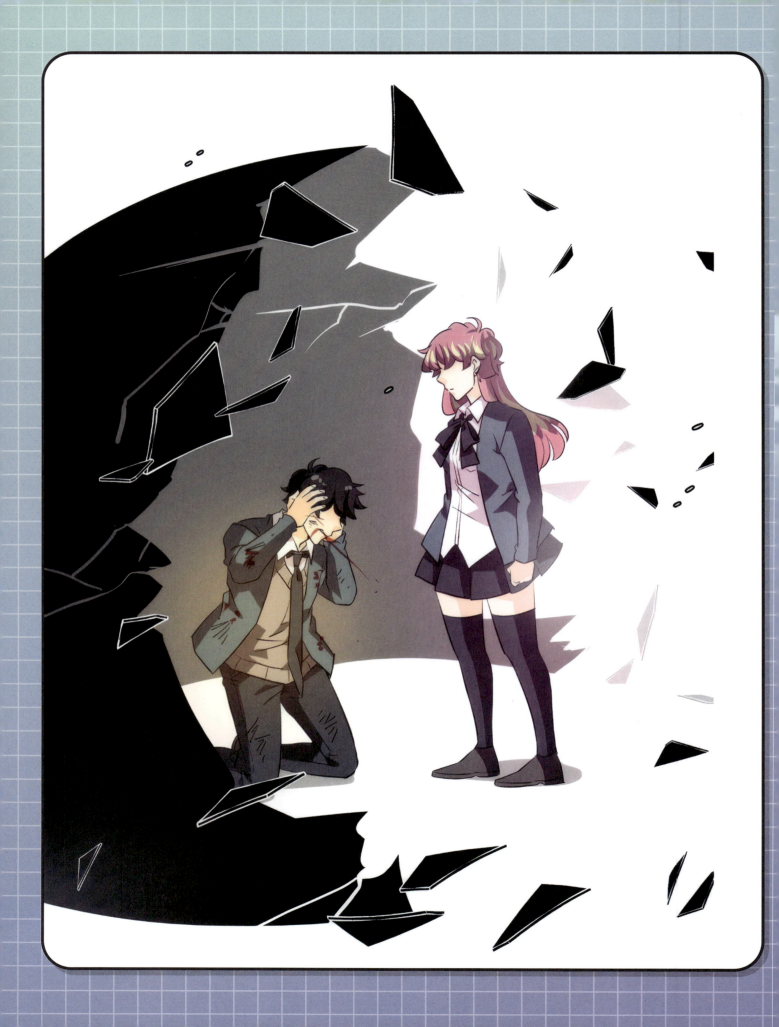

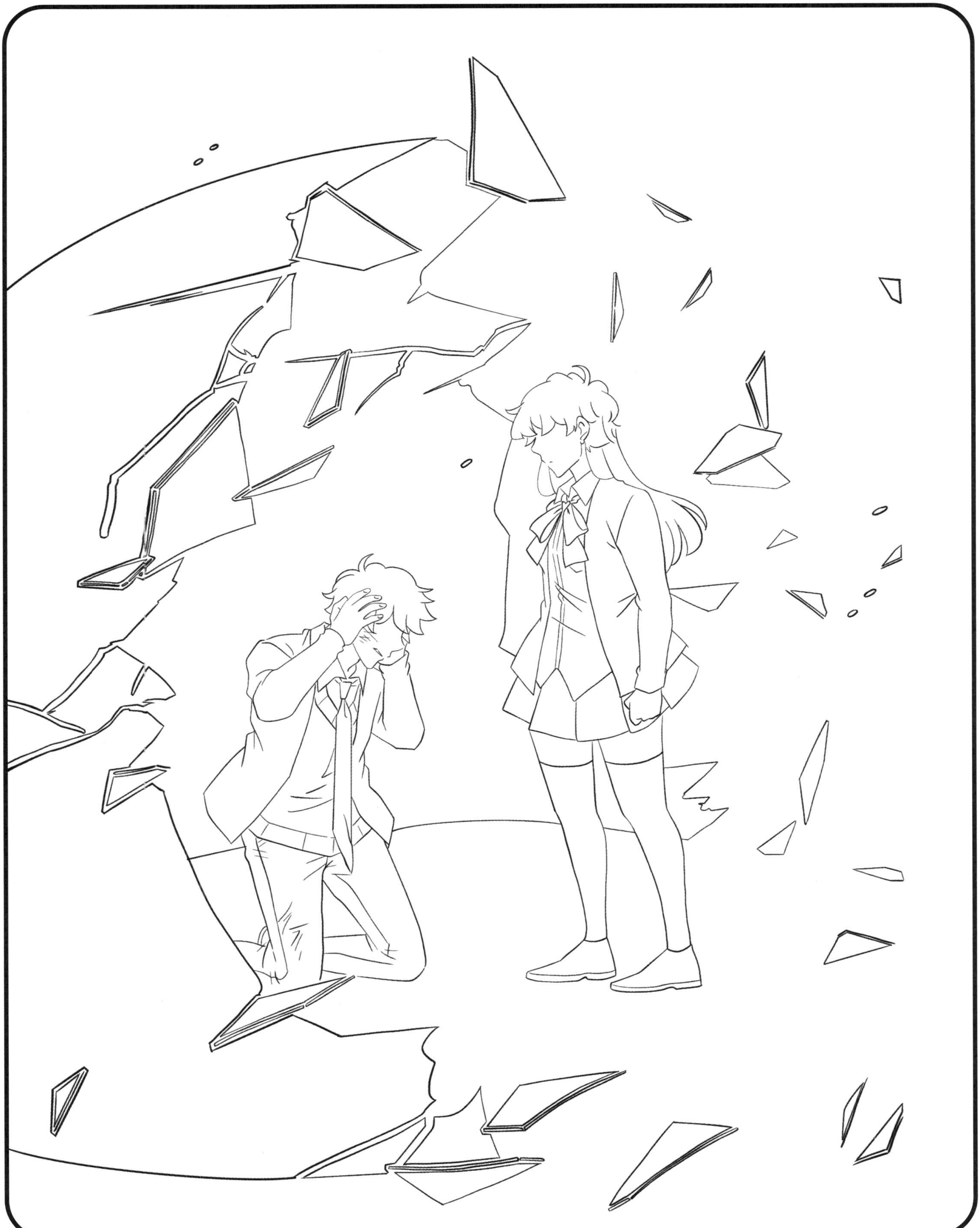

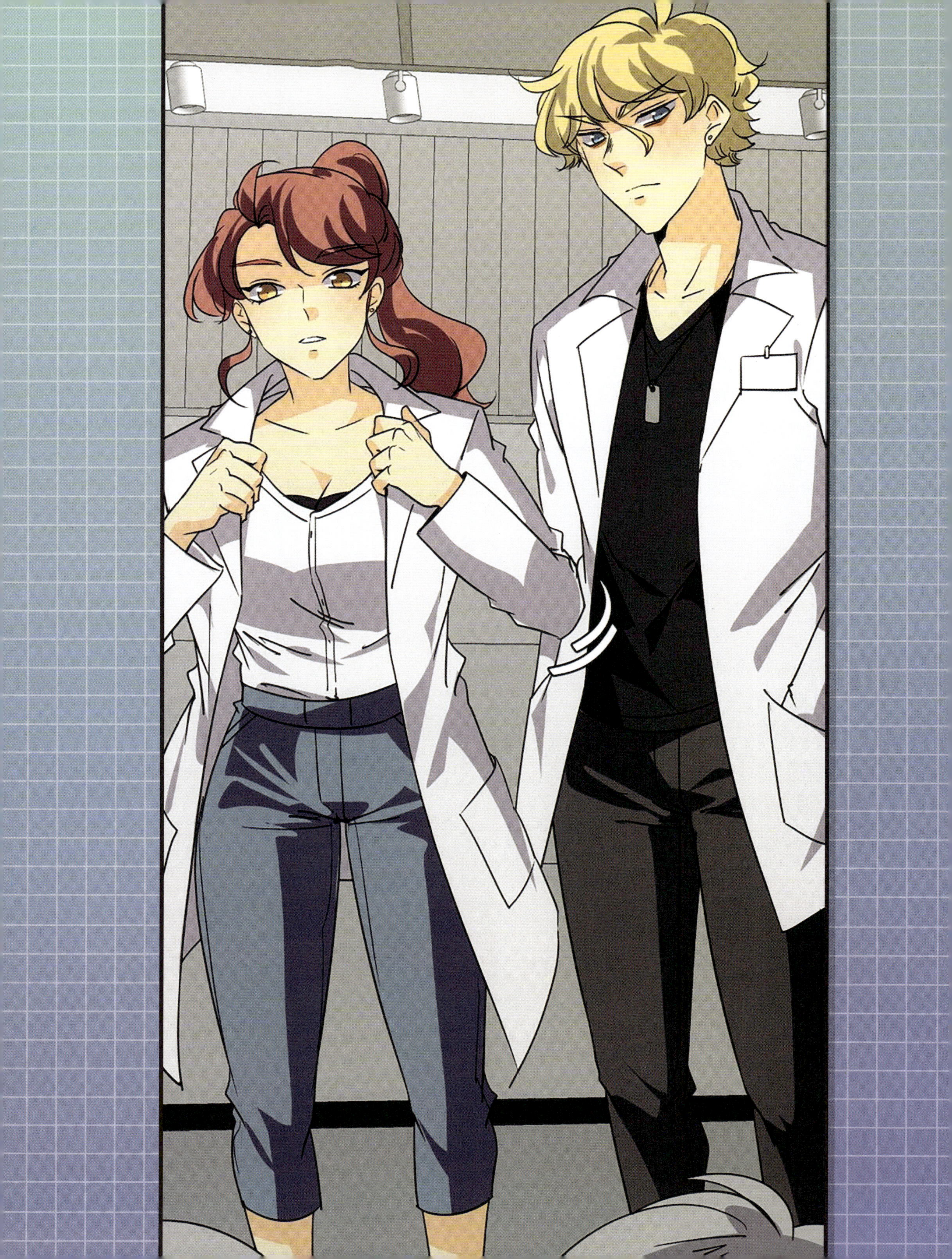

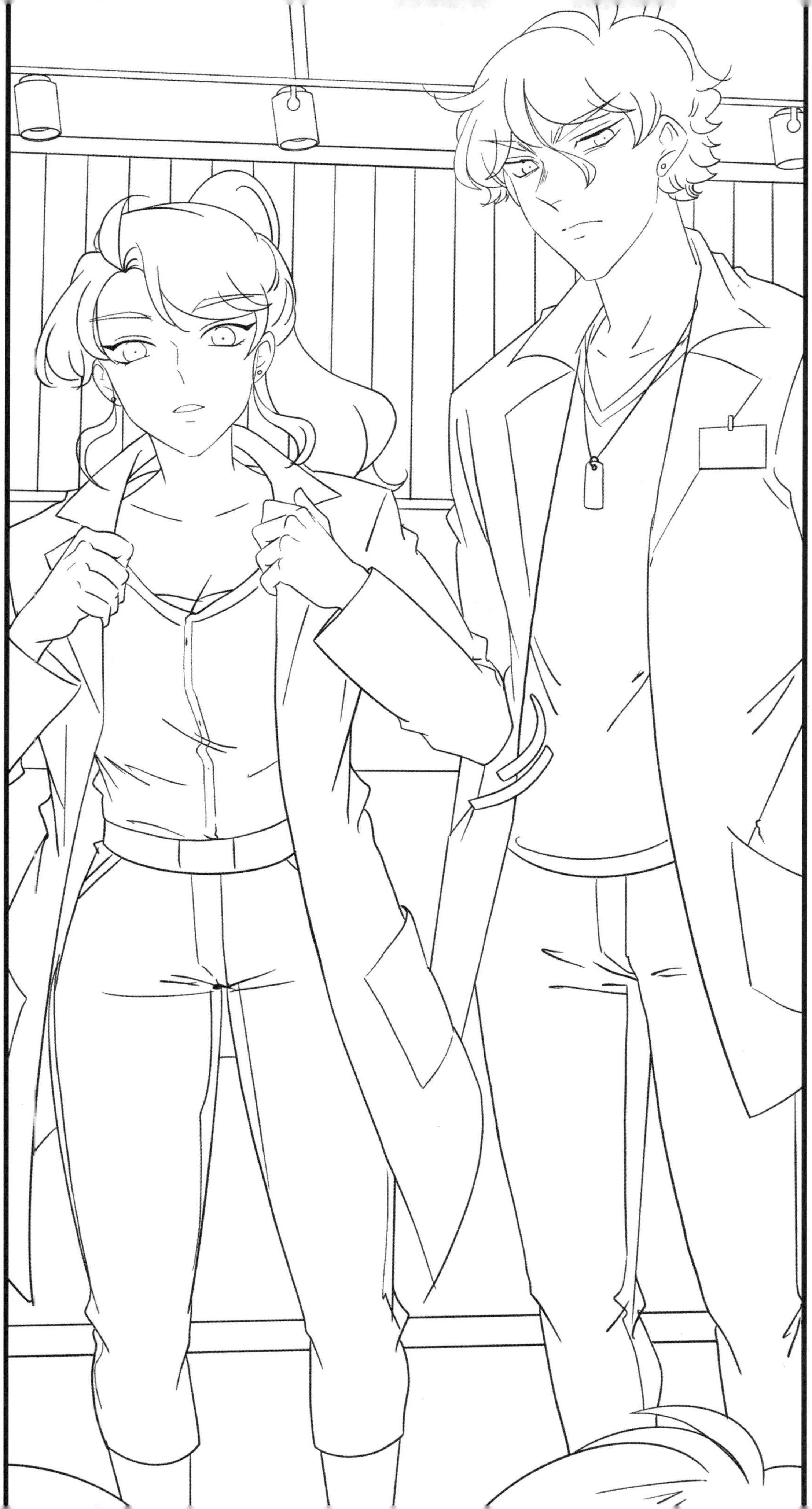

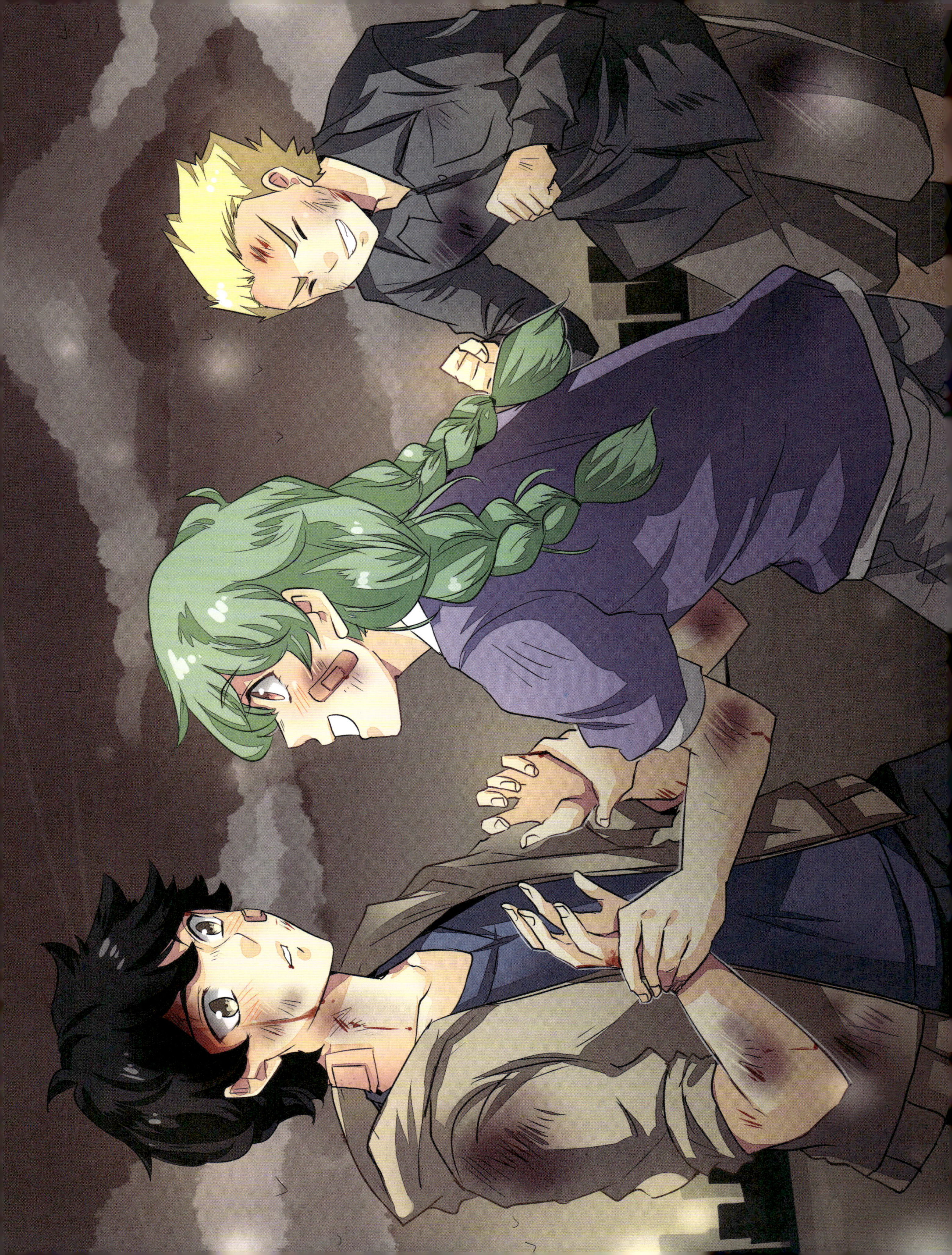

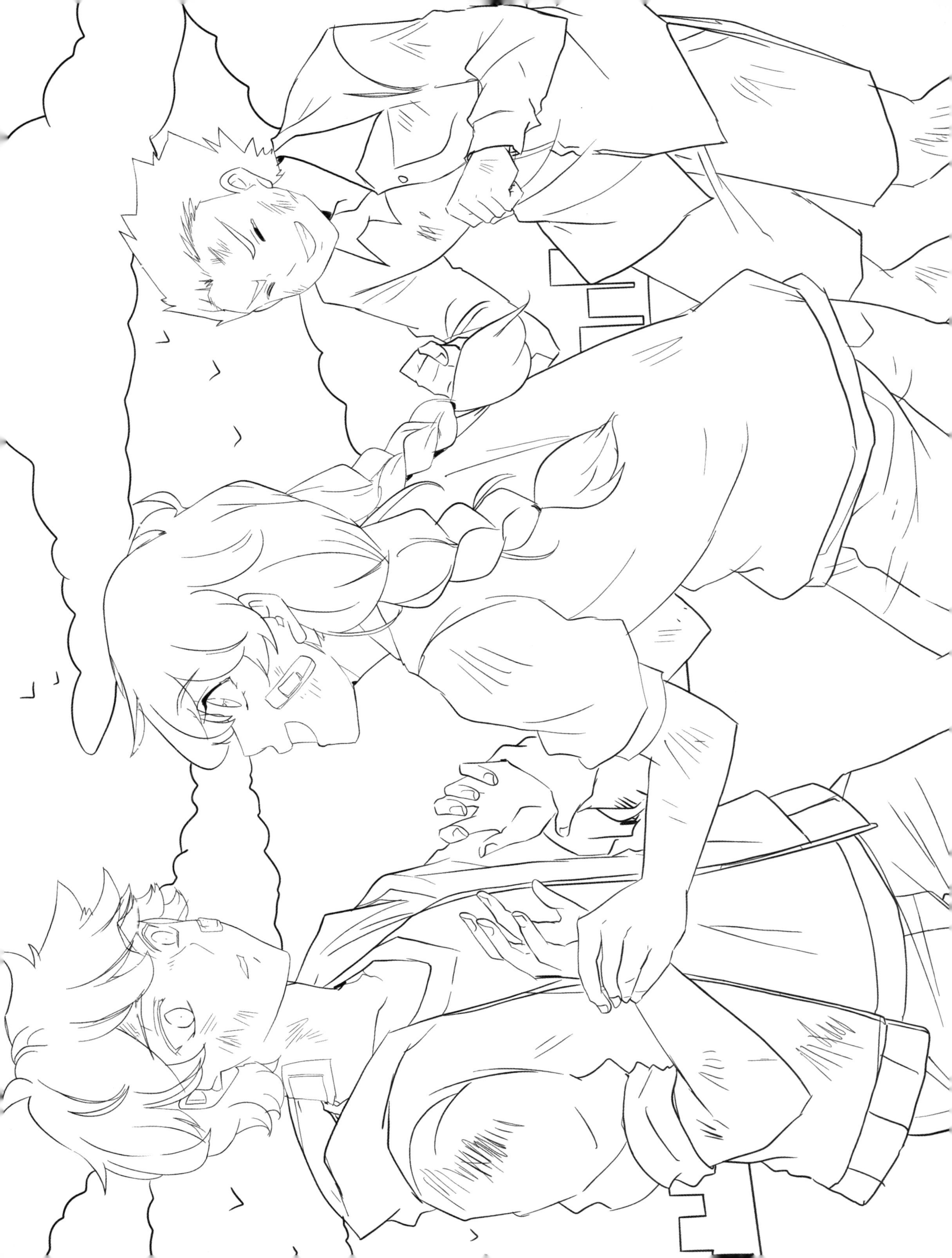

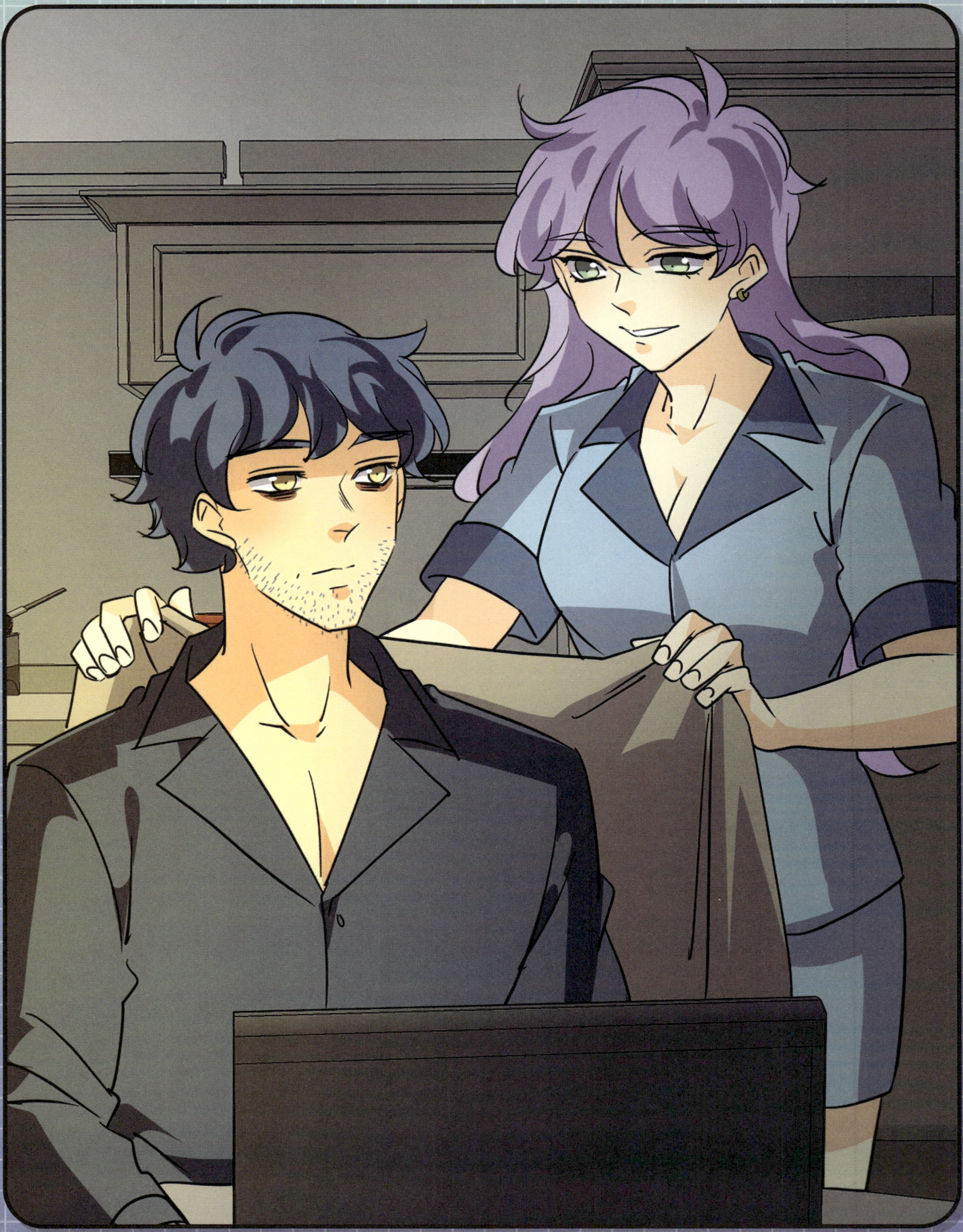

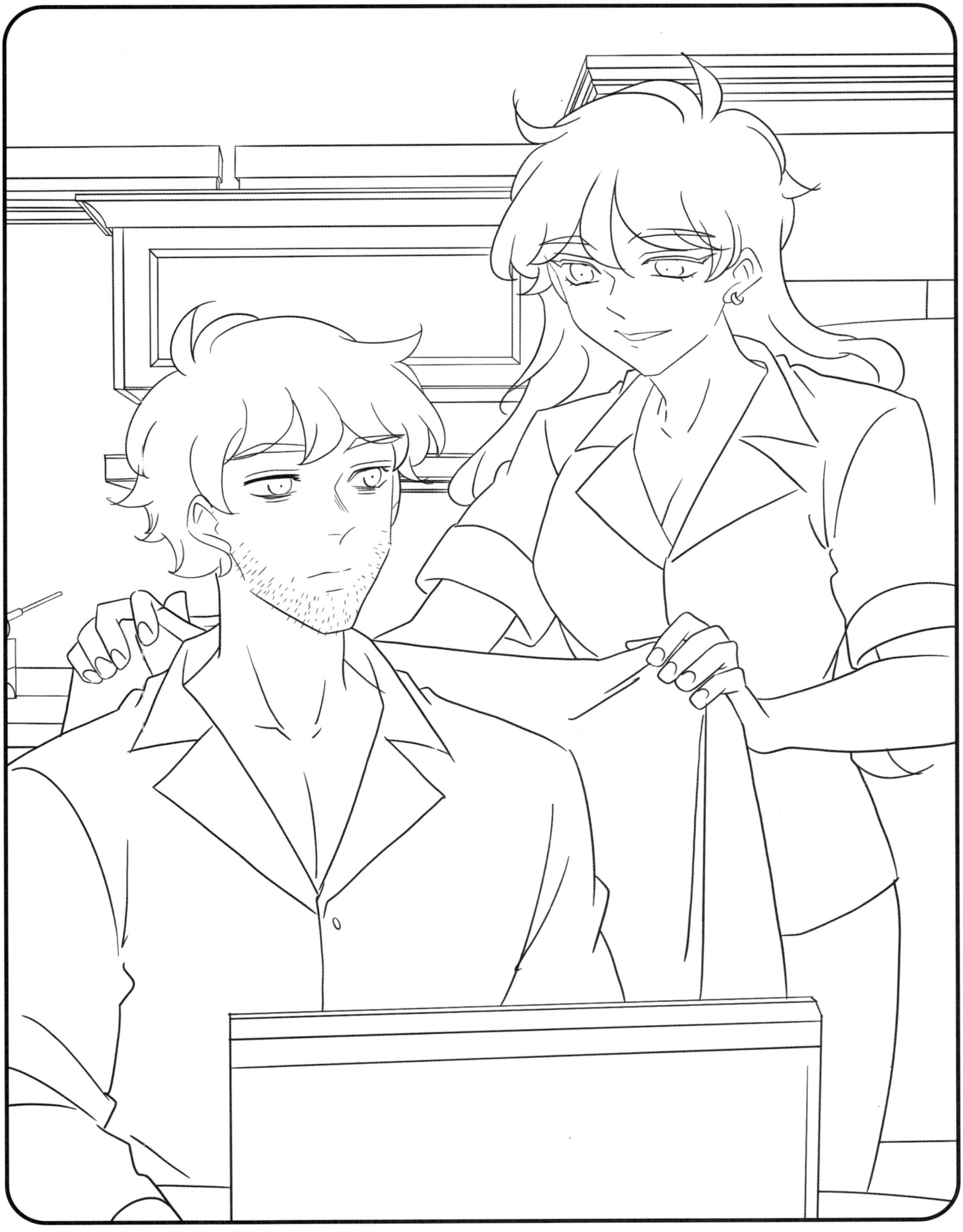

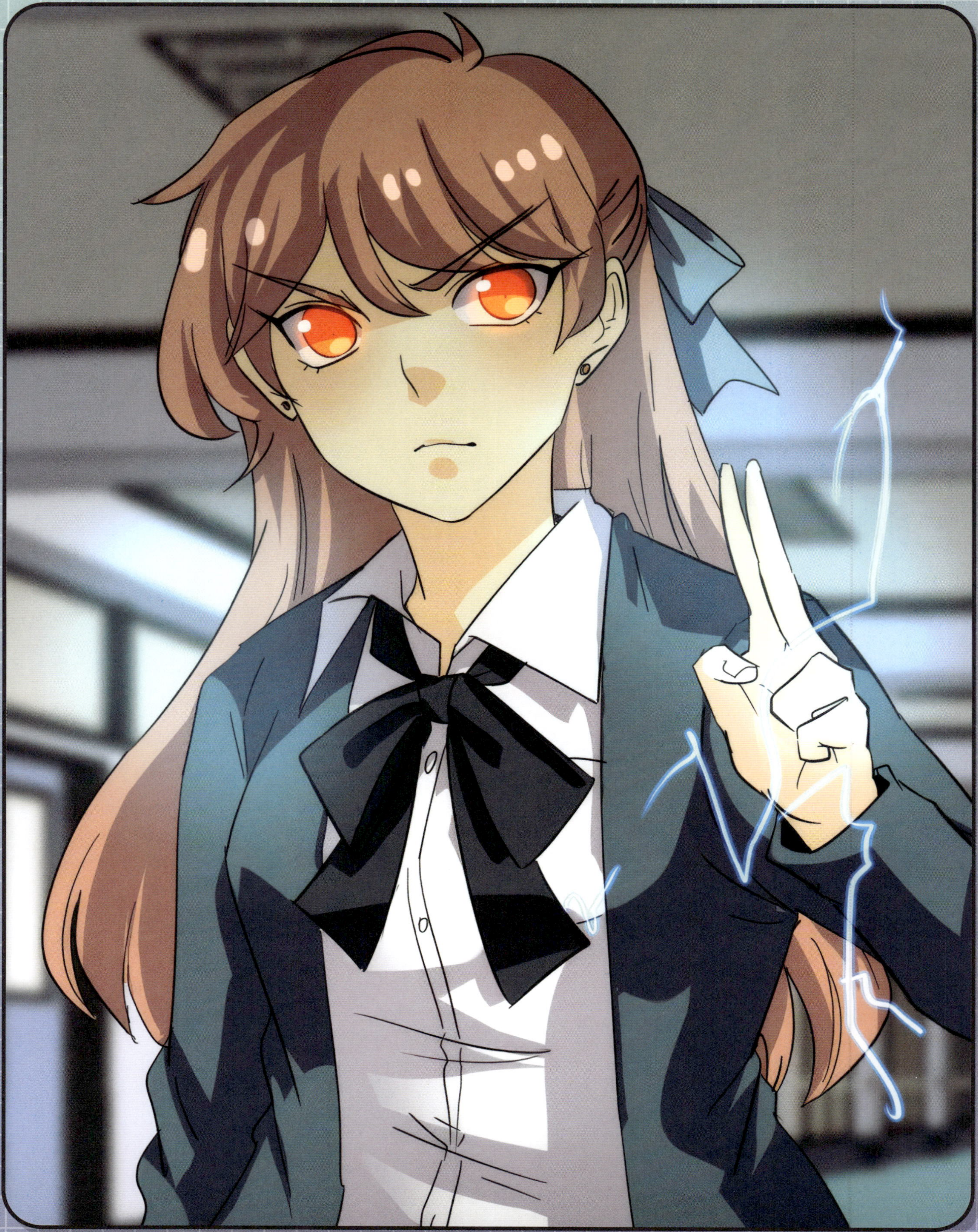

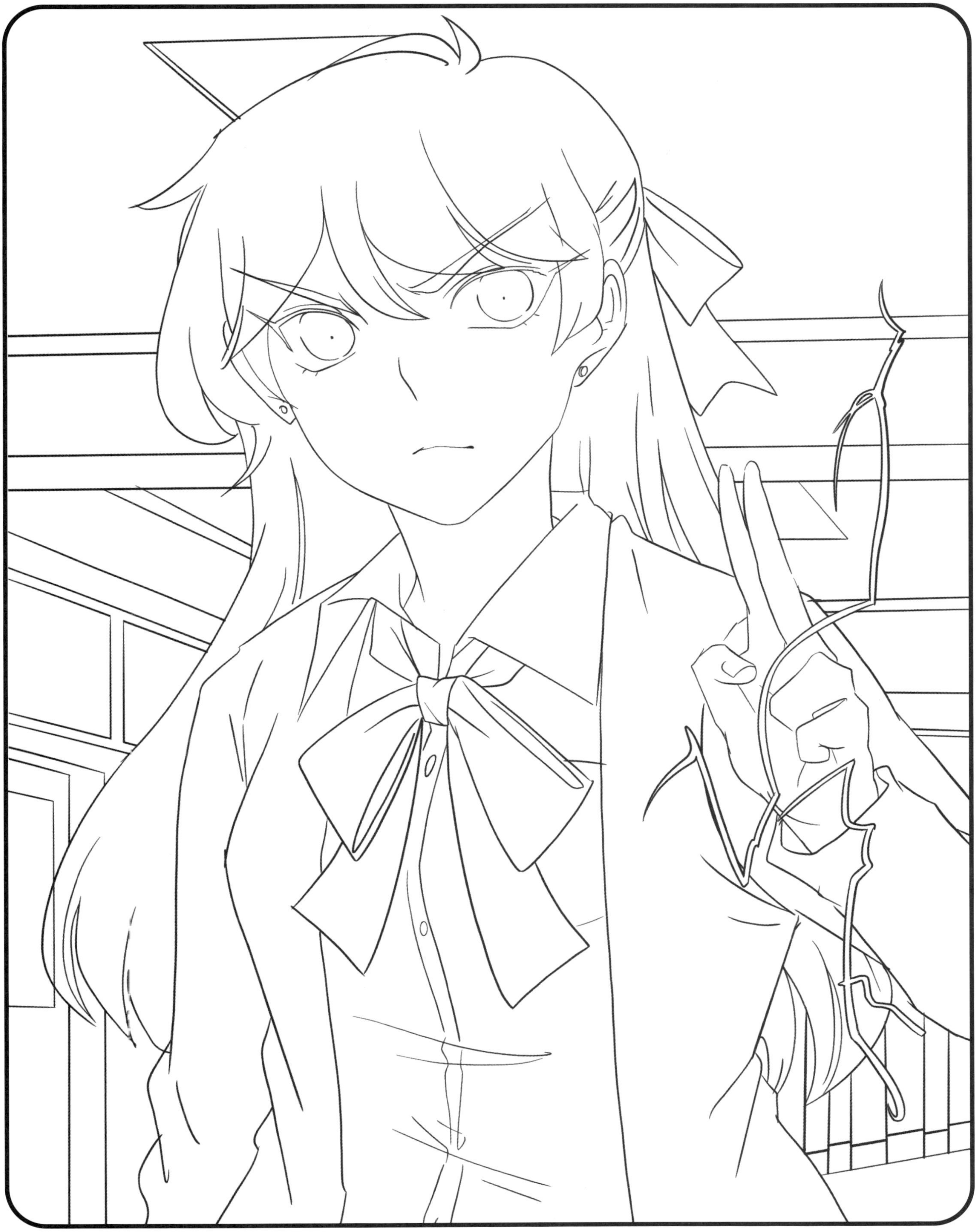

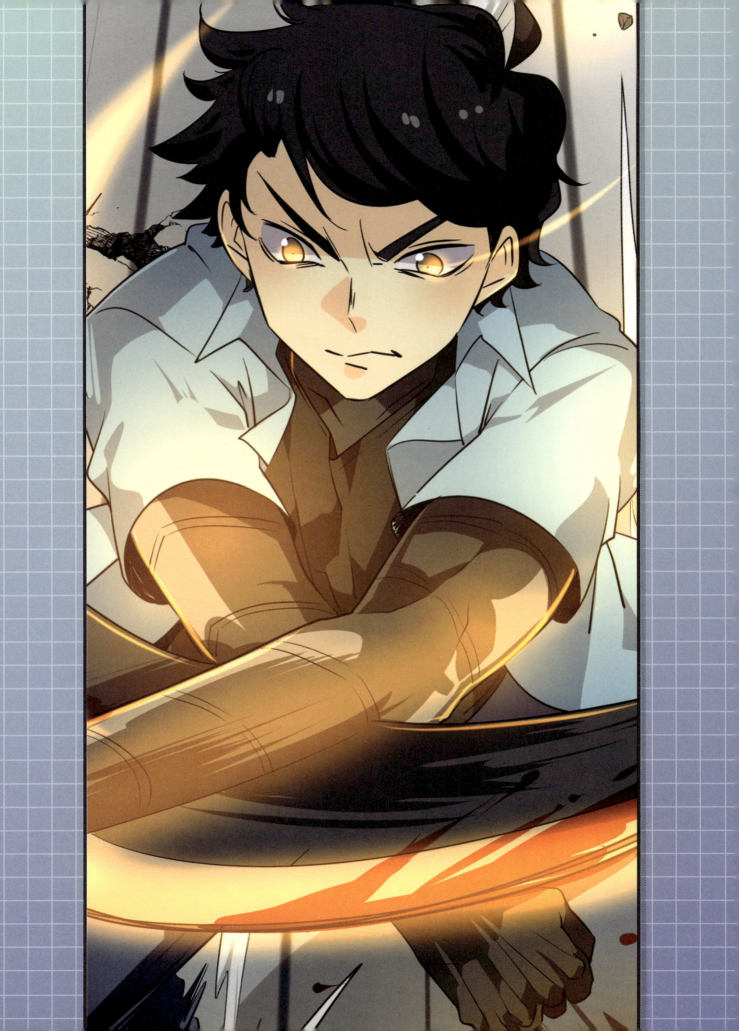

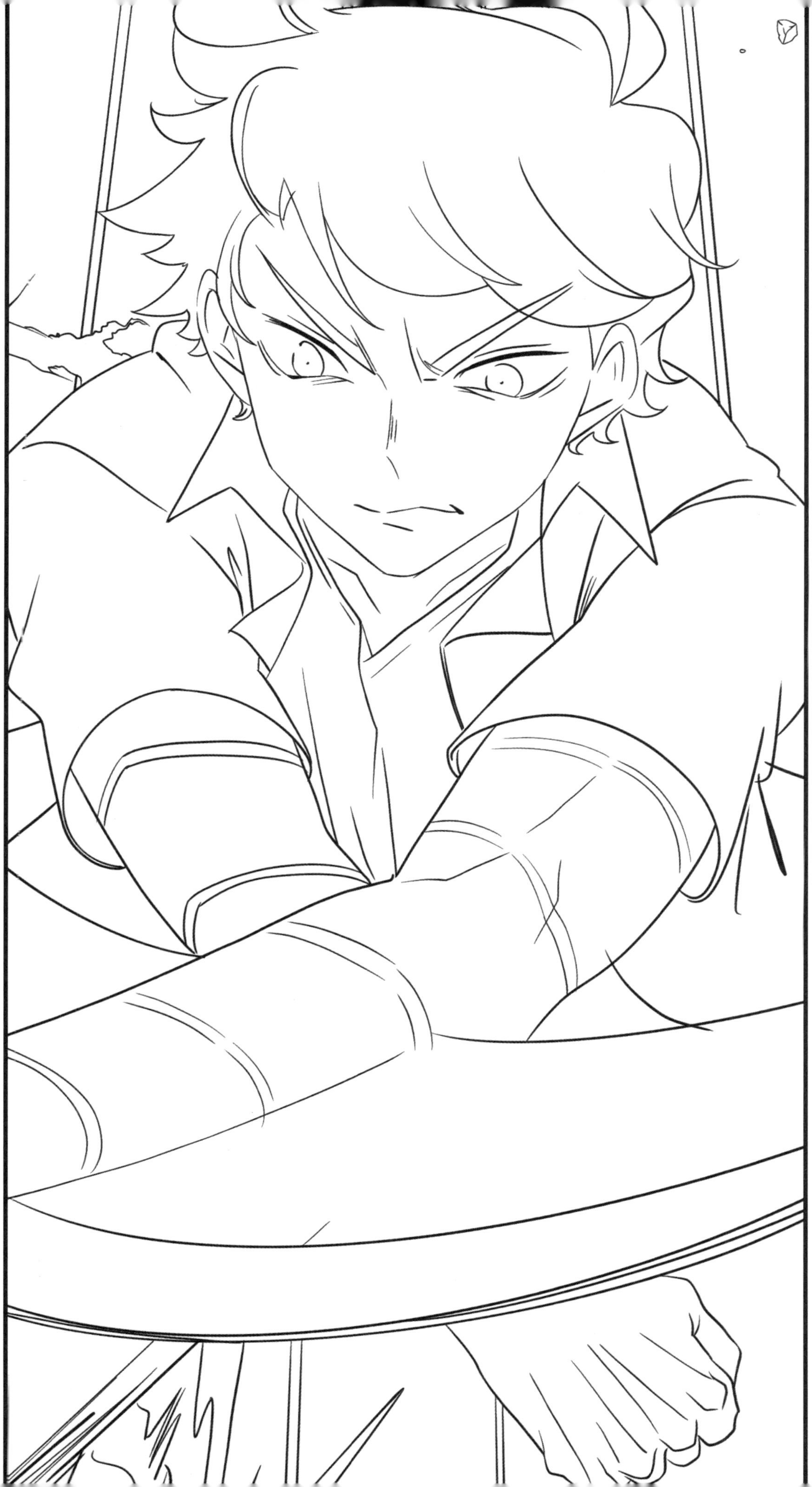

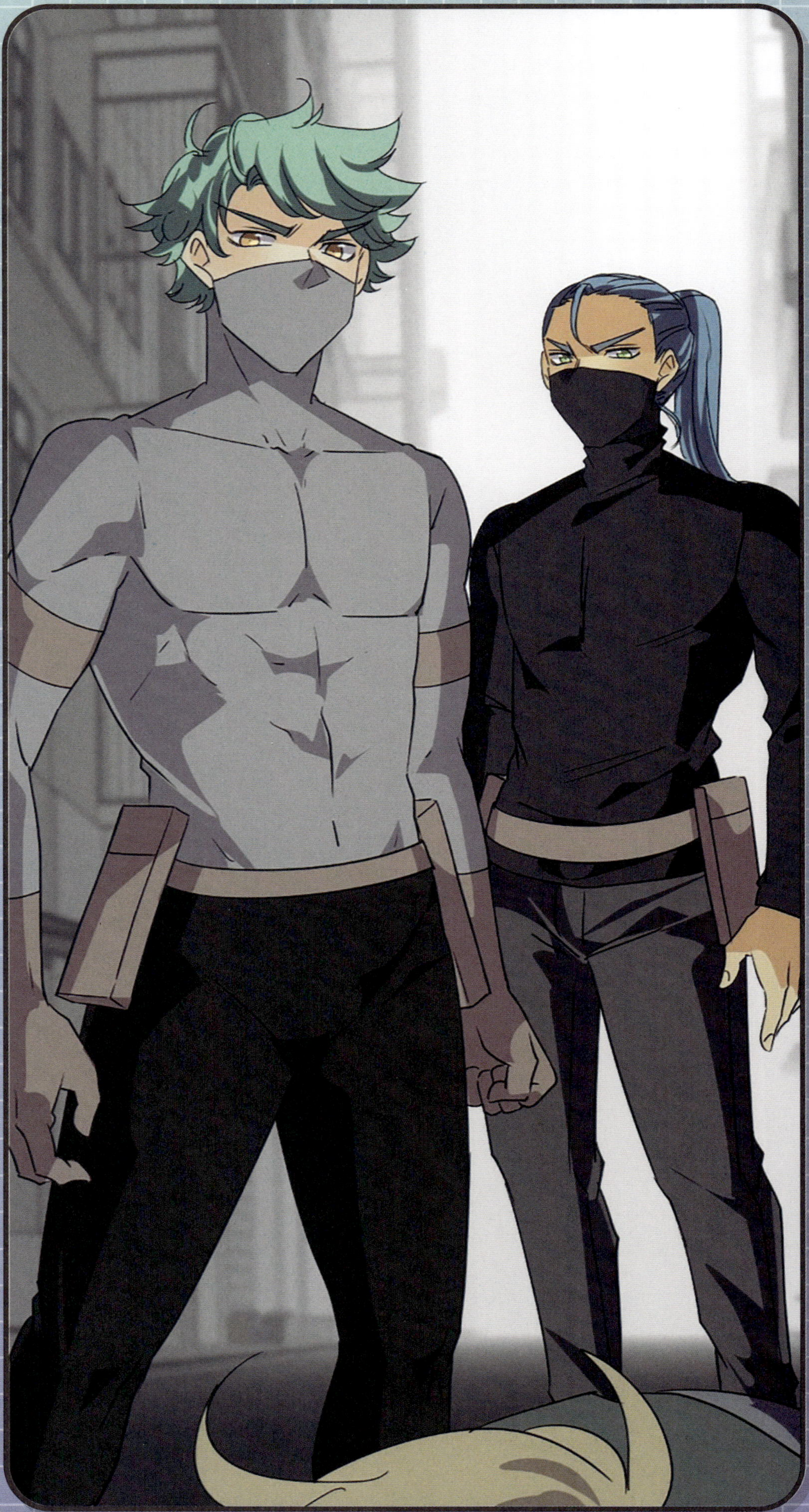

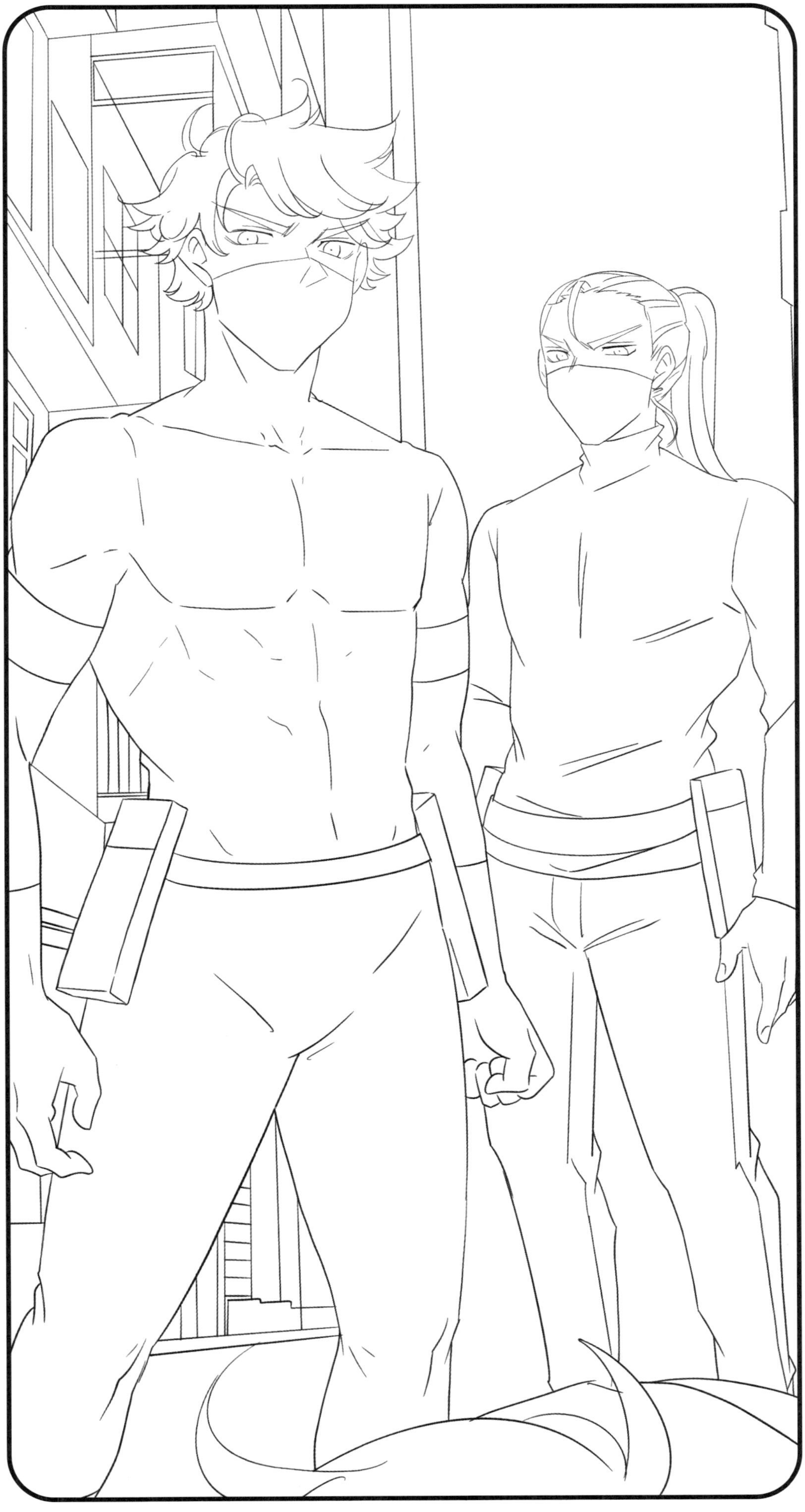

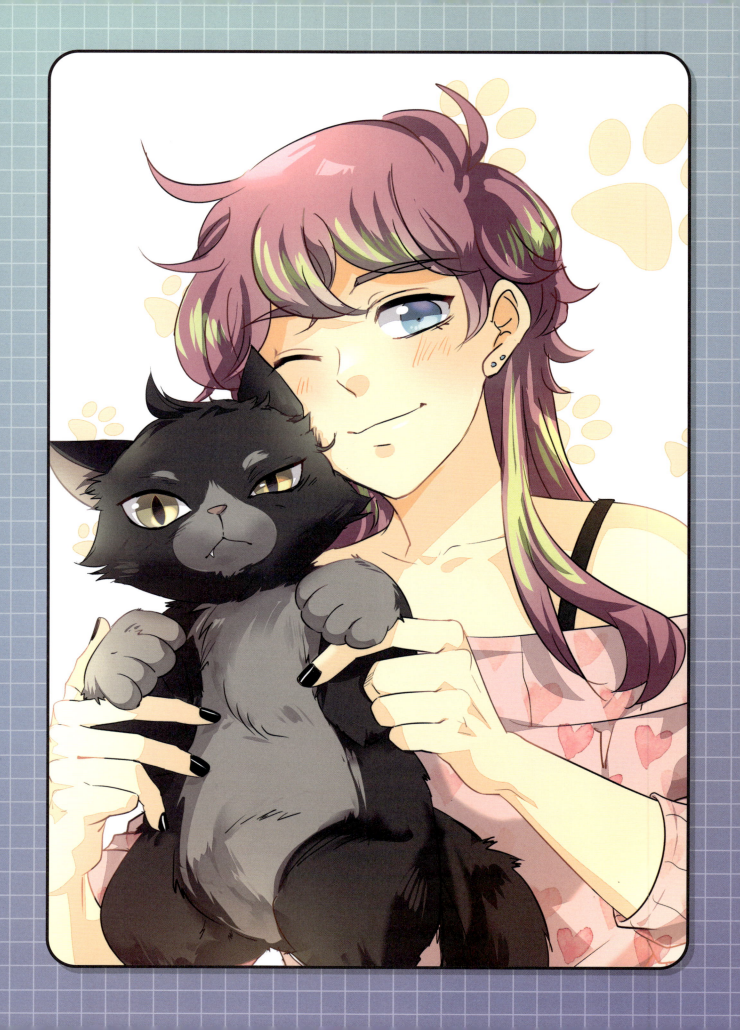

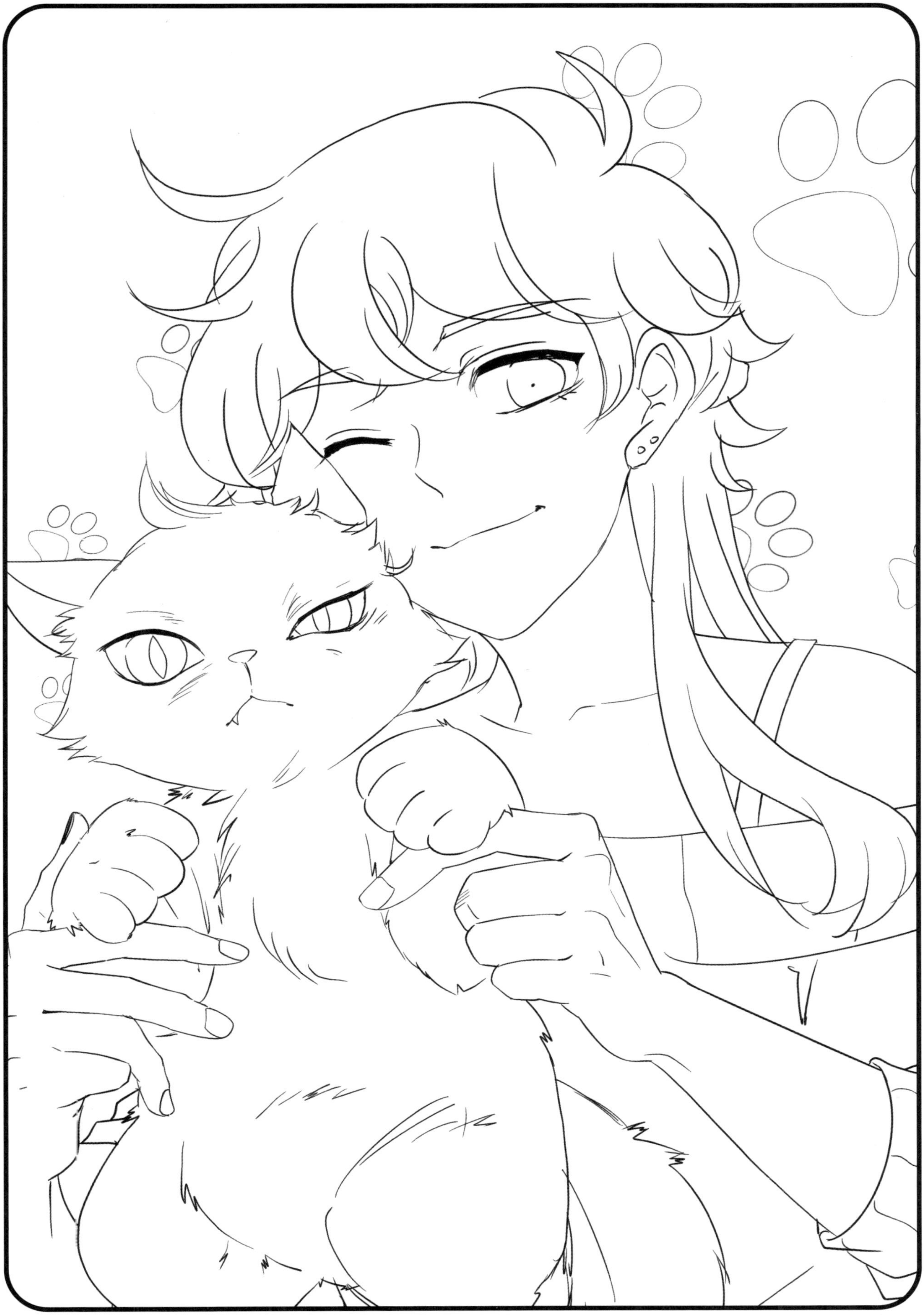

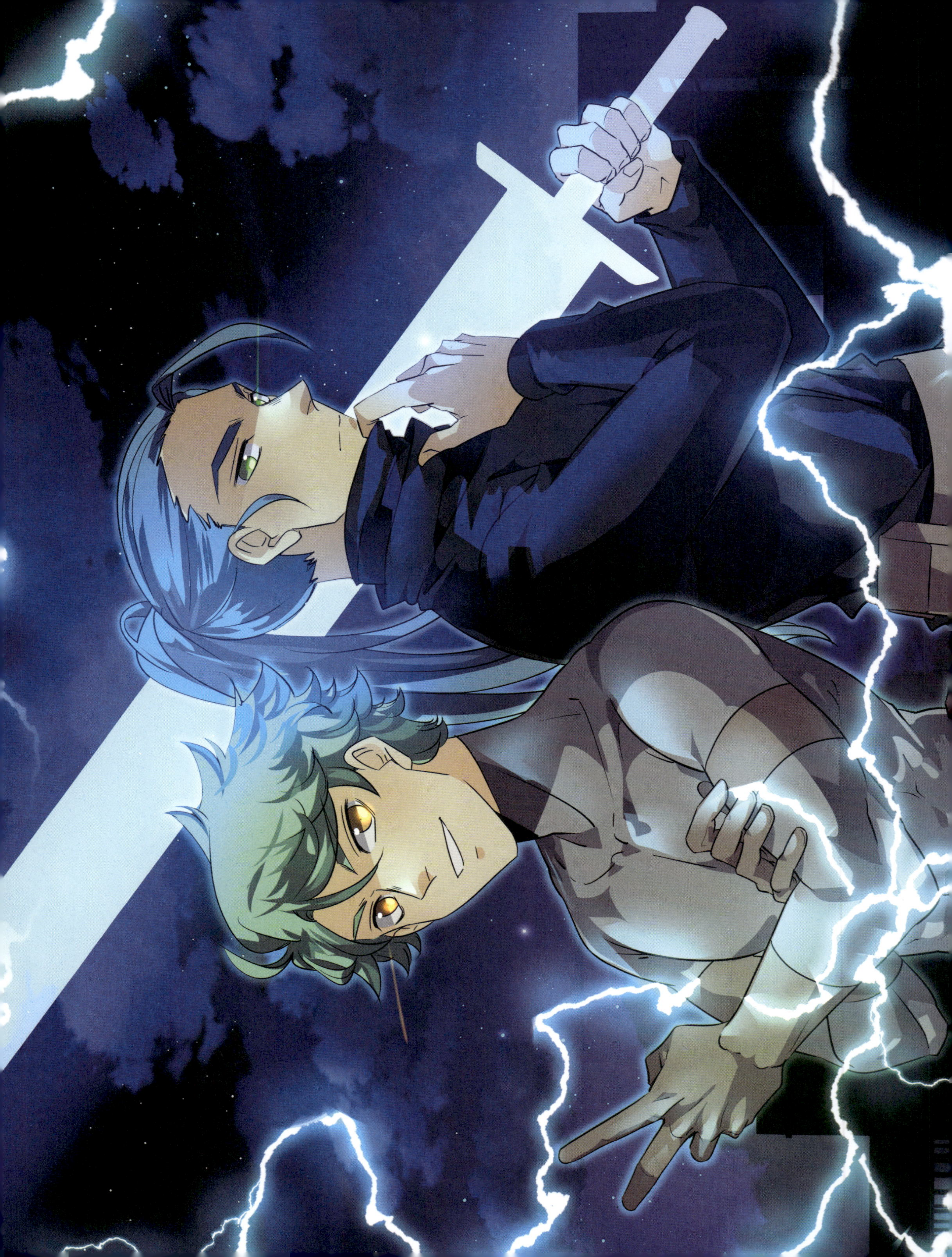

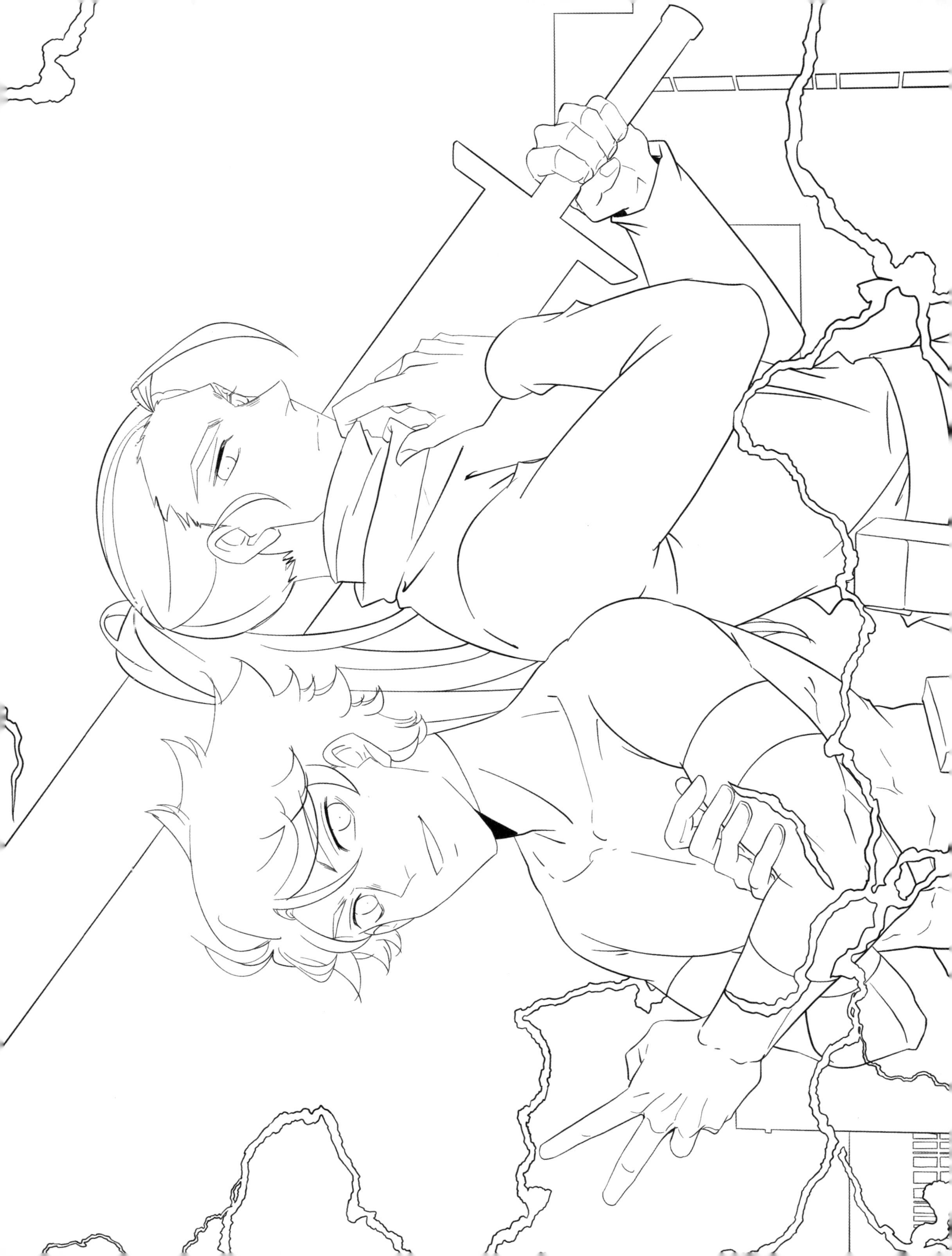

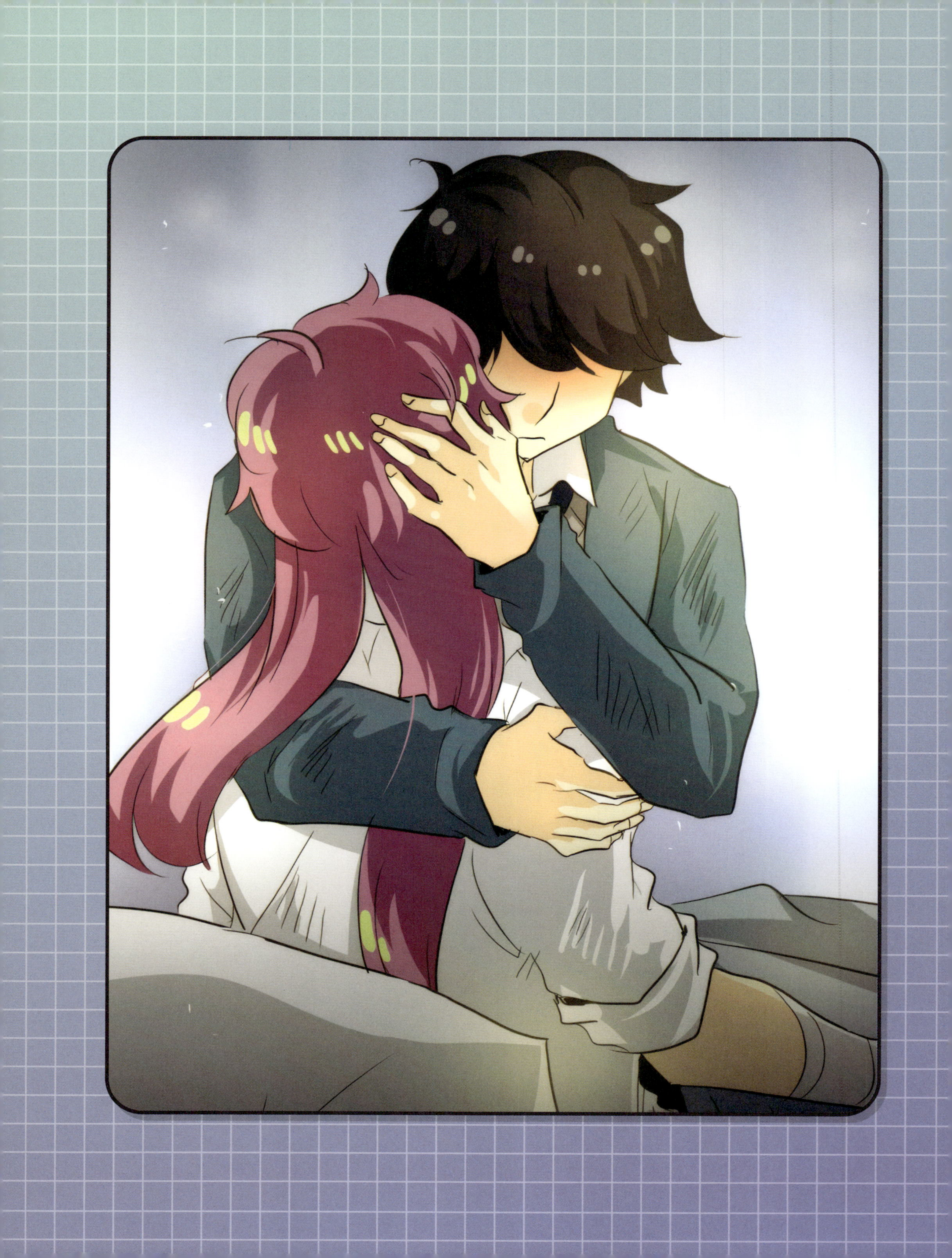

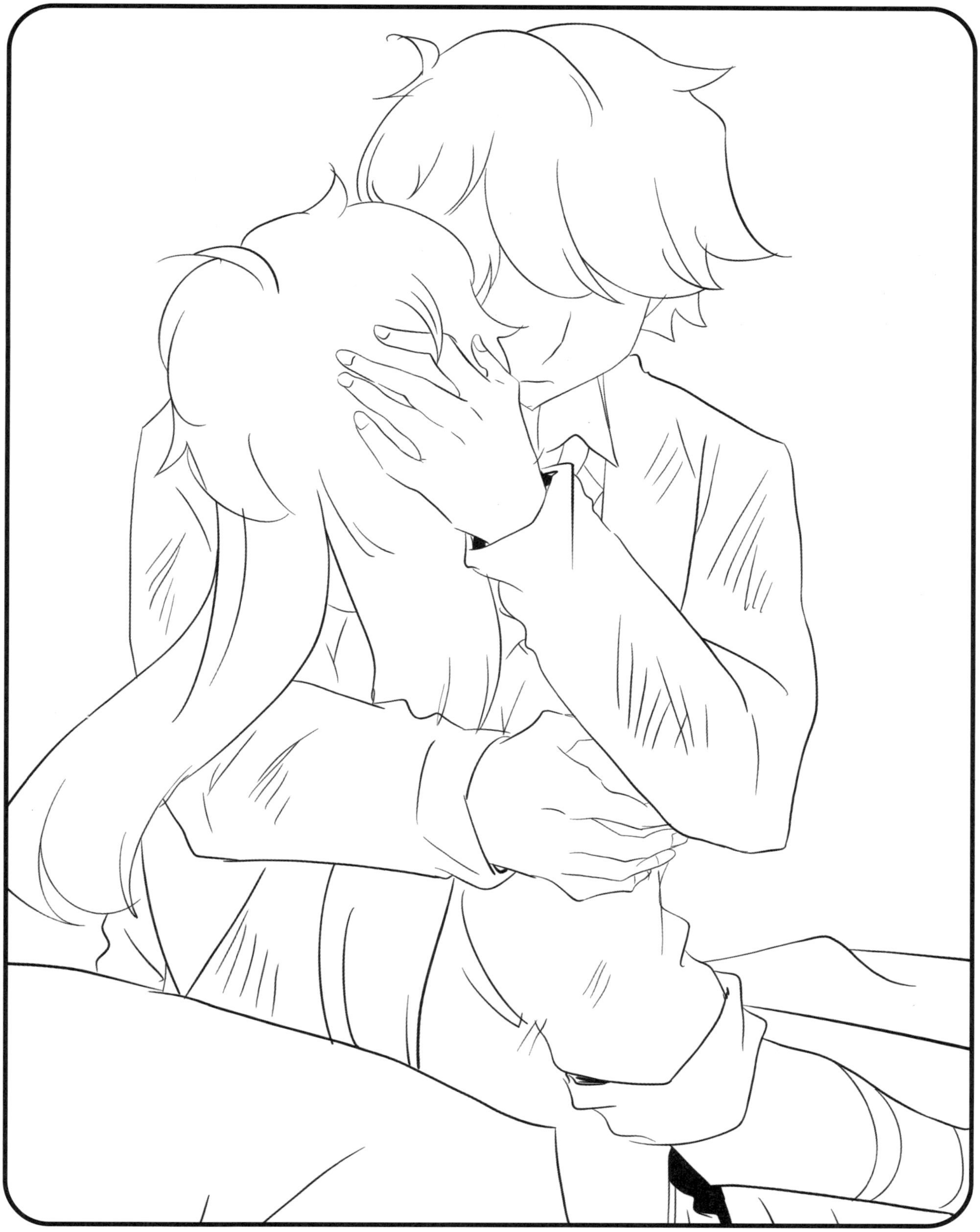

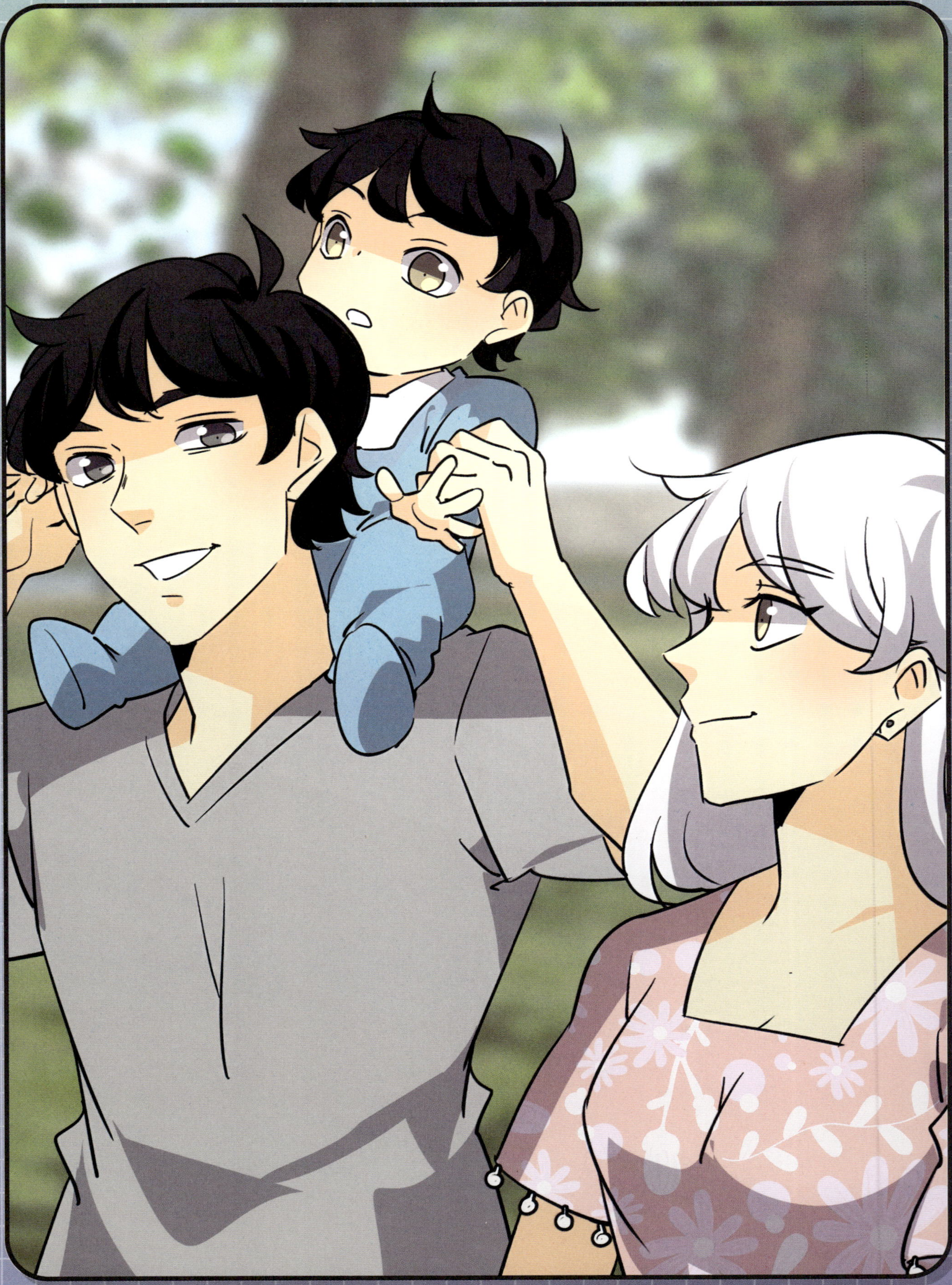

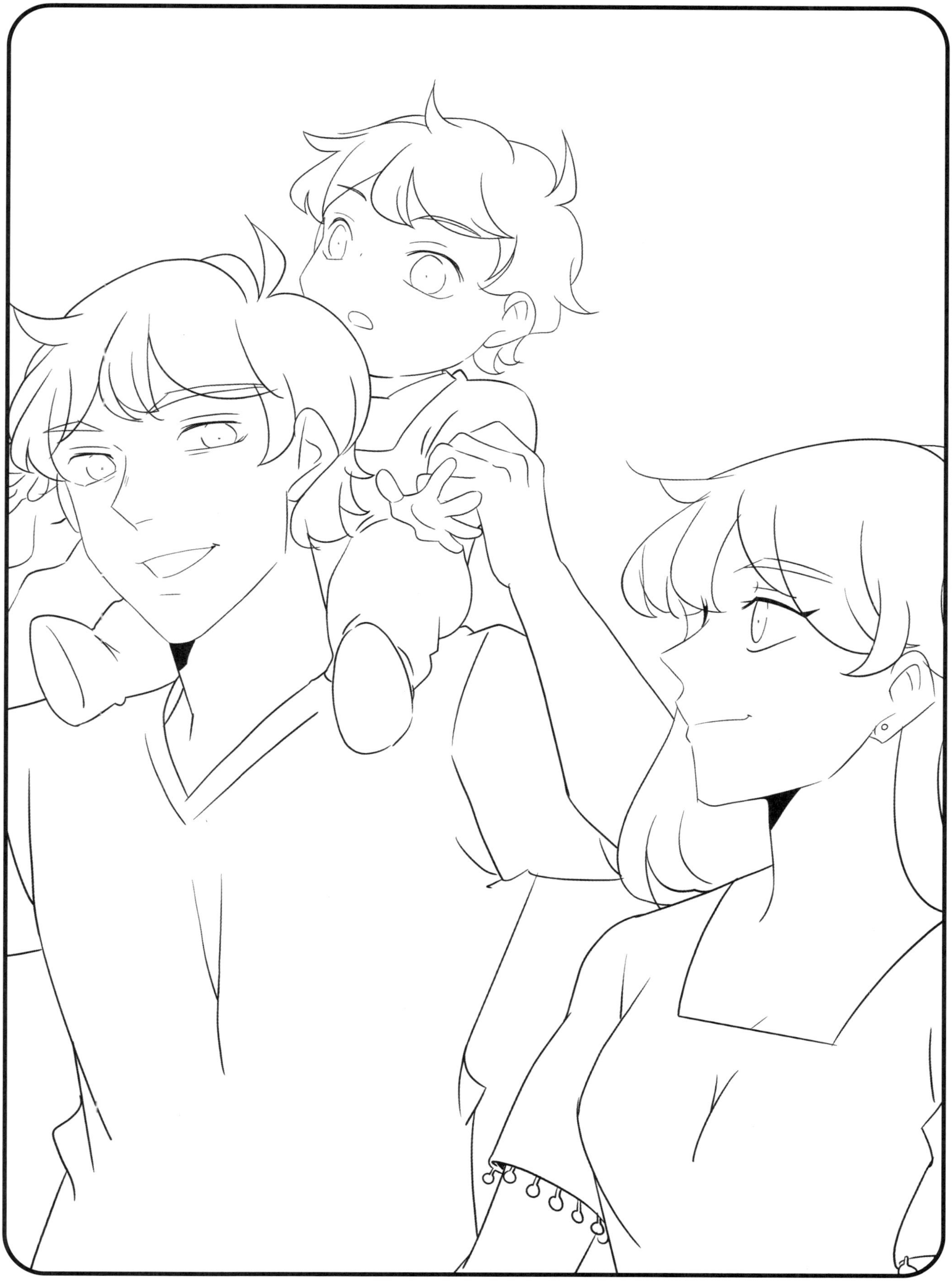

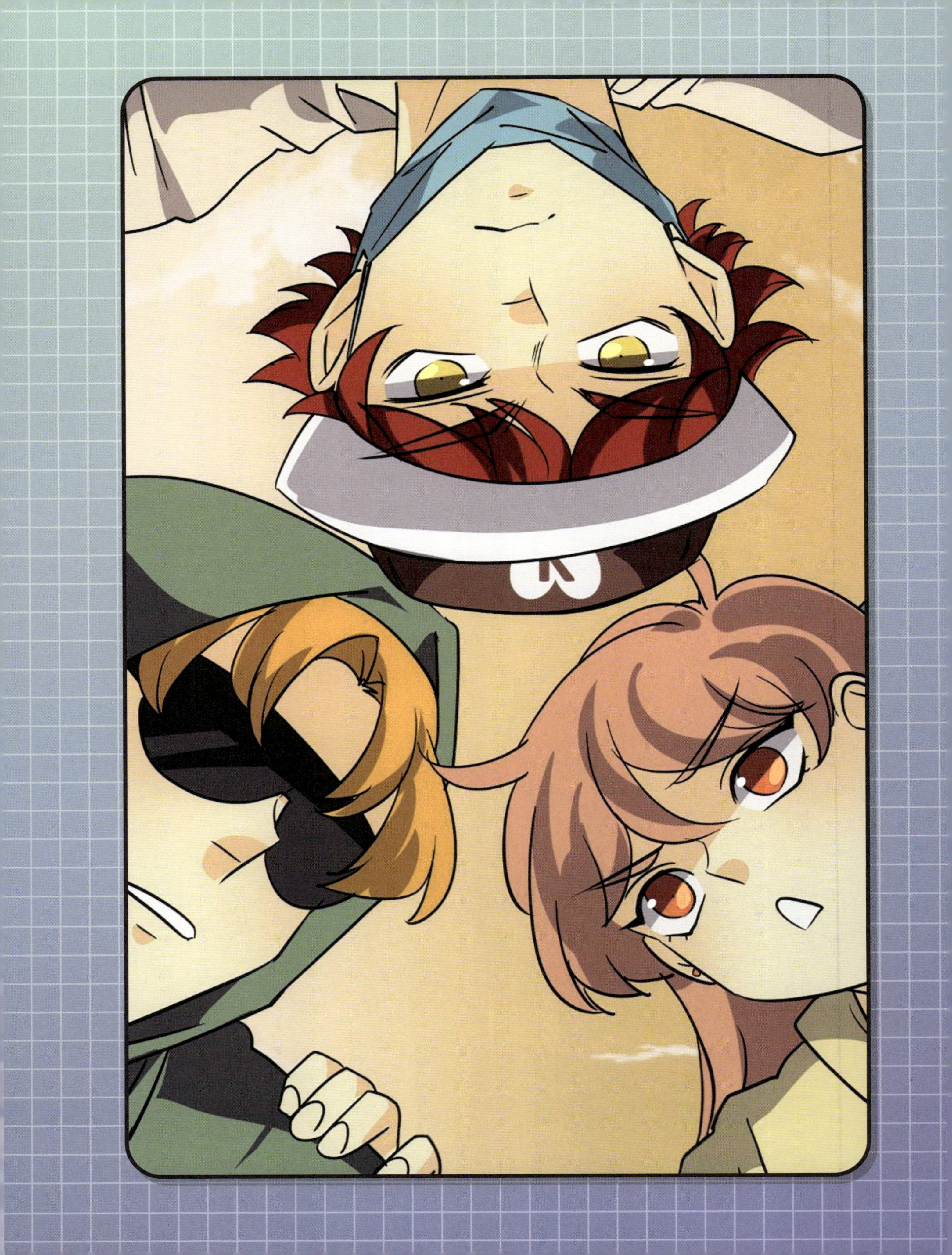

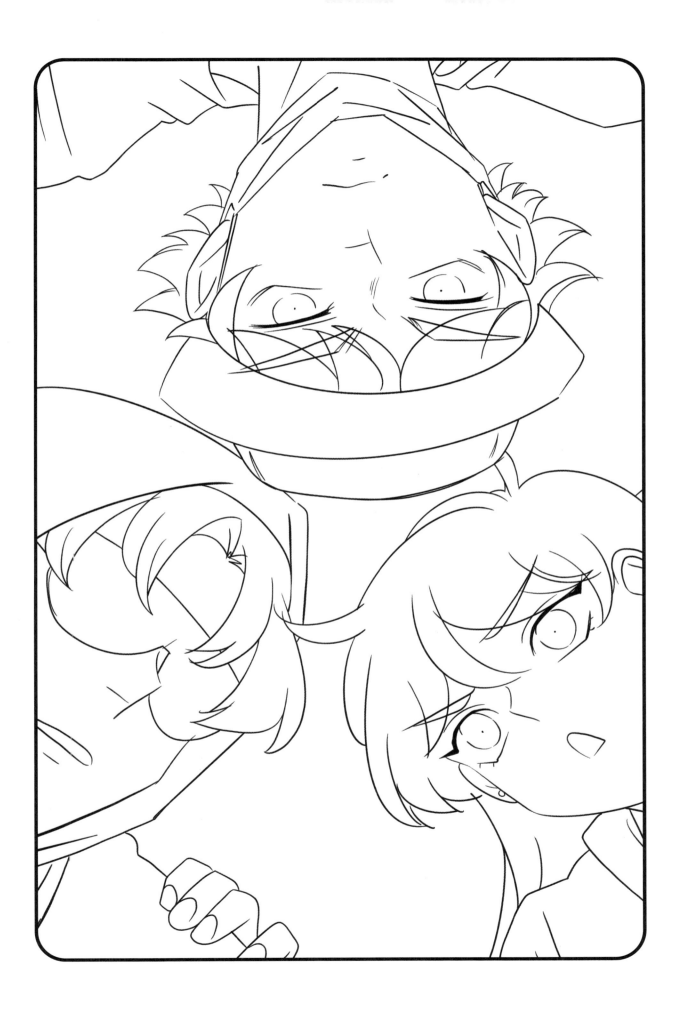

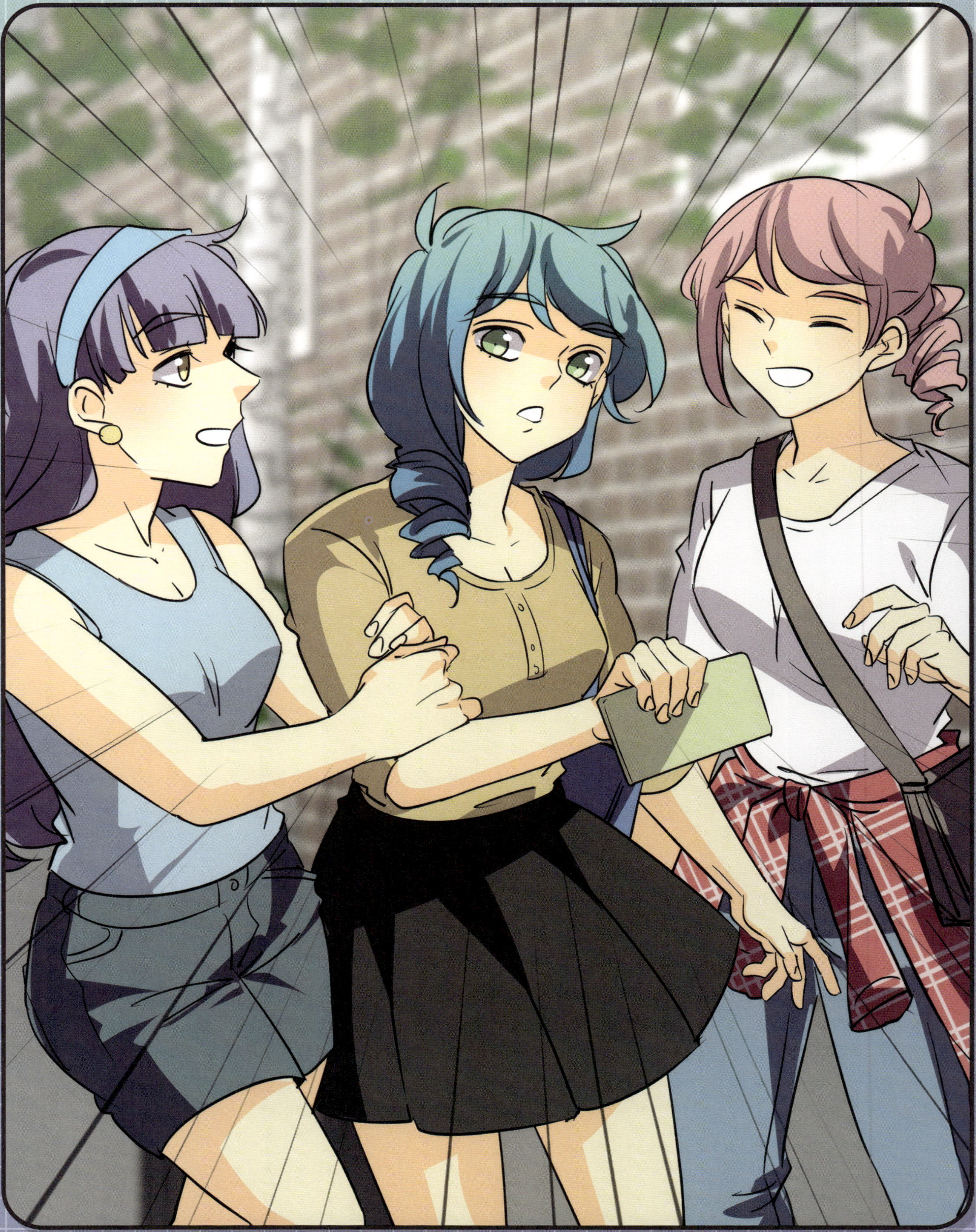

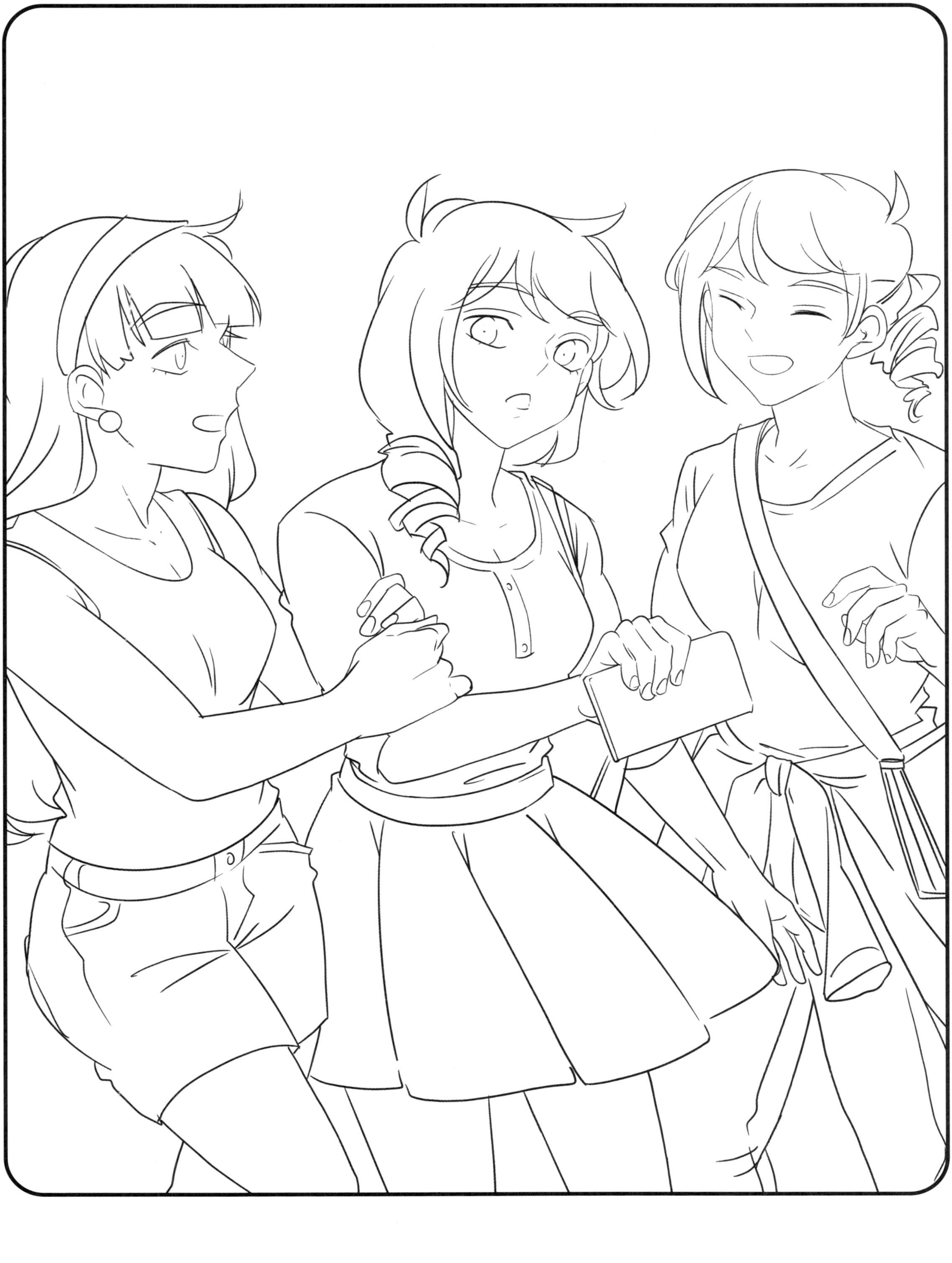

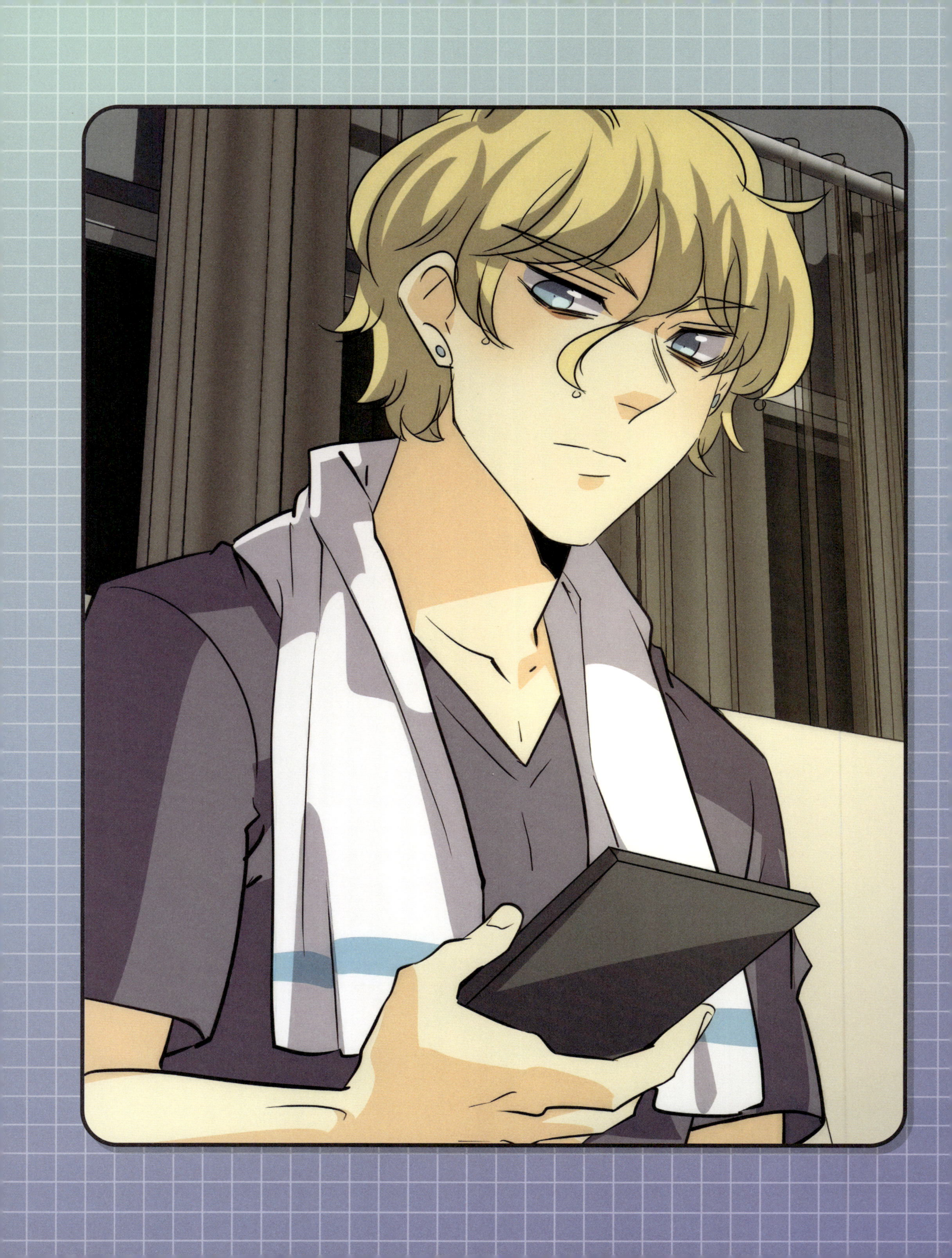

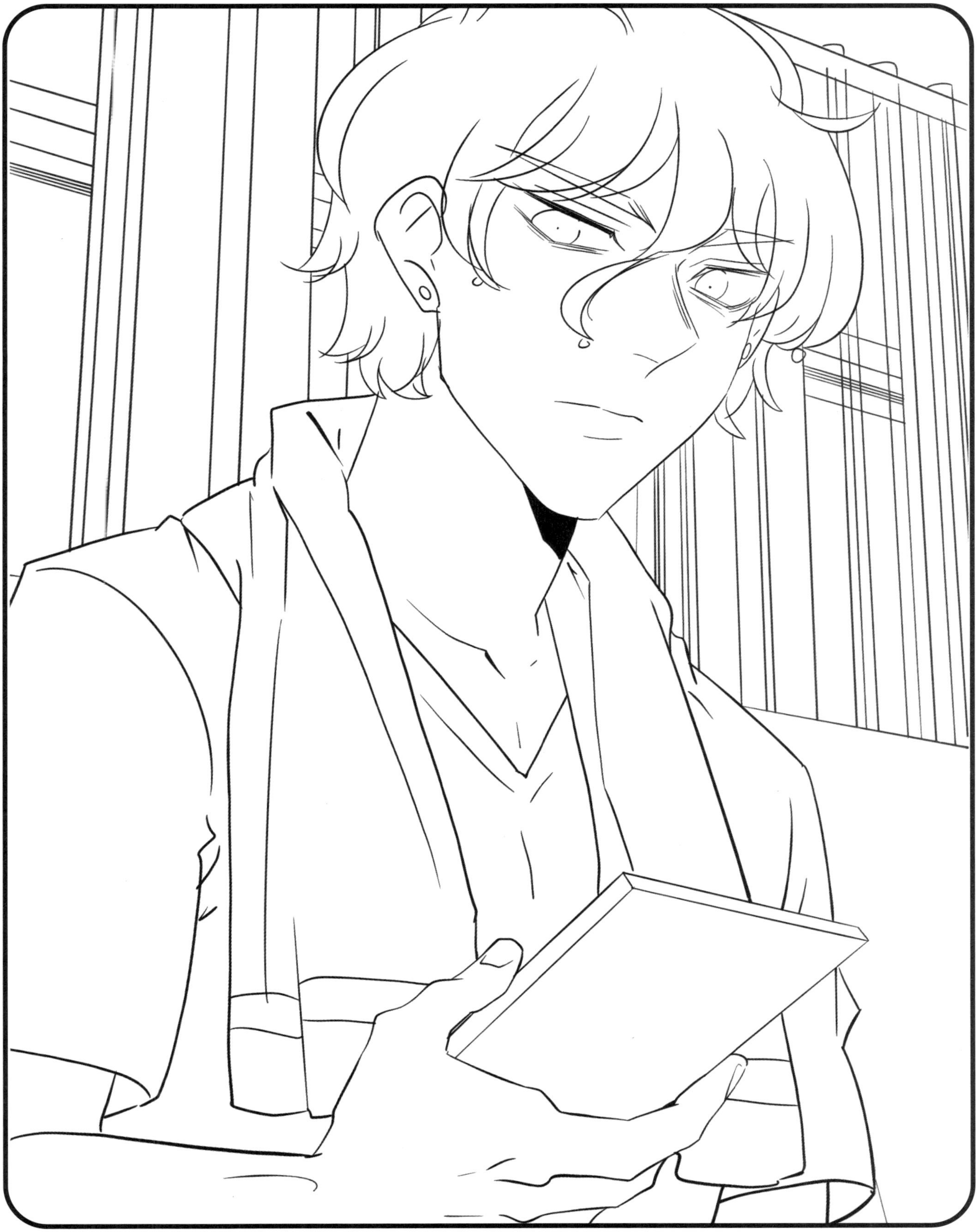

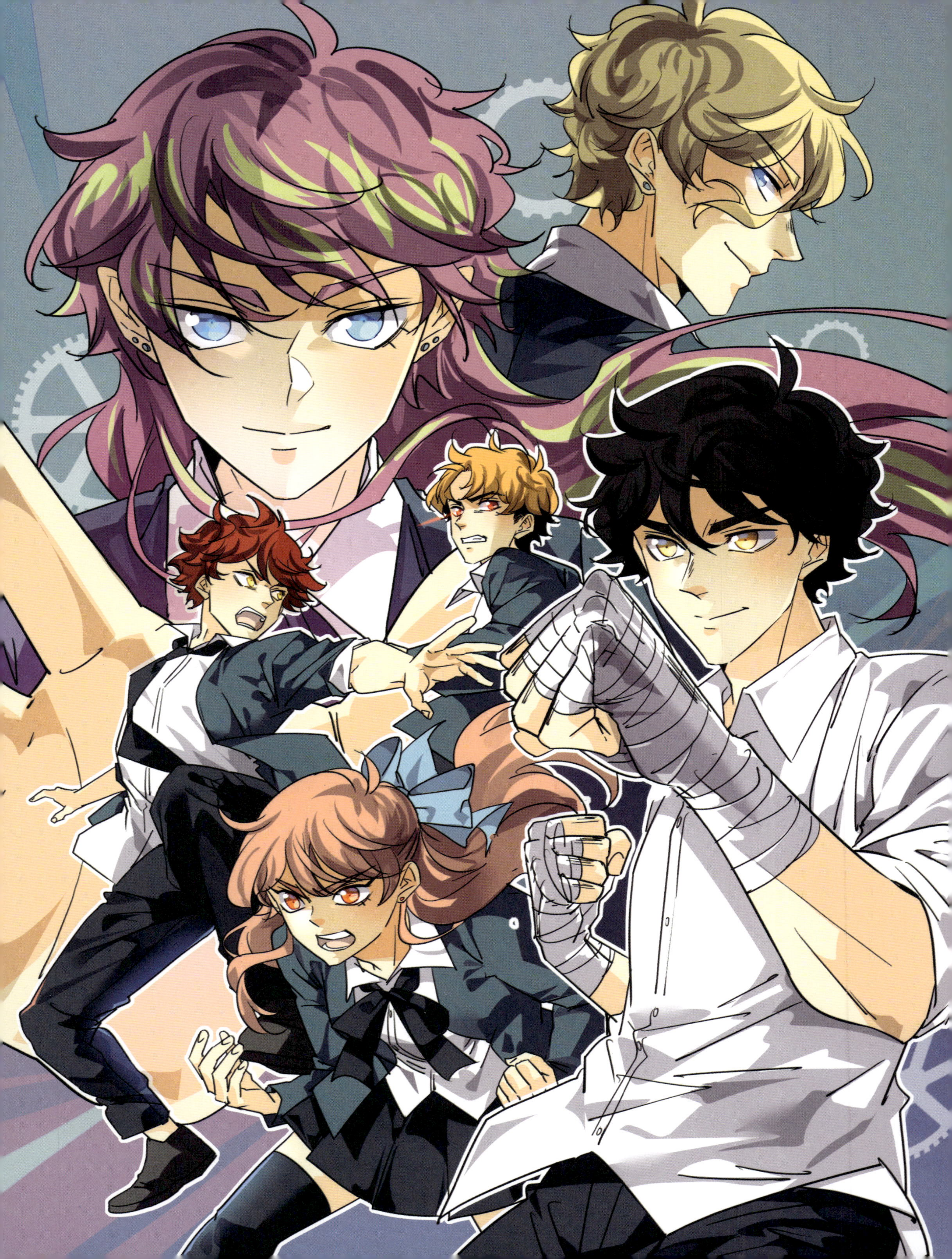

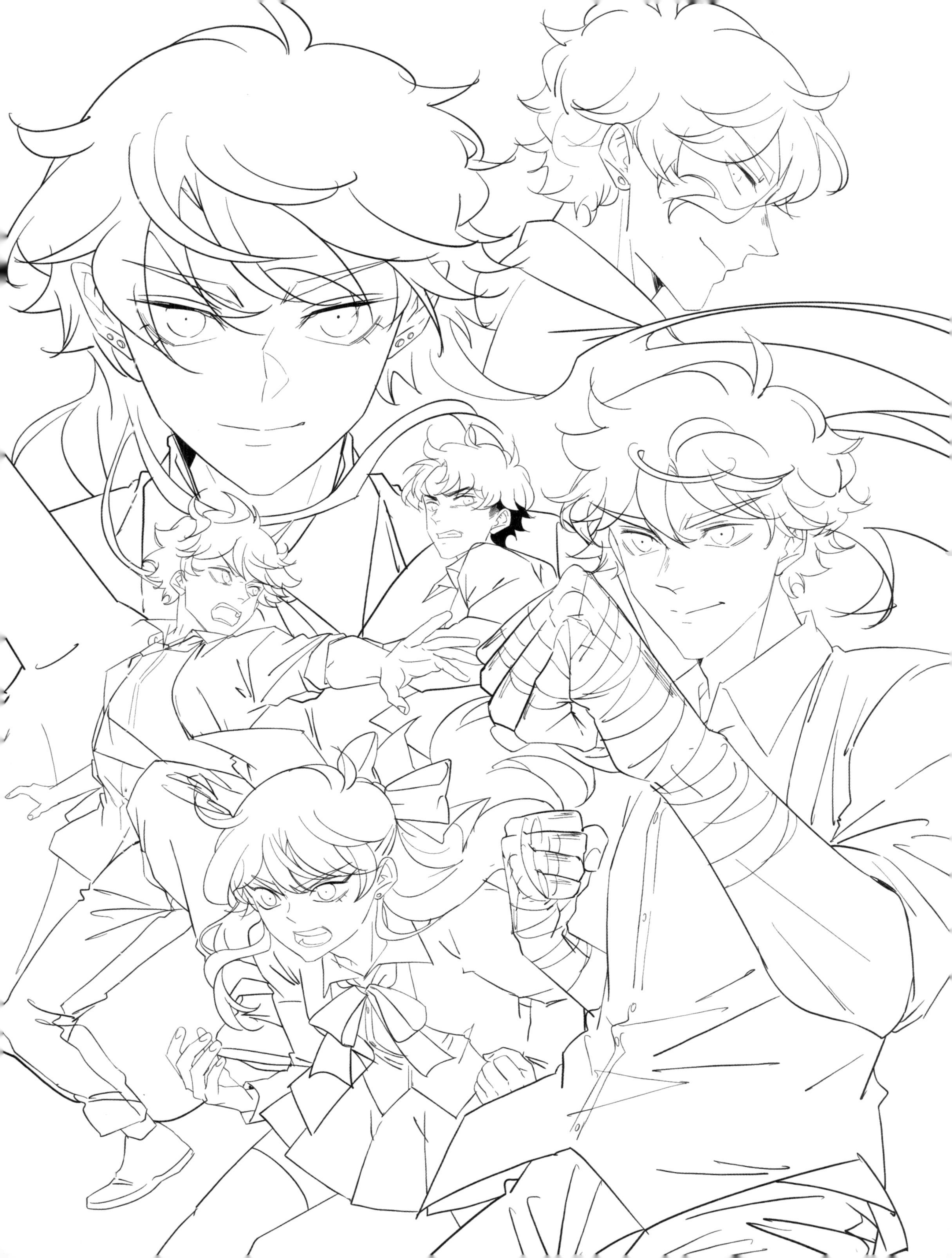

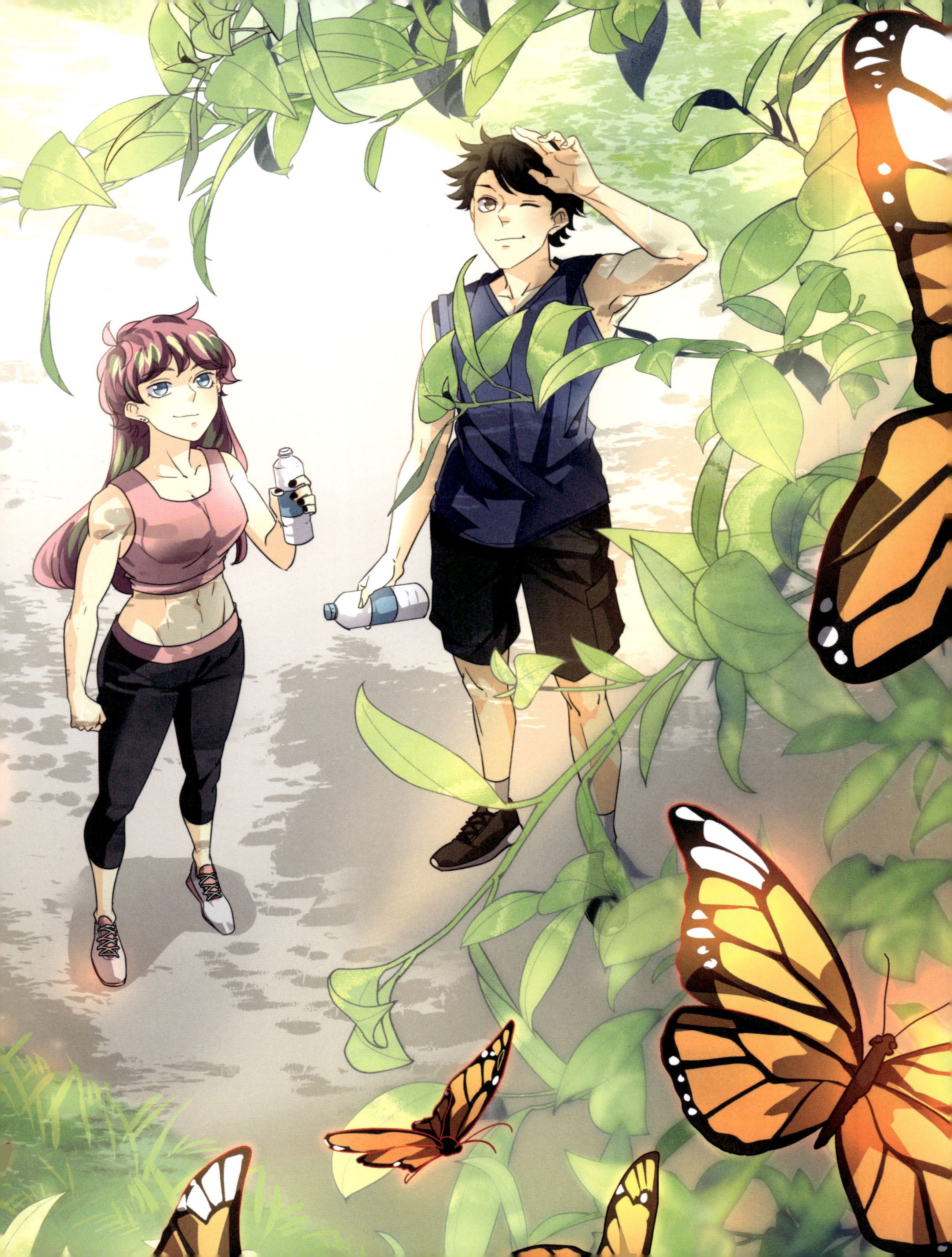

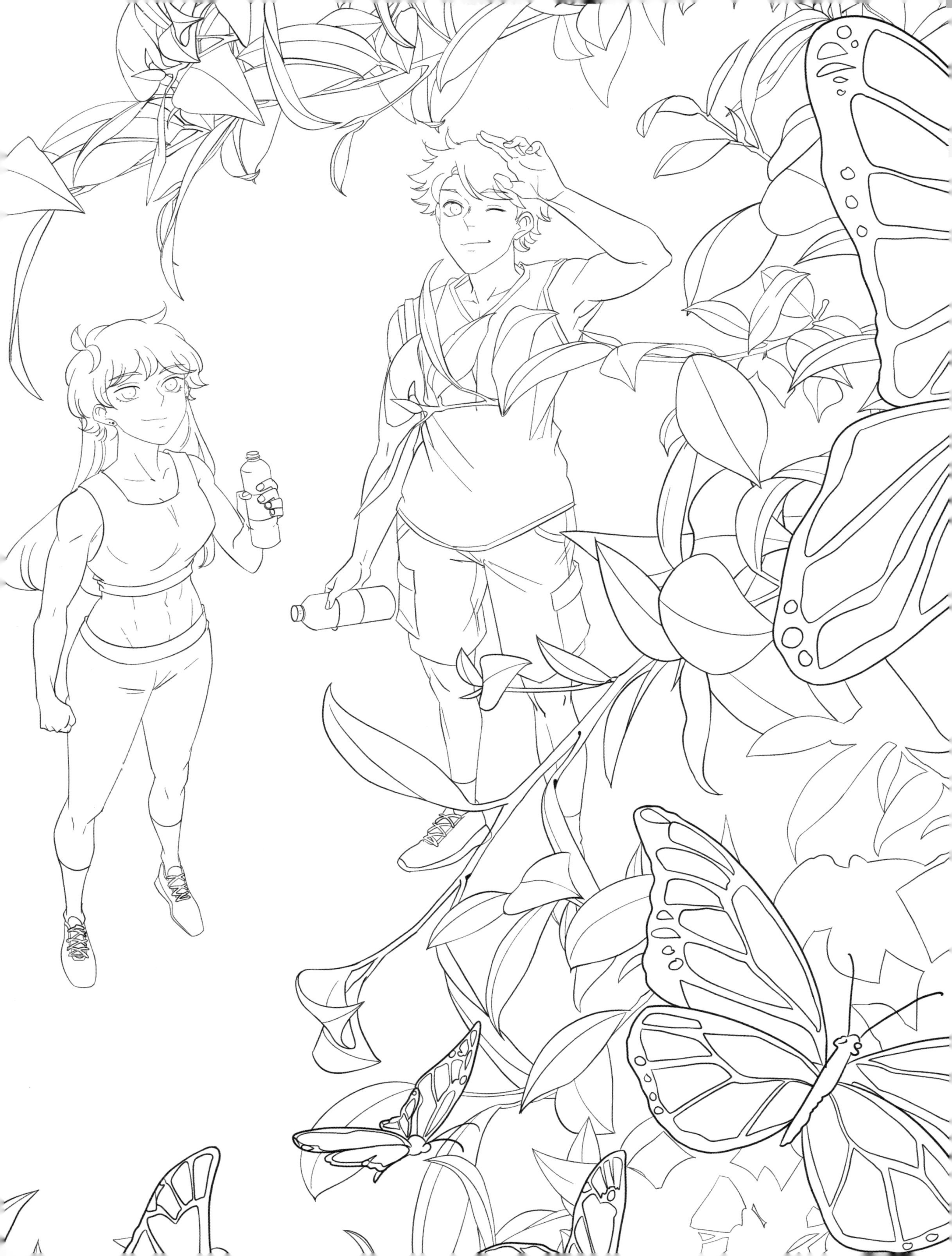

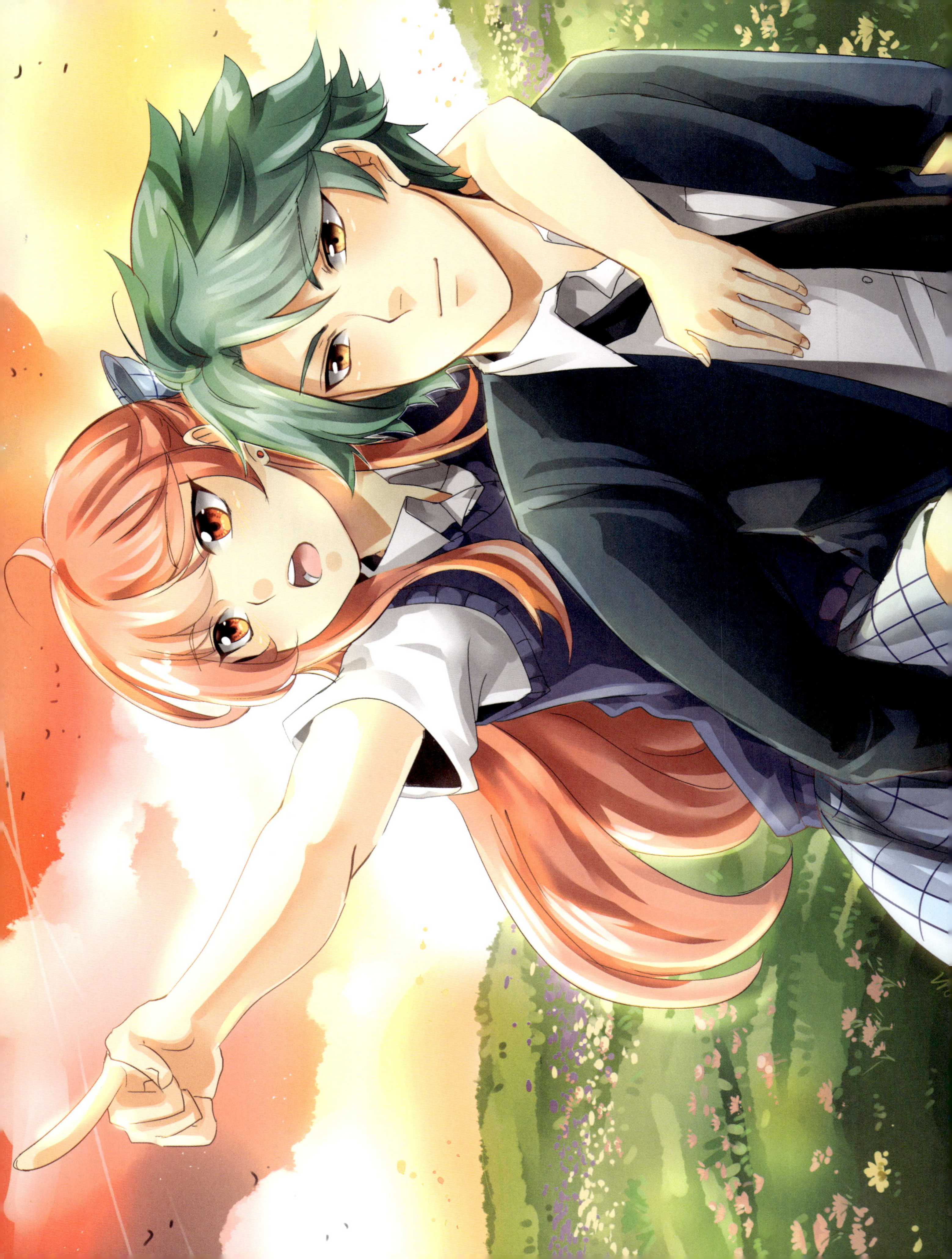

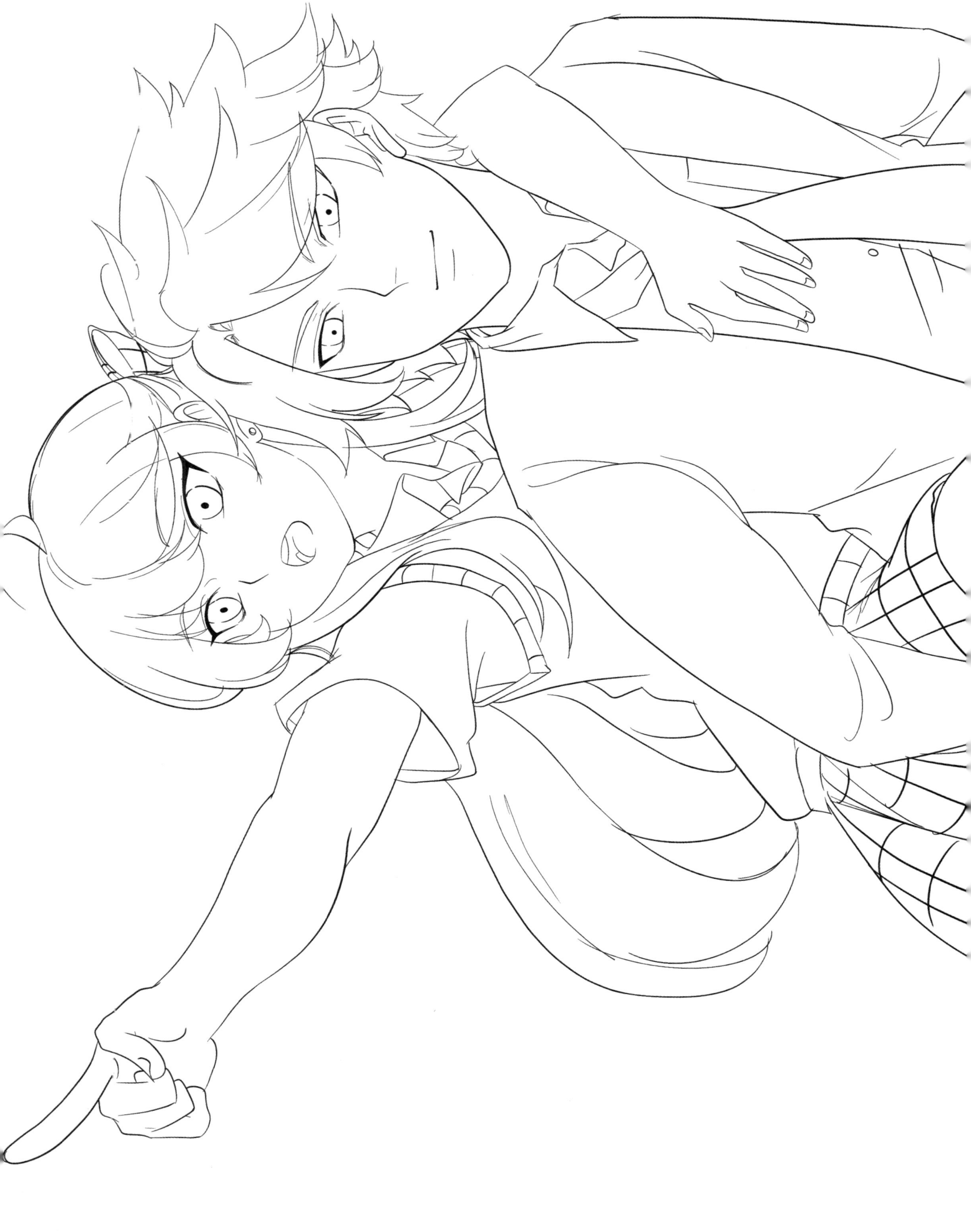

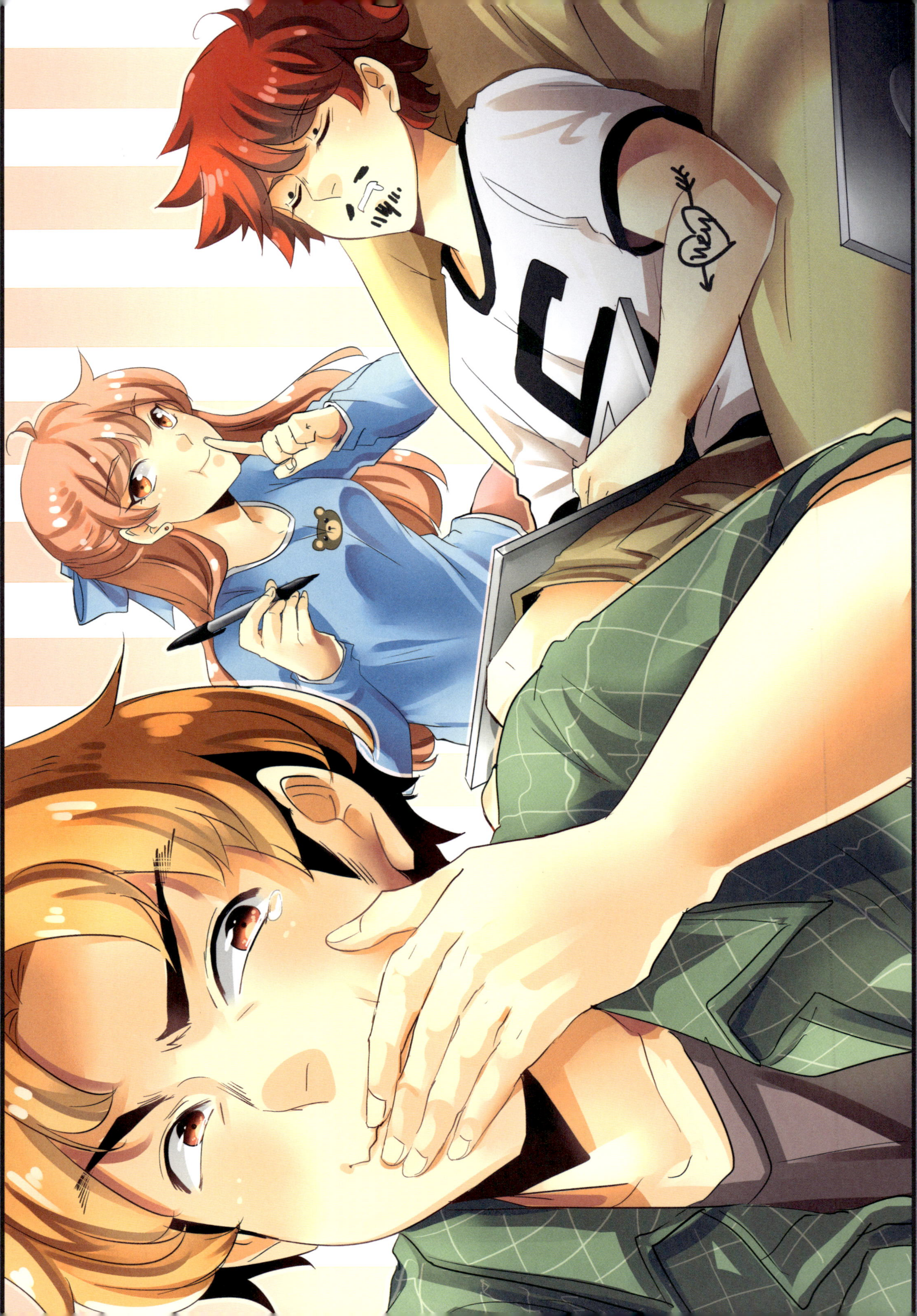

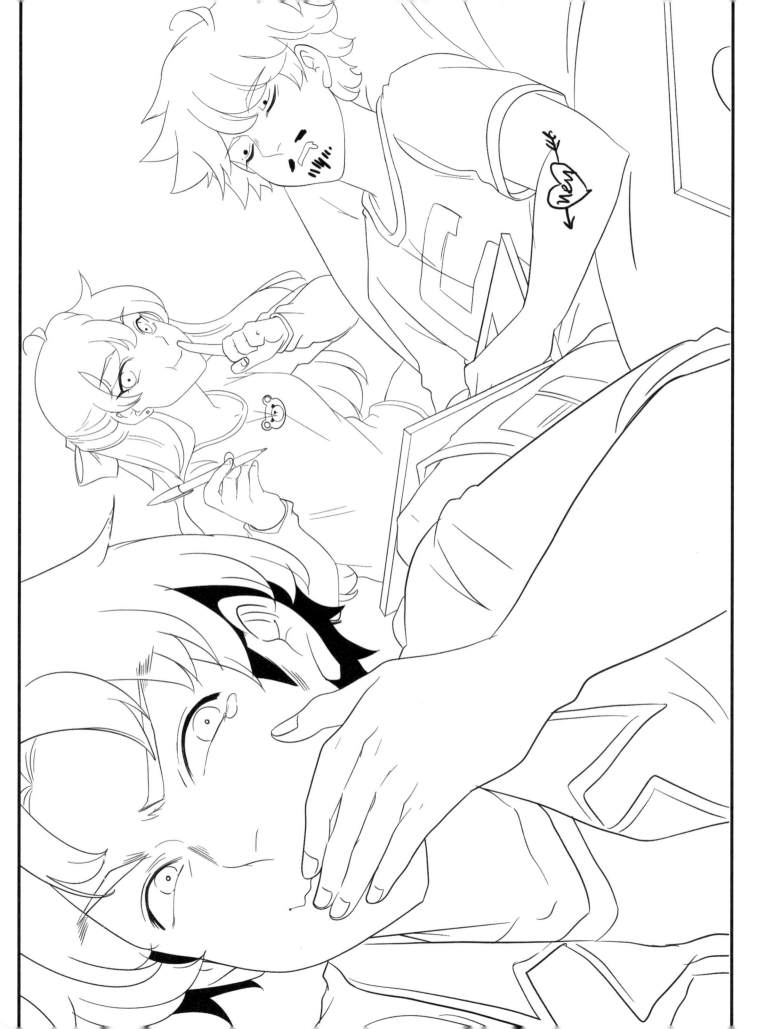

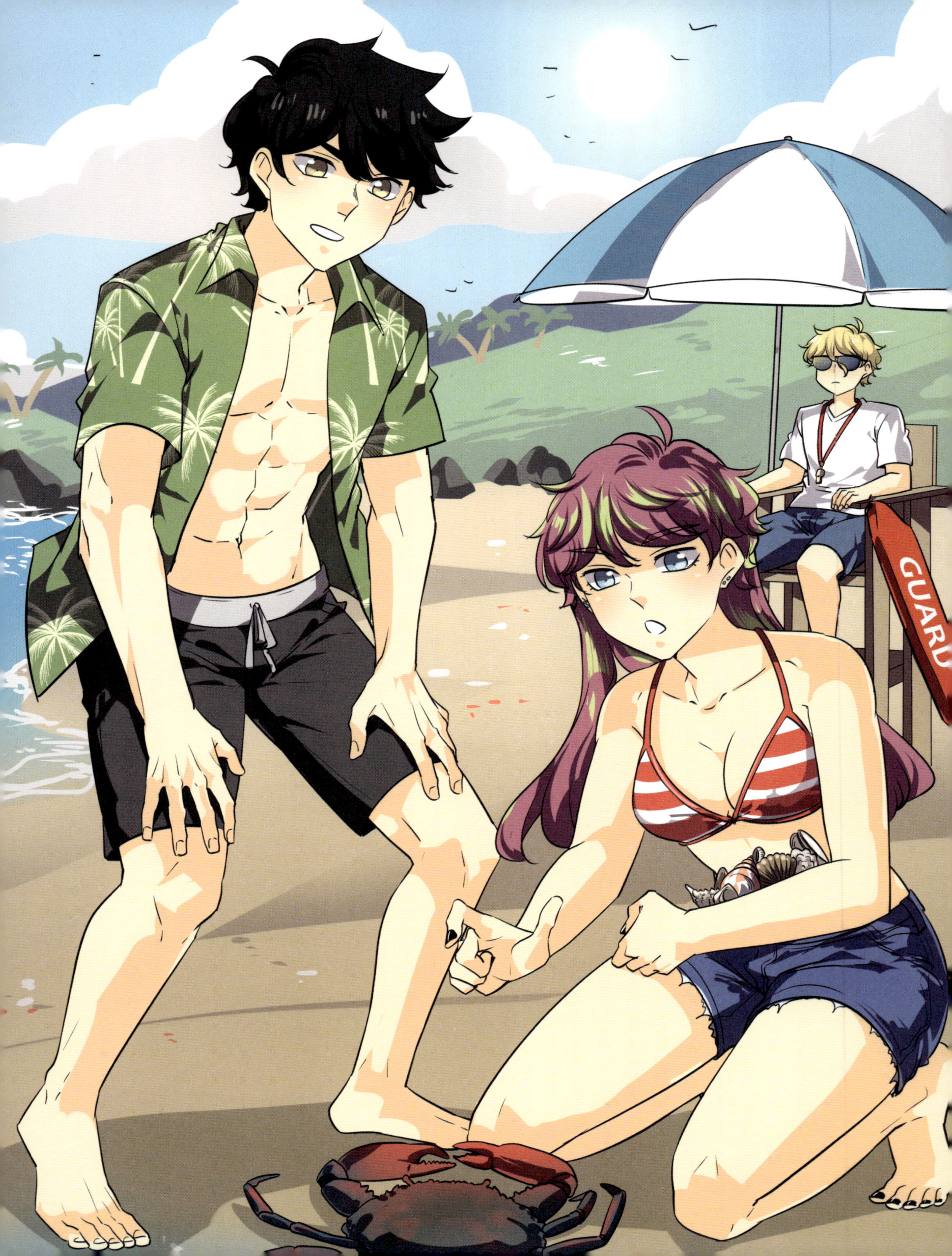
GUARD

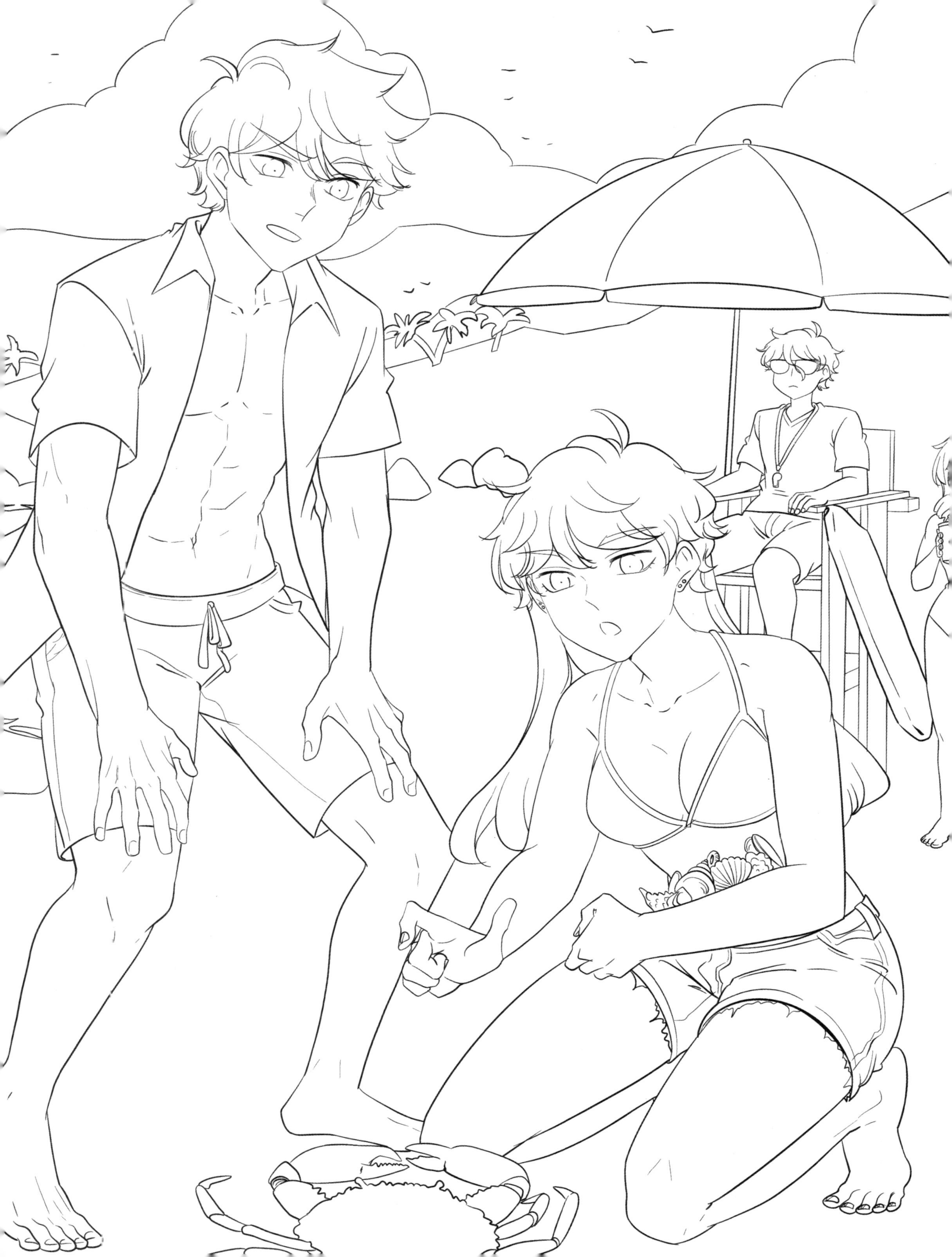

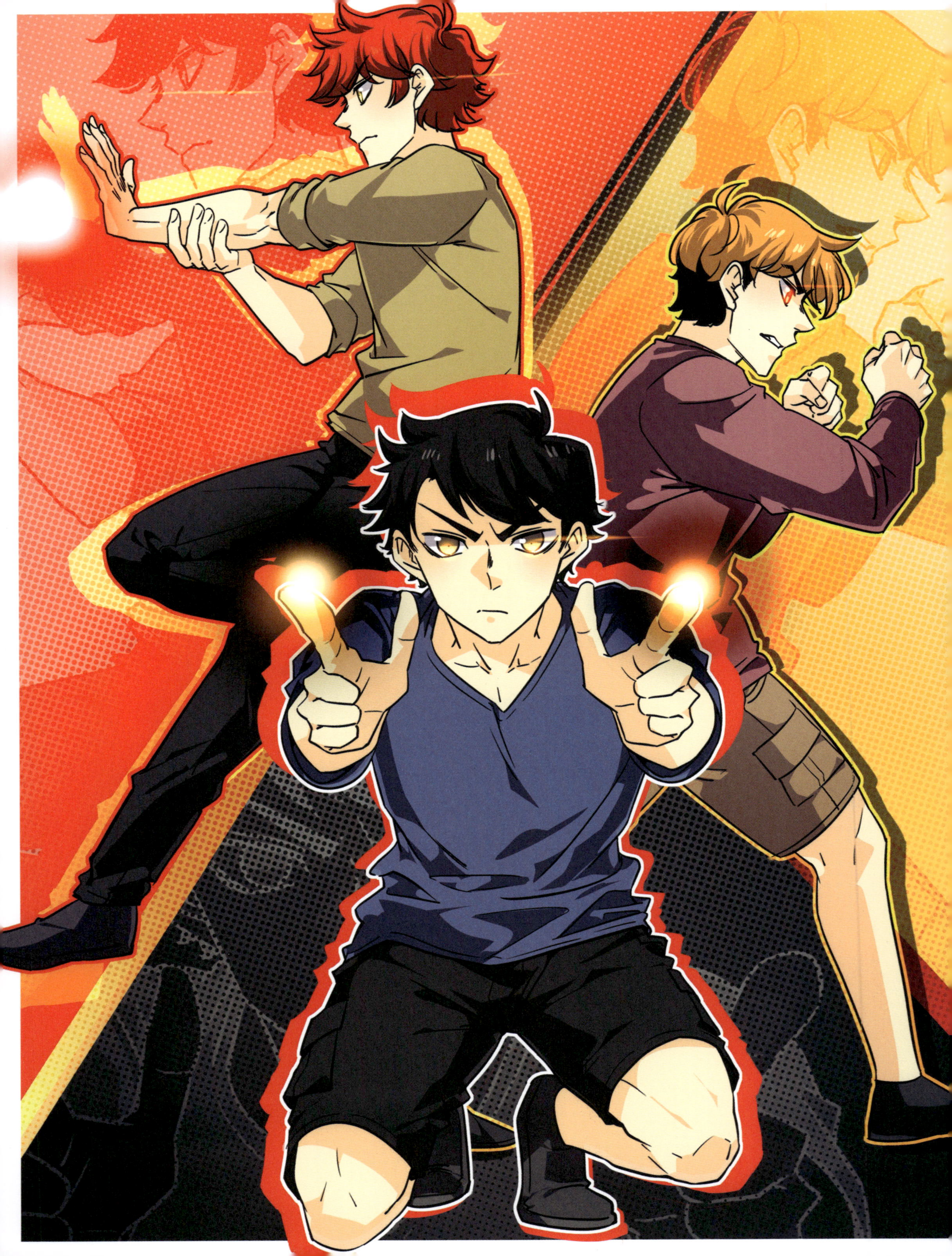

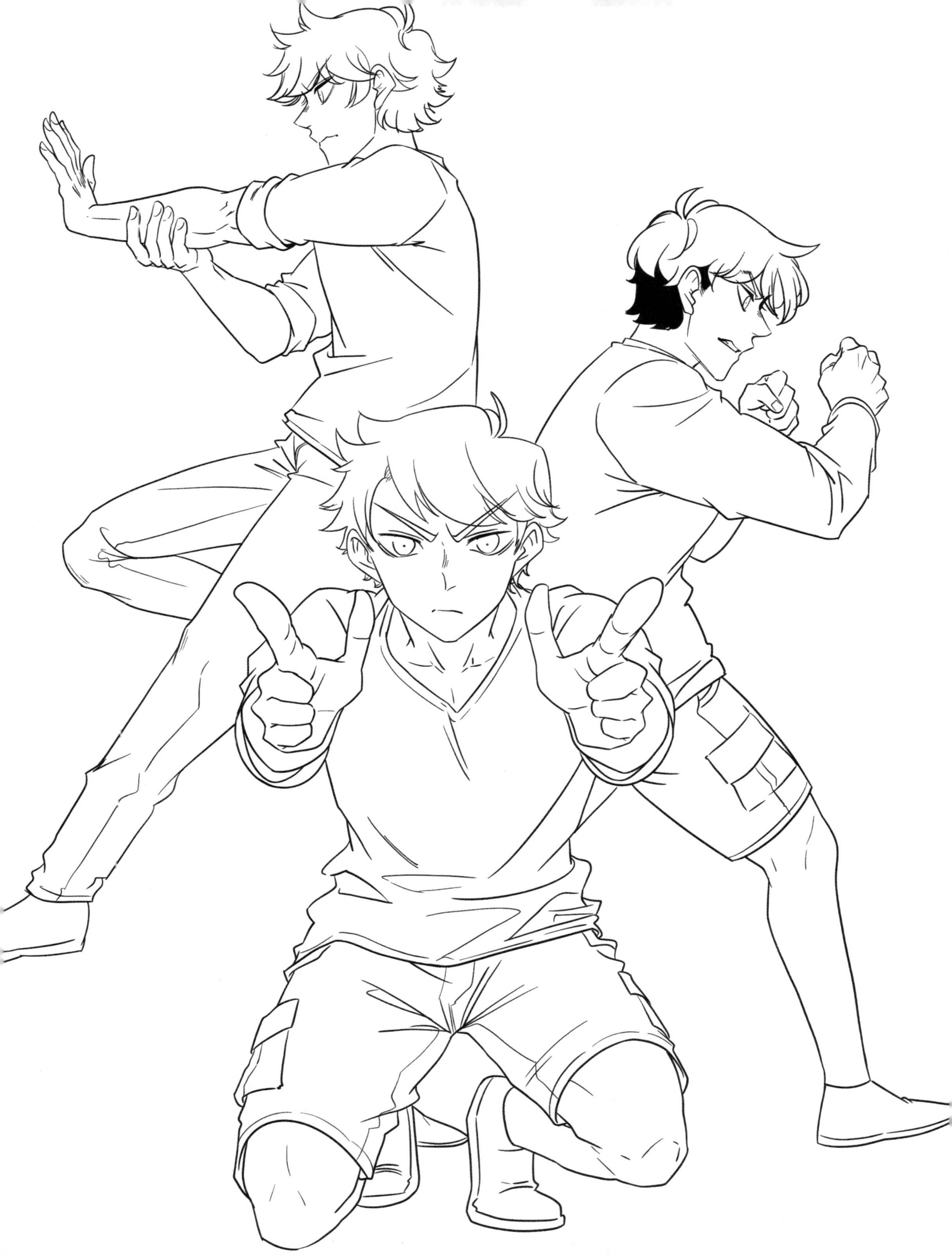

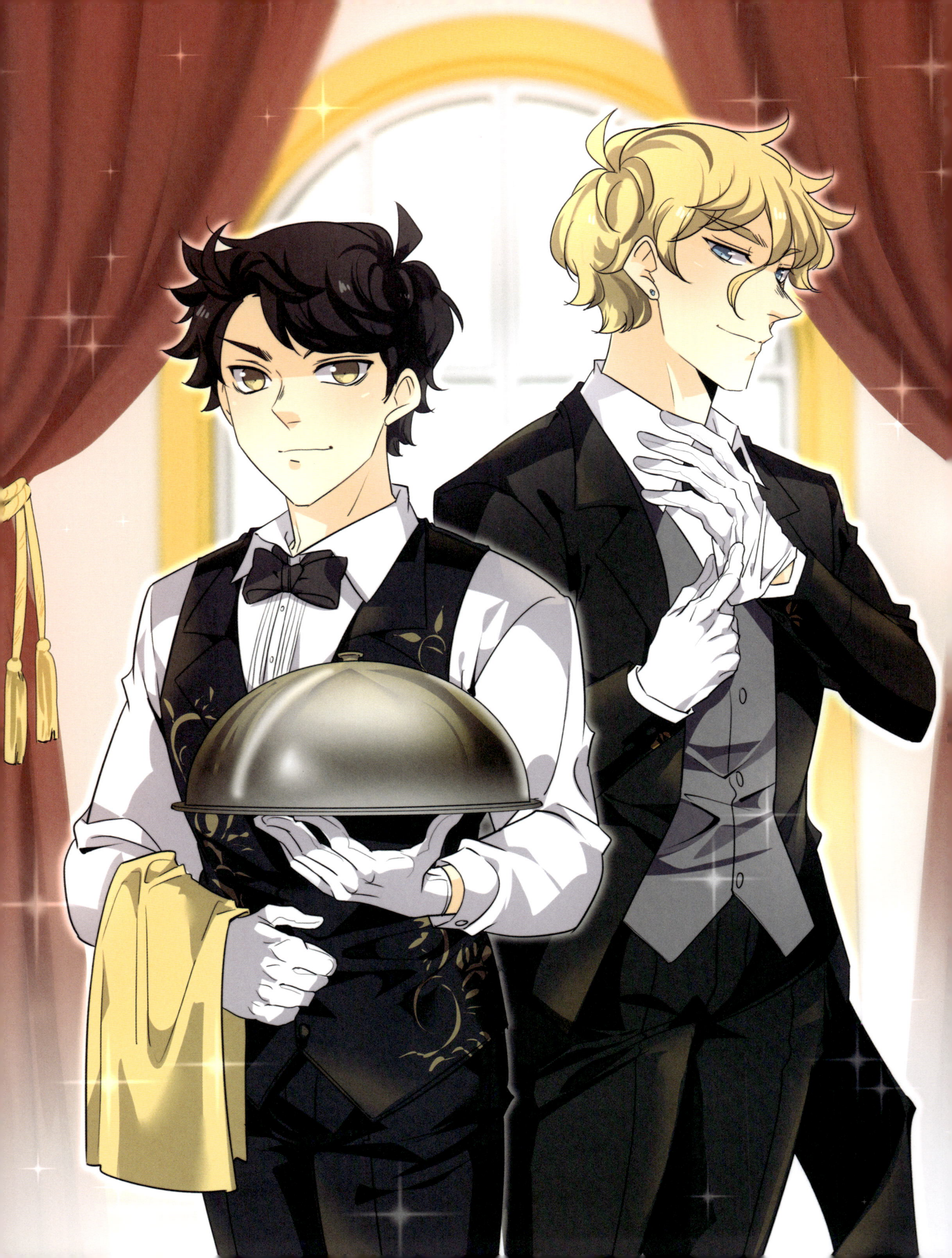

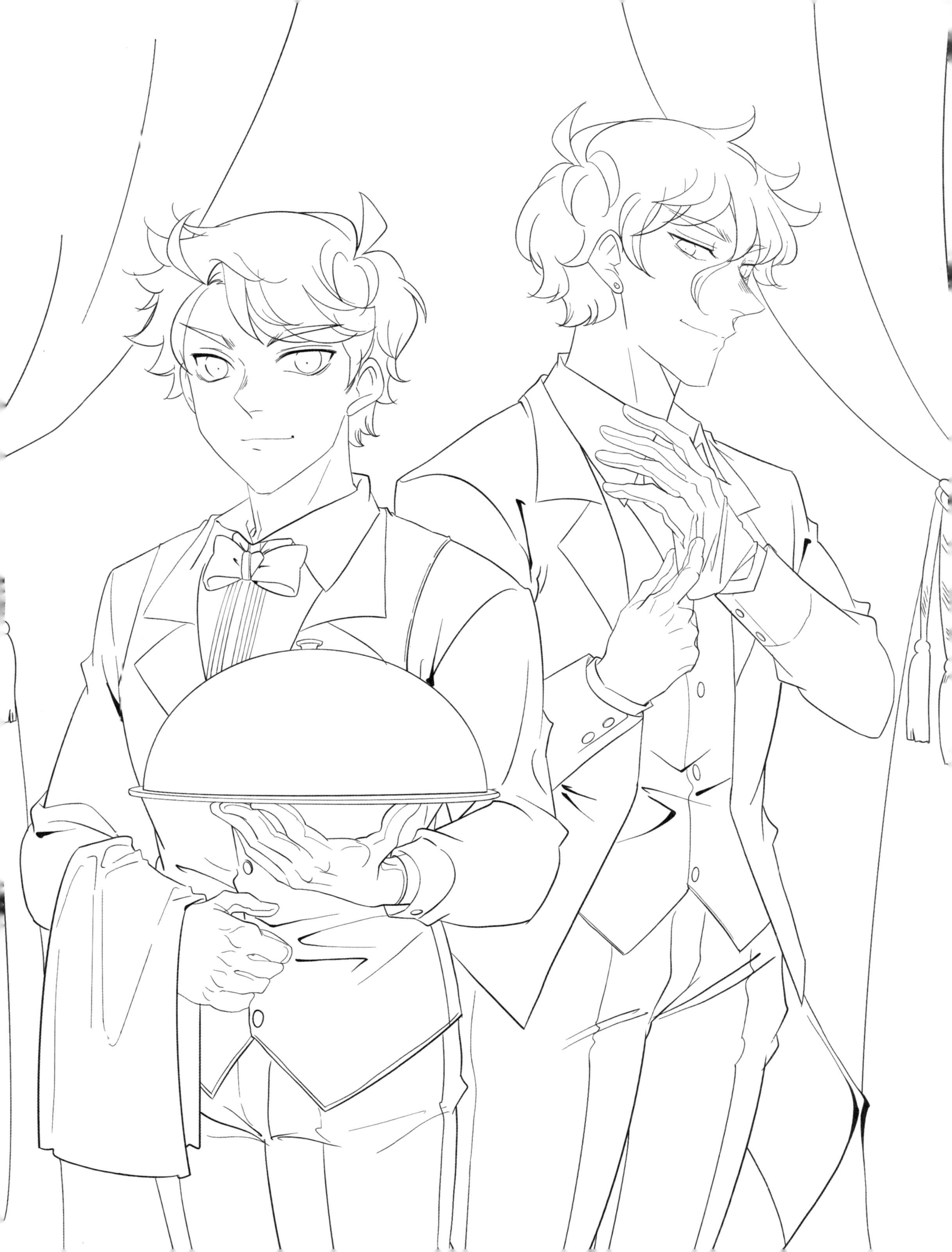

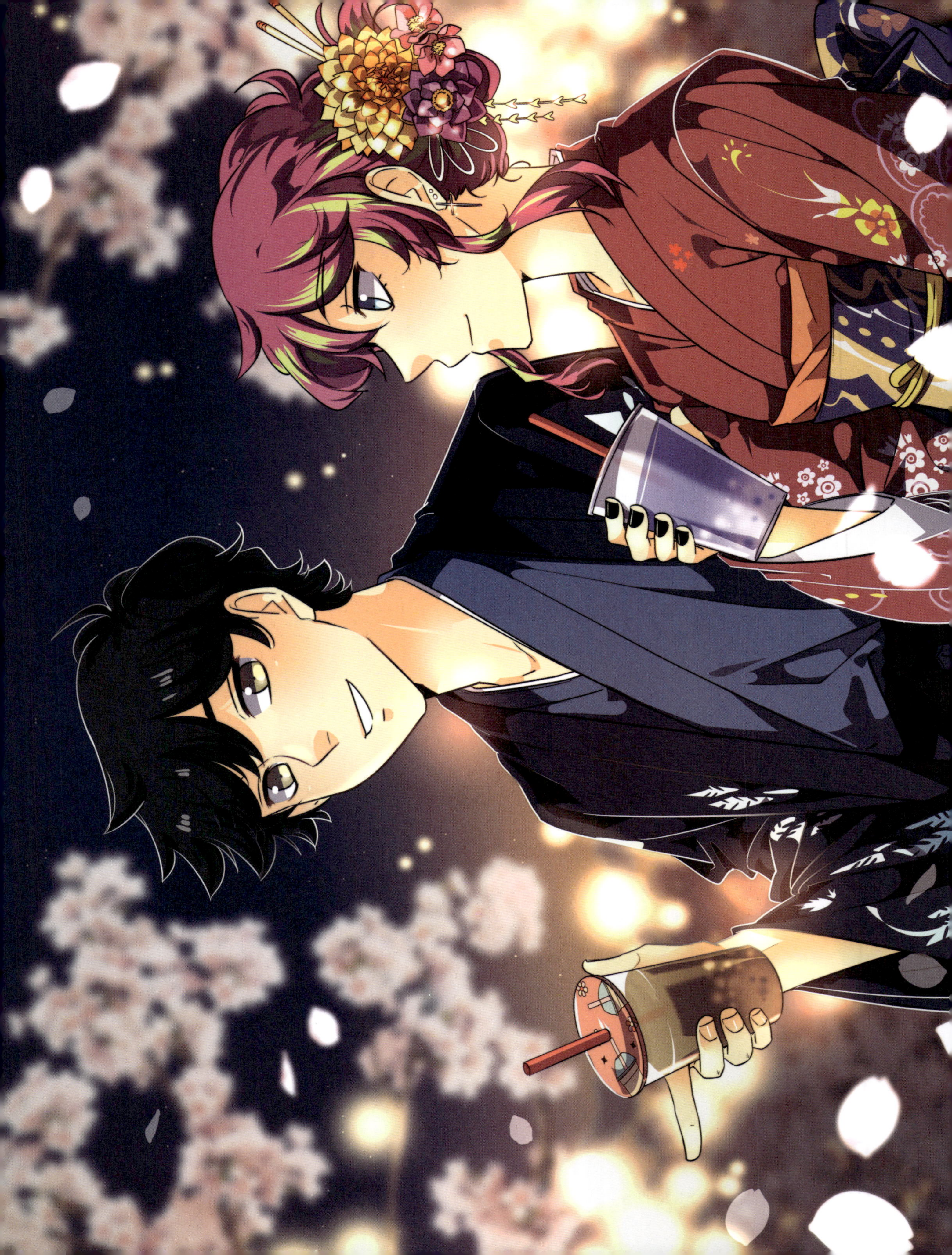

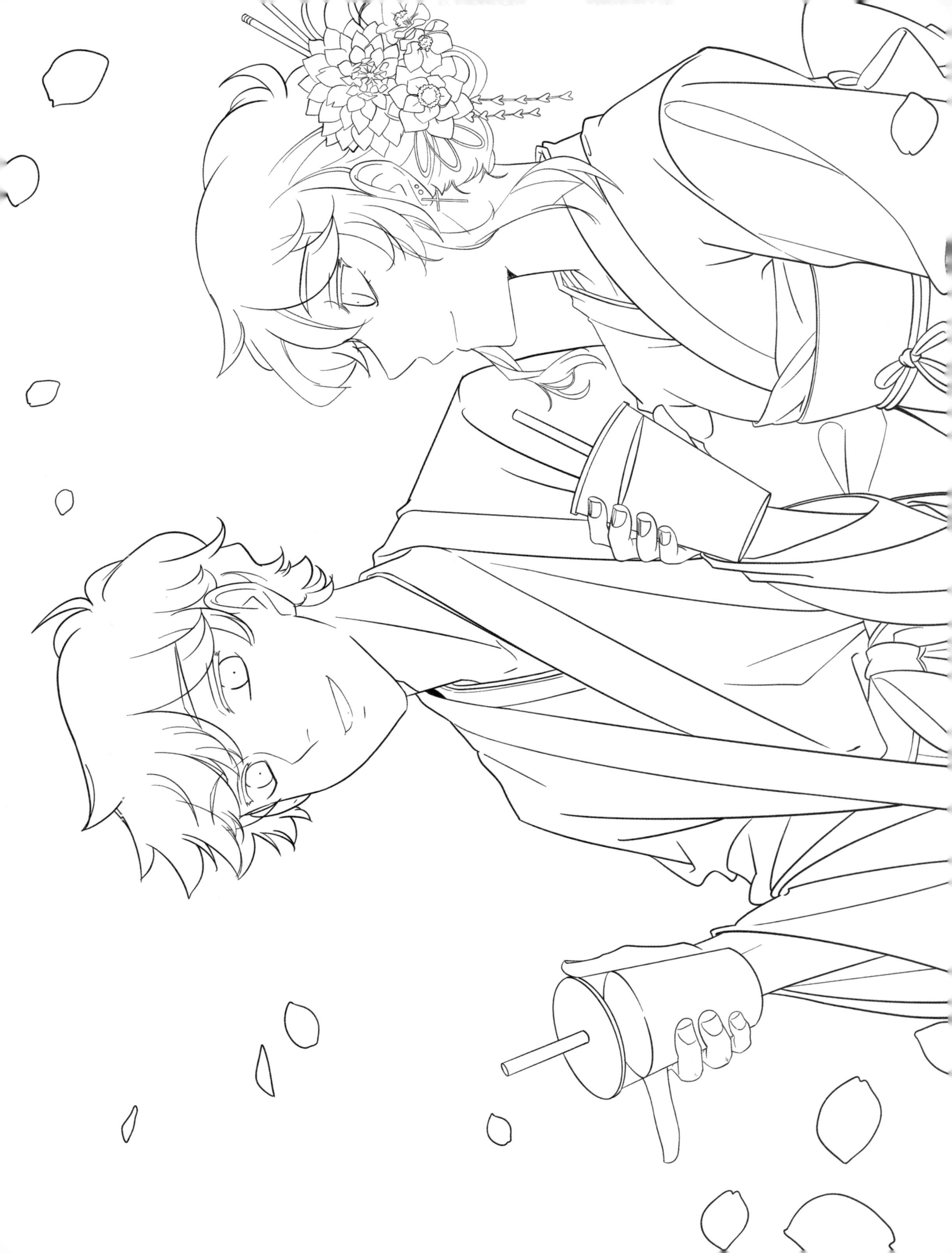

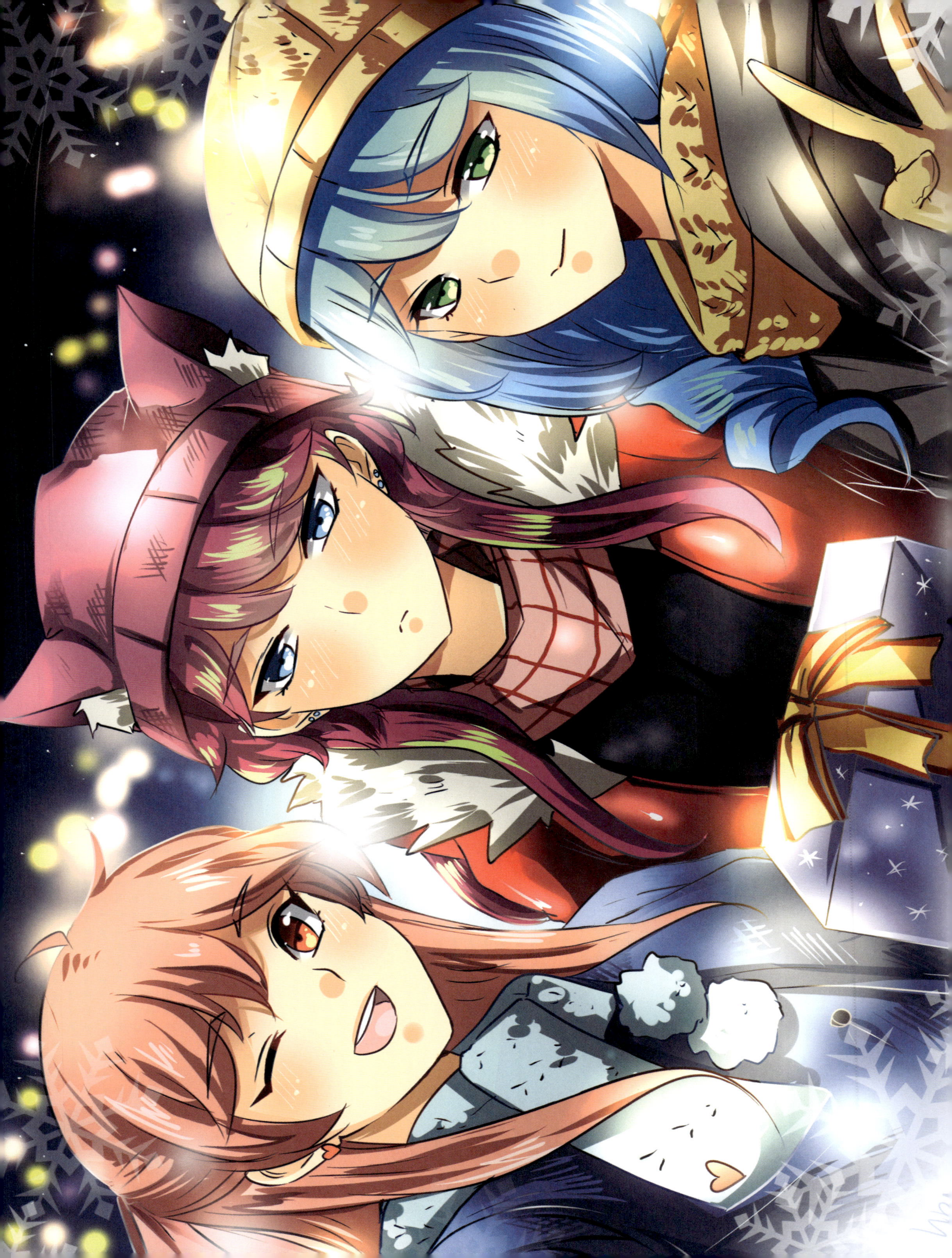

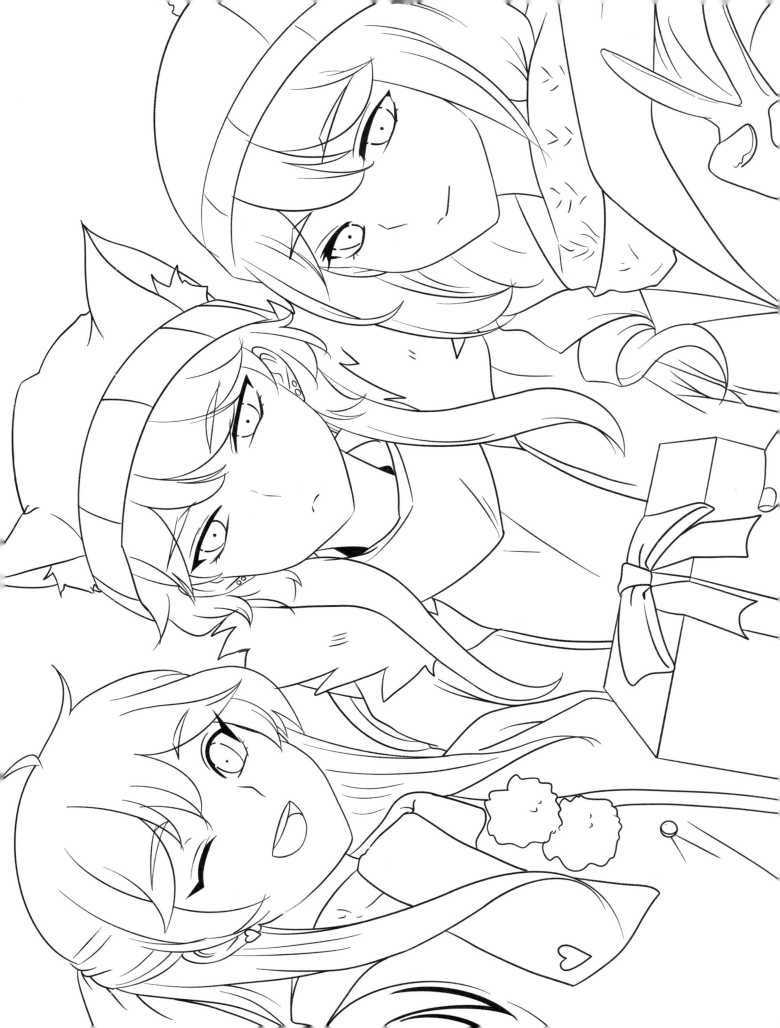

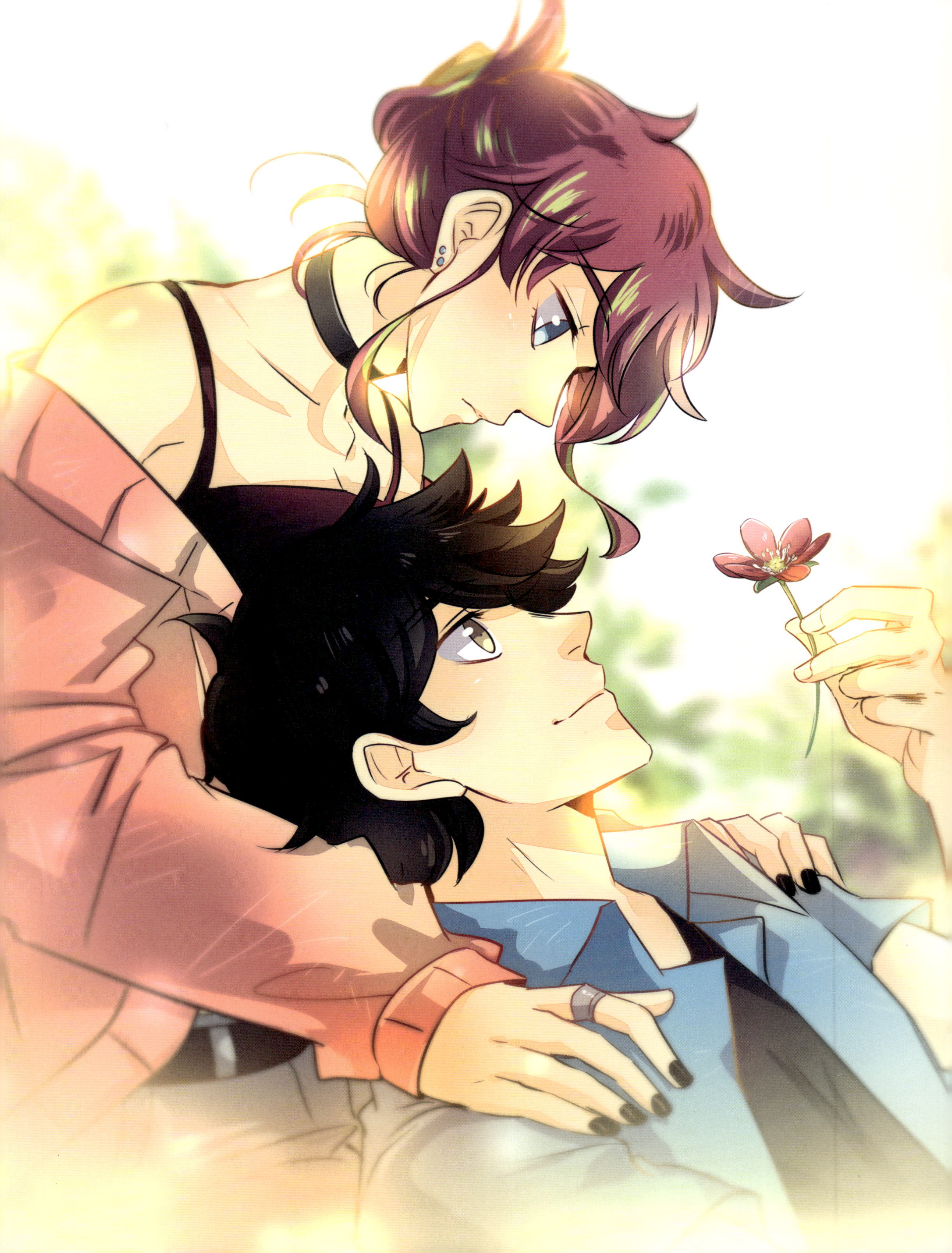

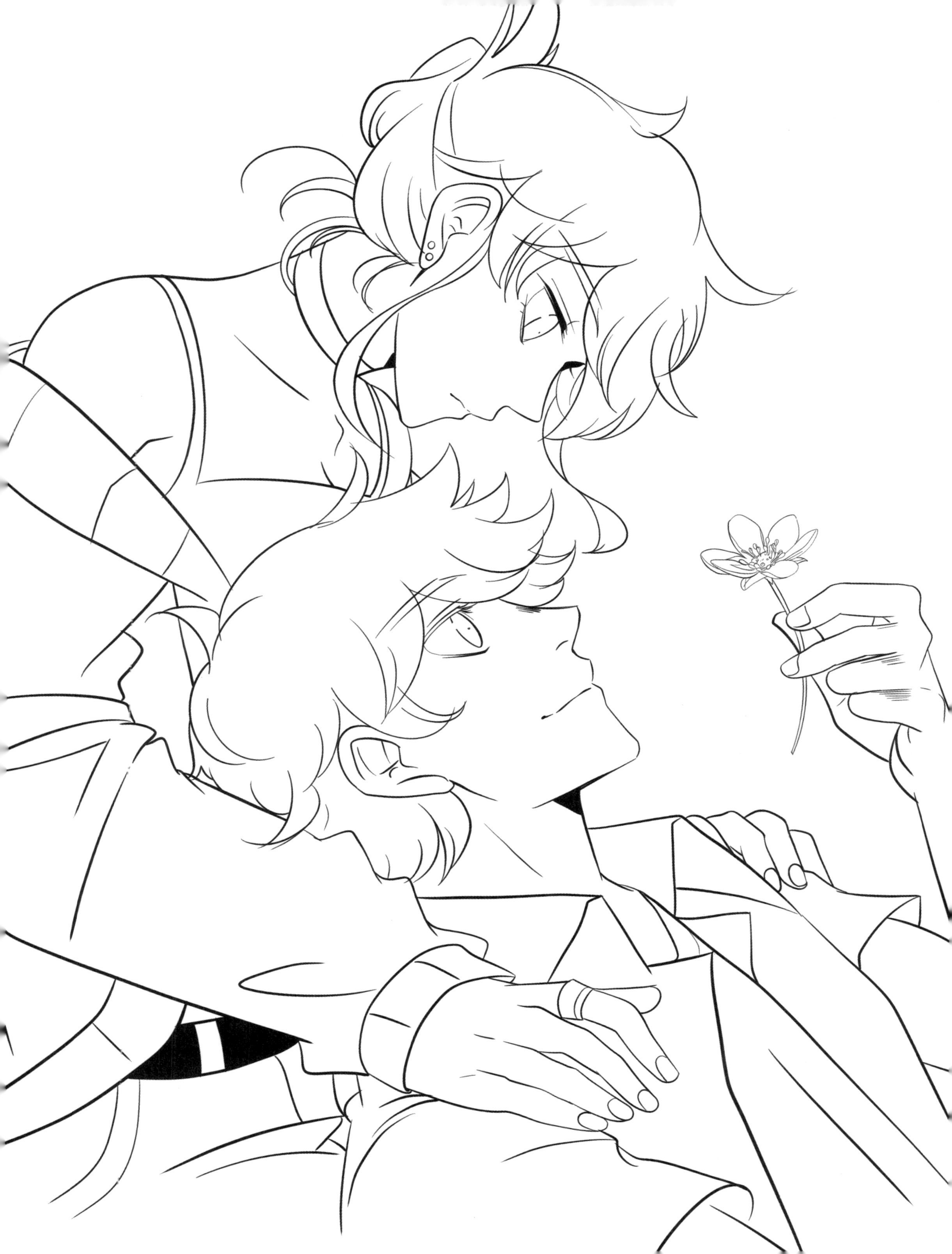

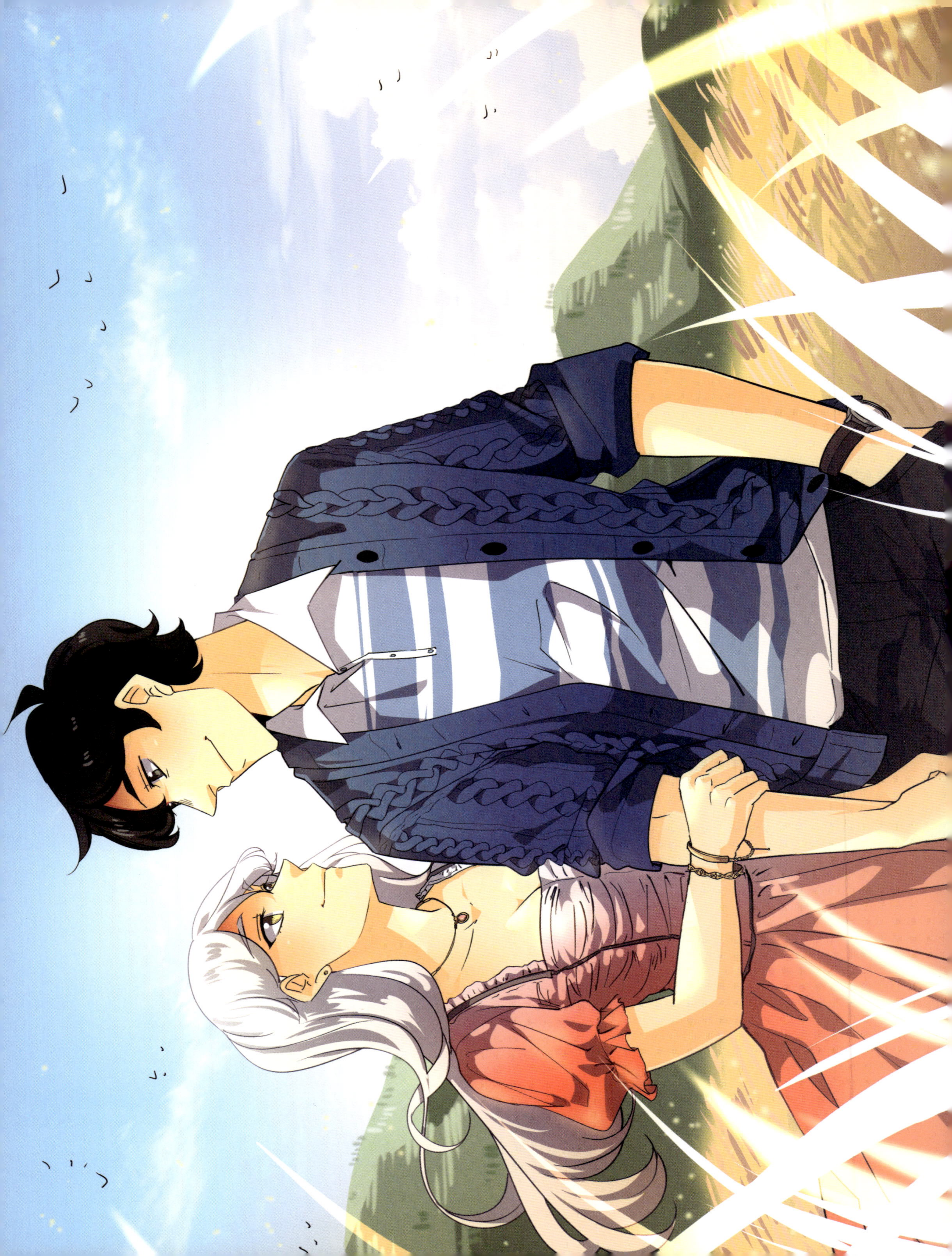

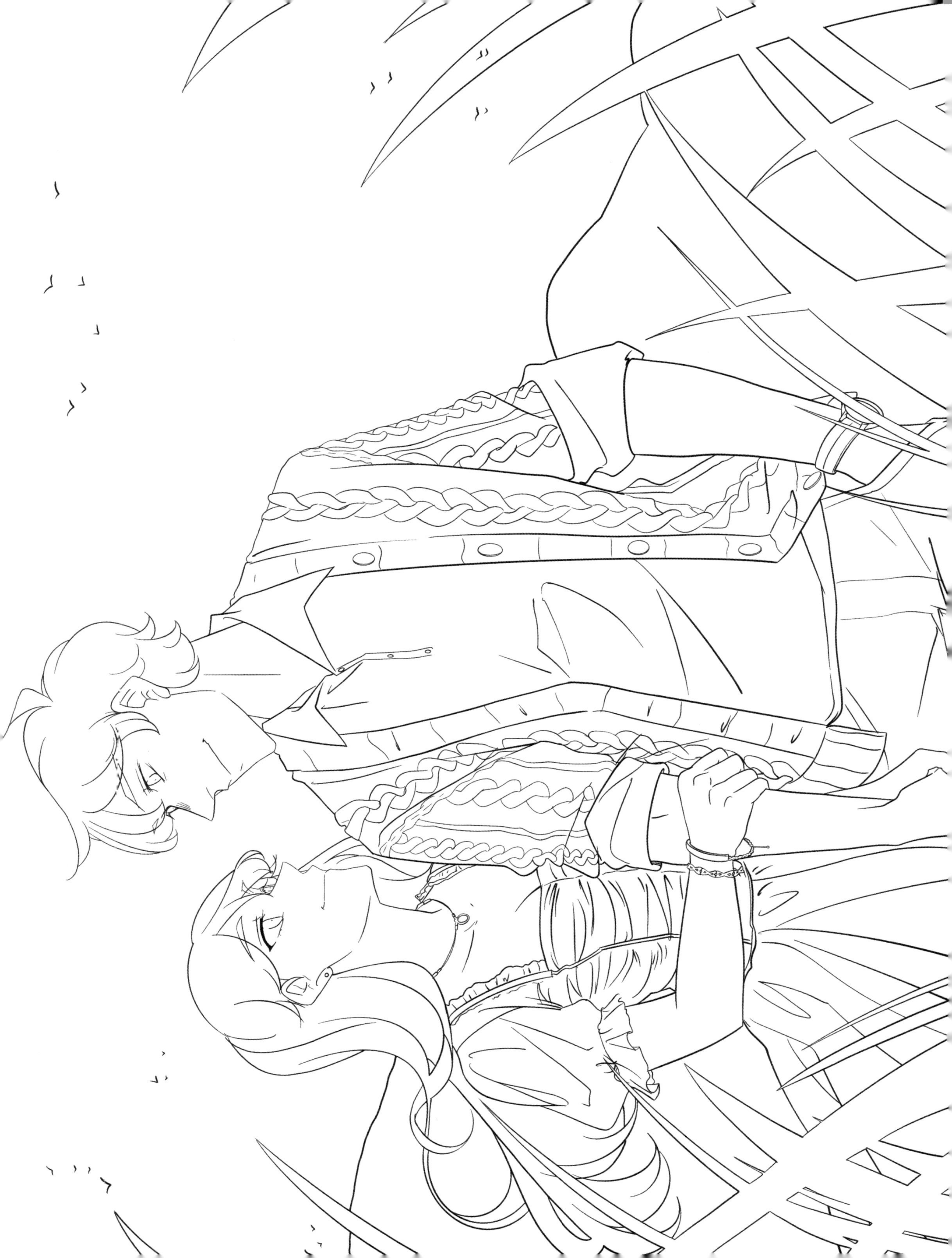

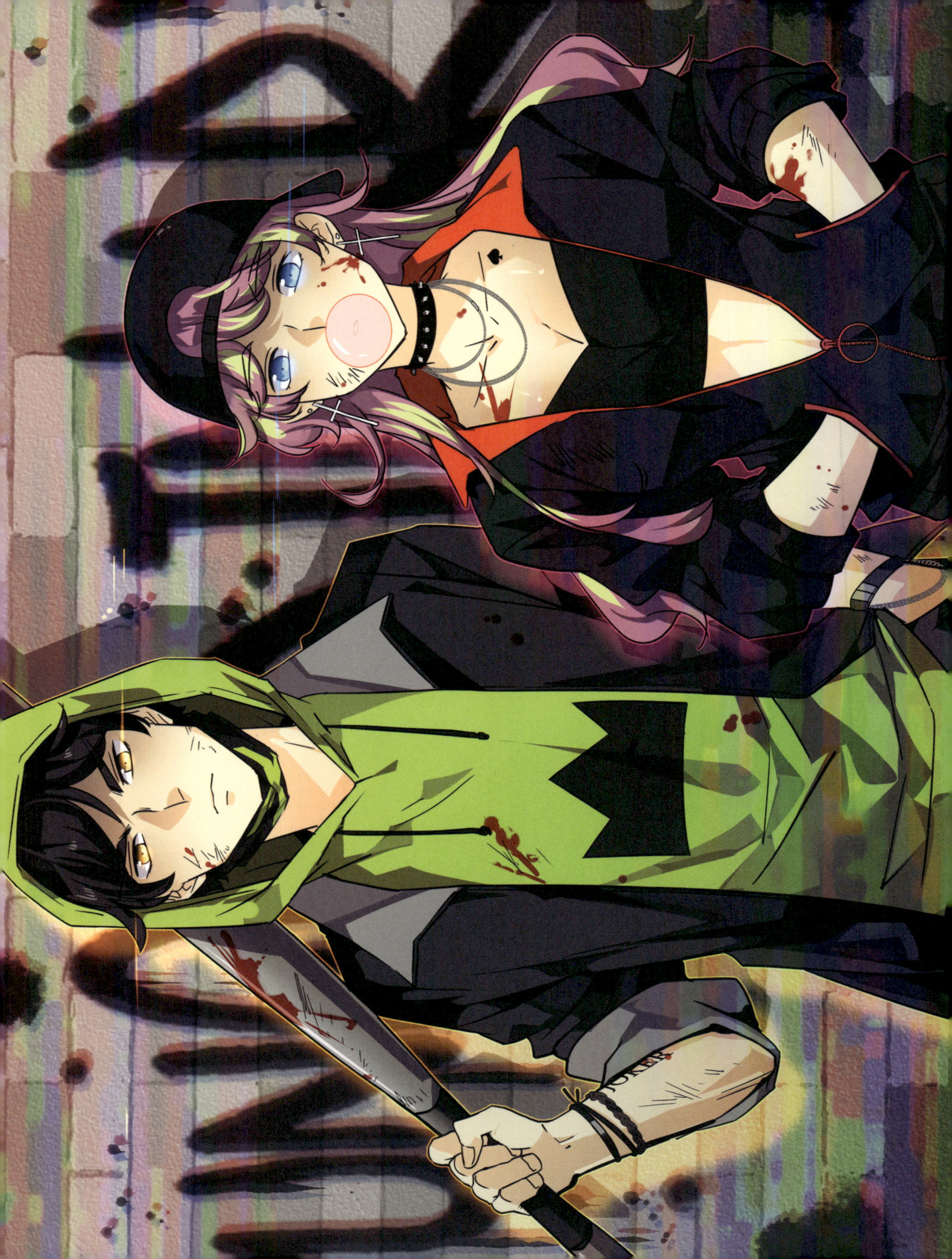

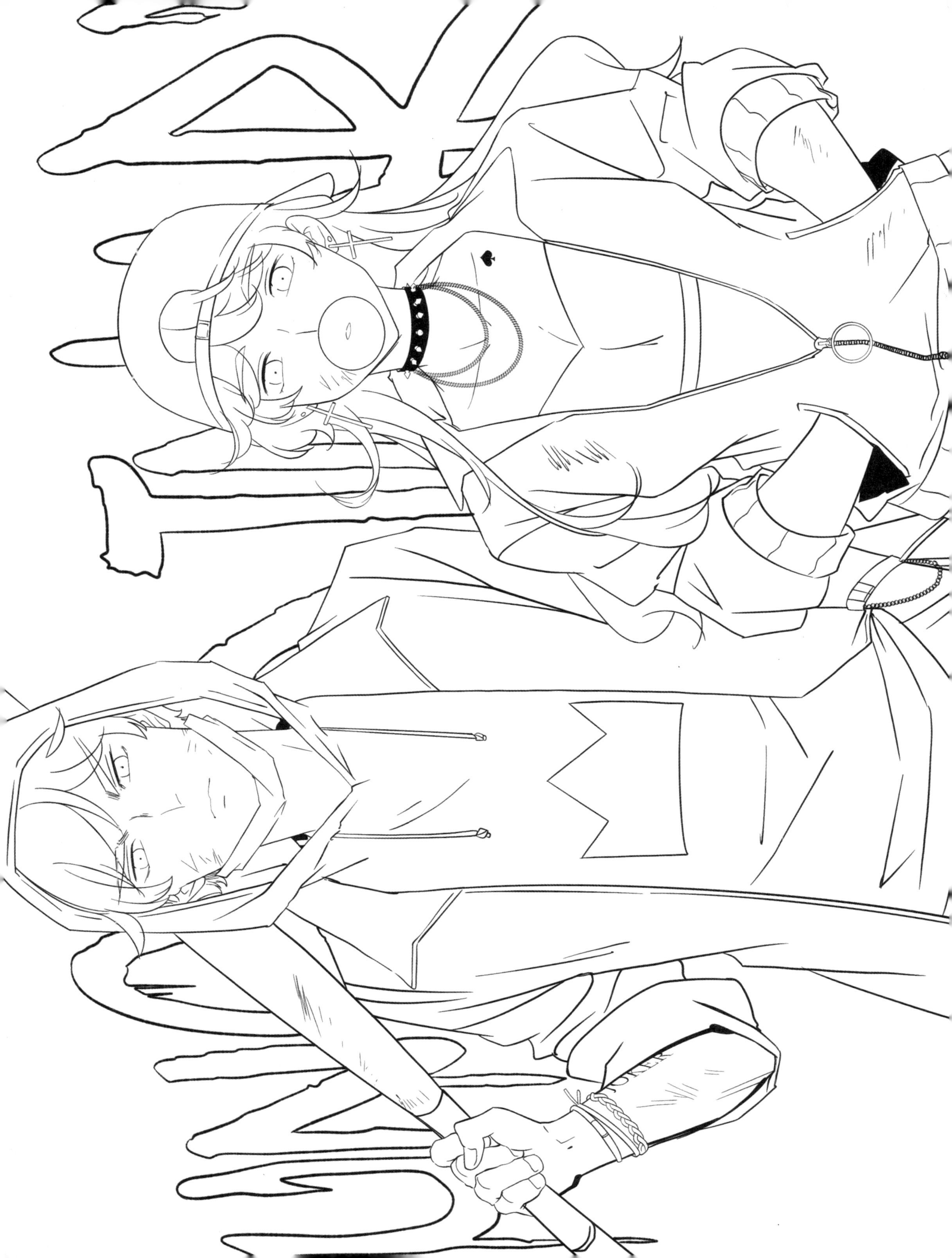

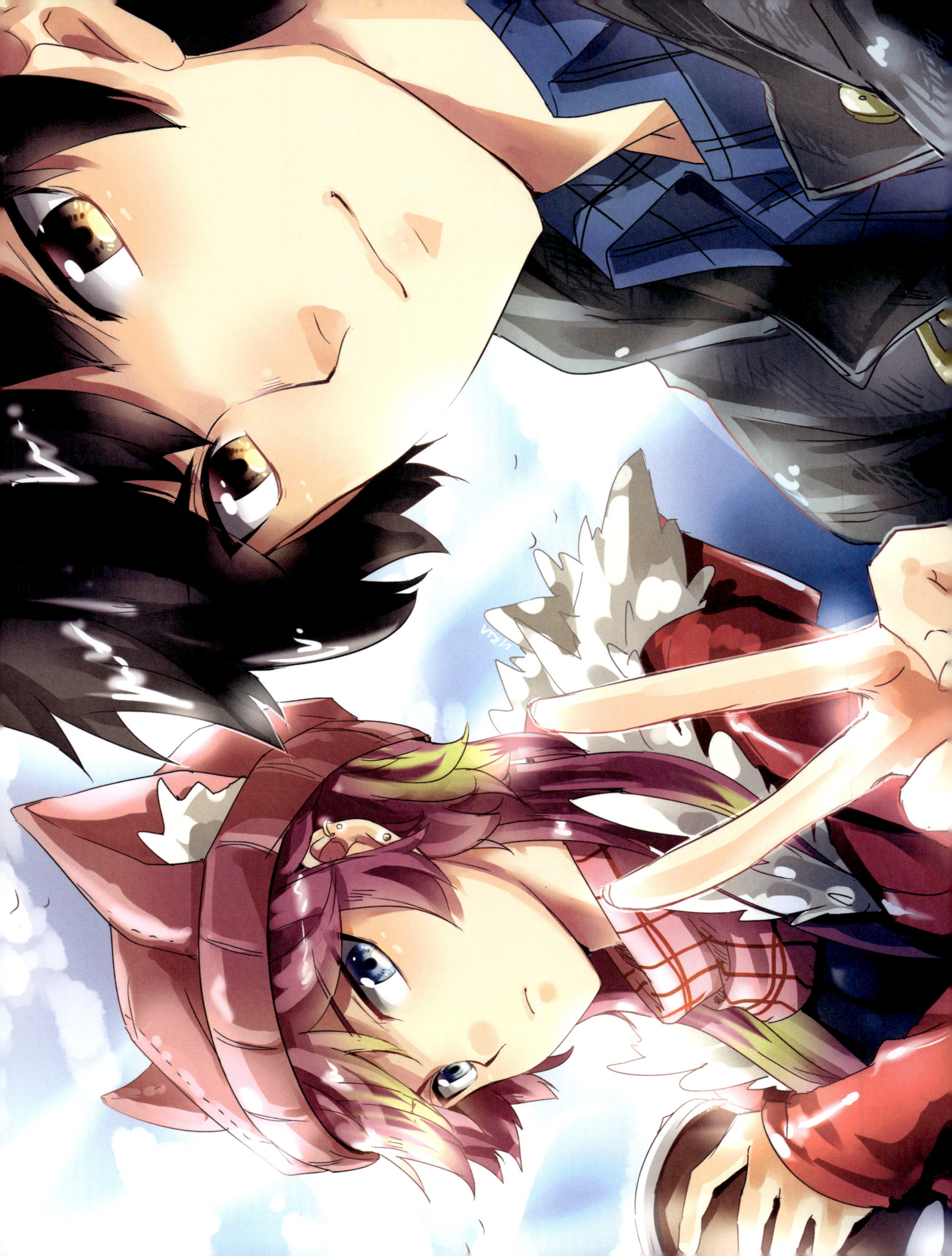

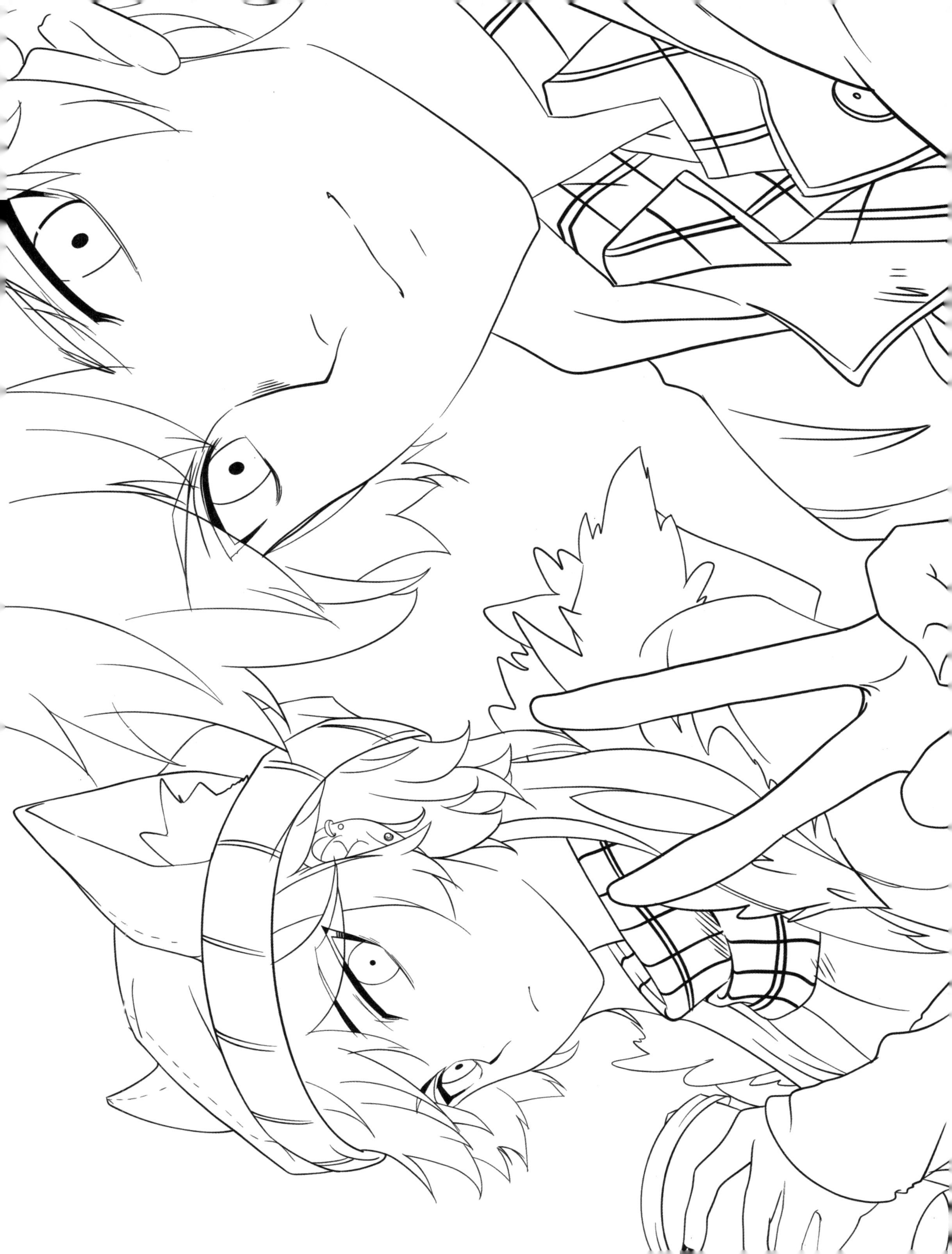

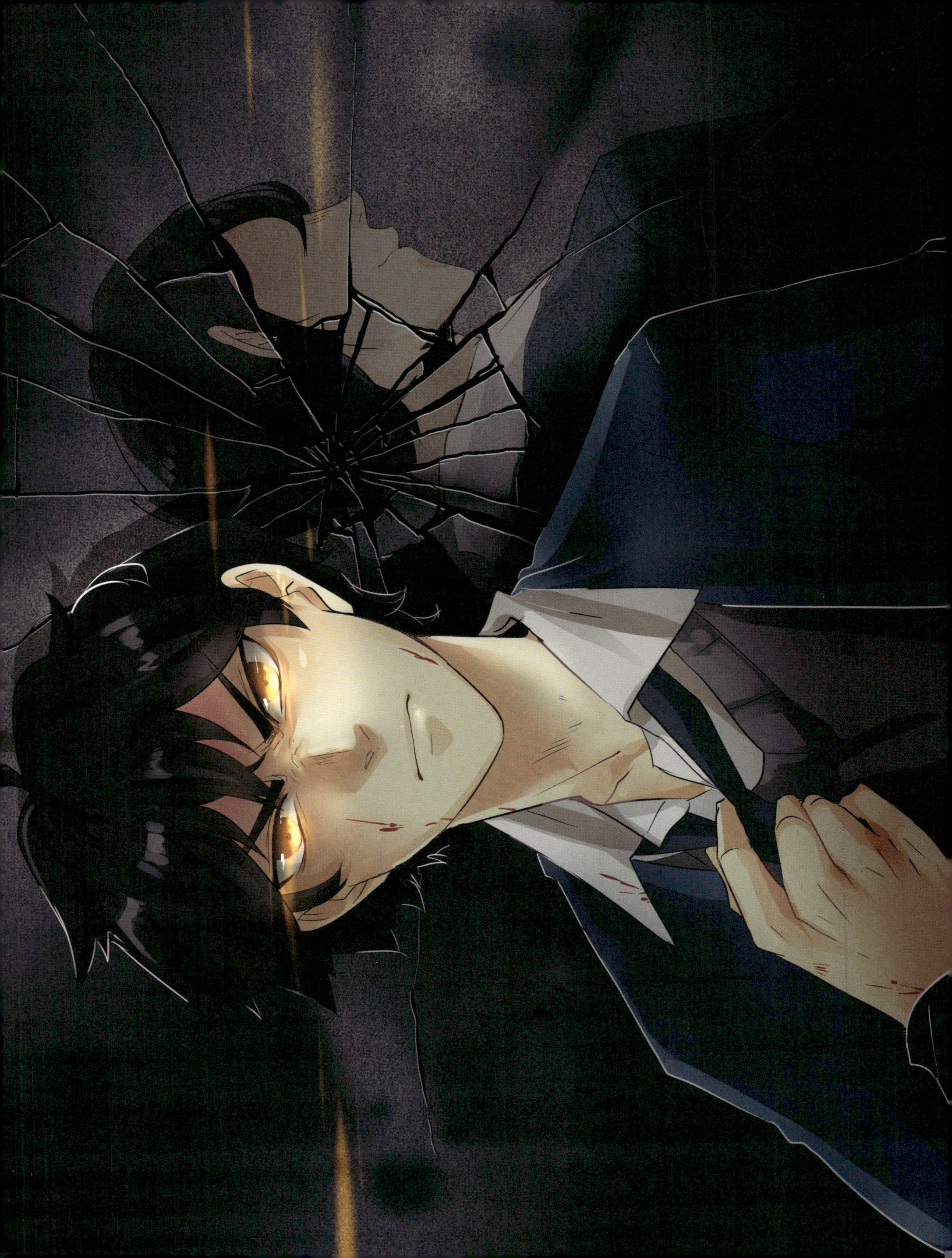

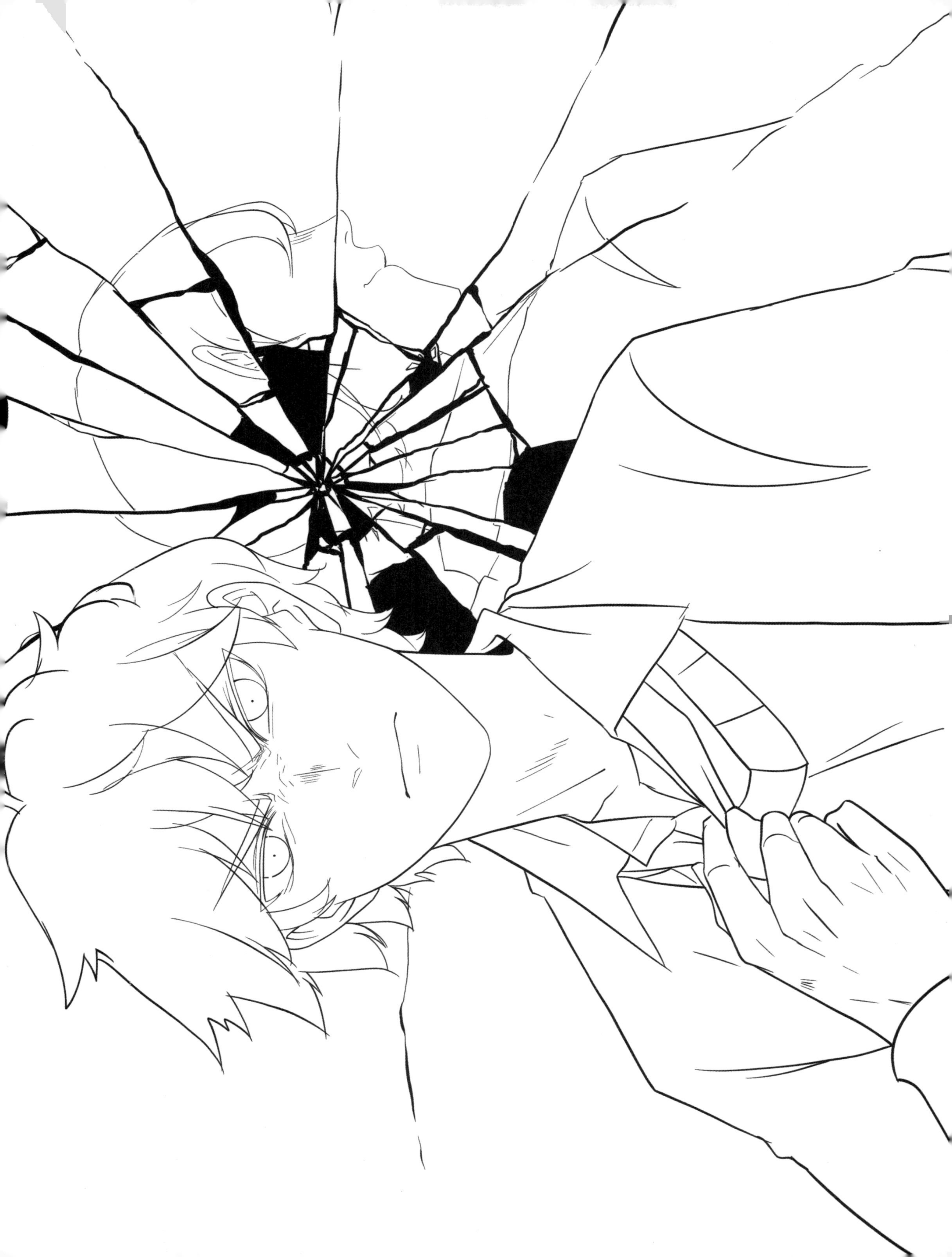

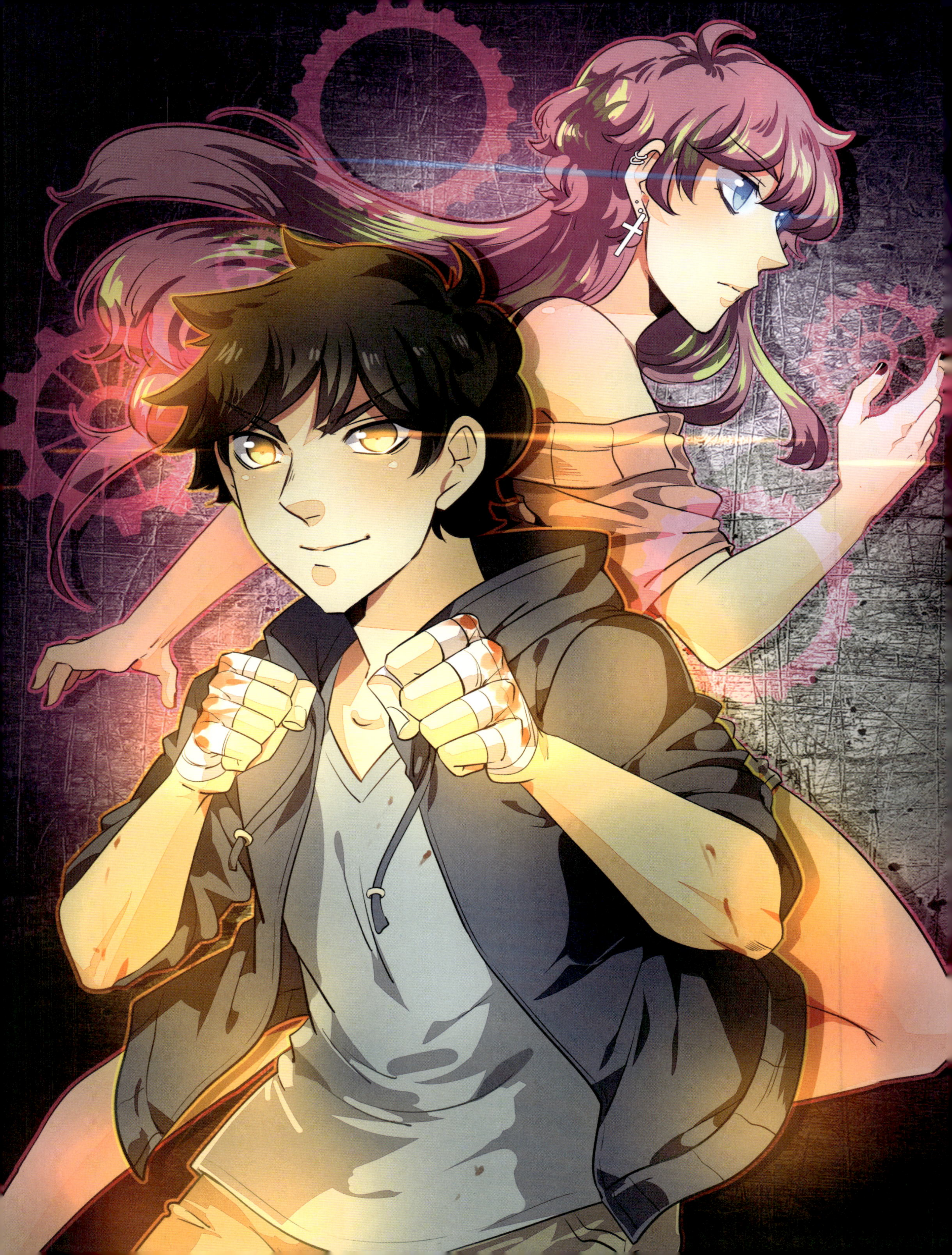

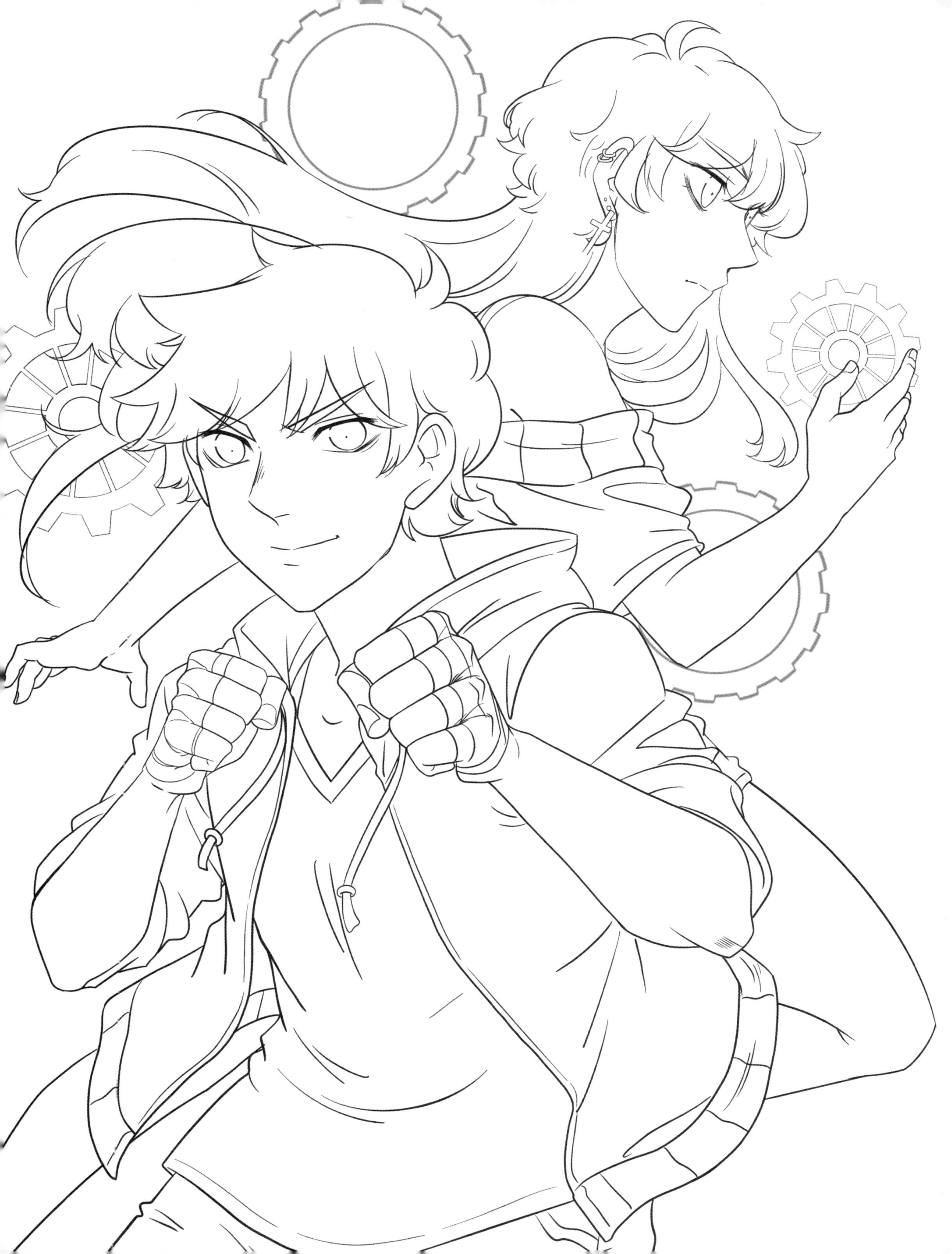

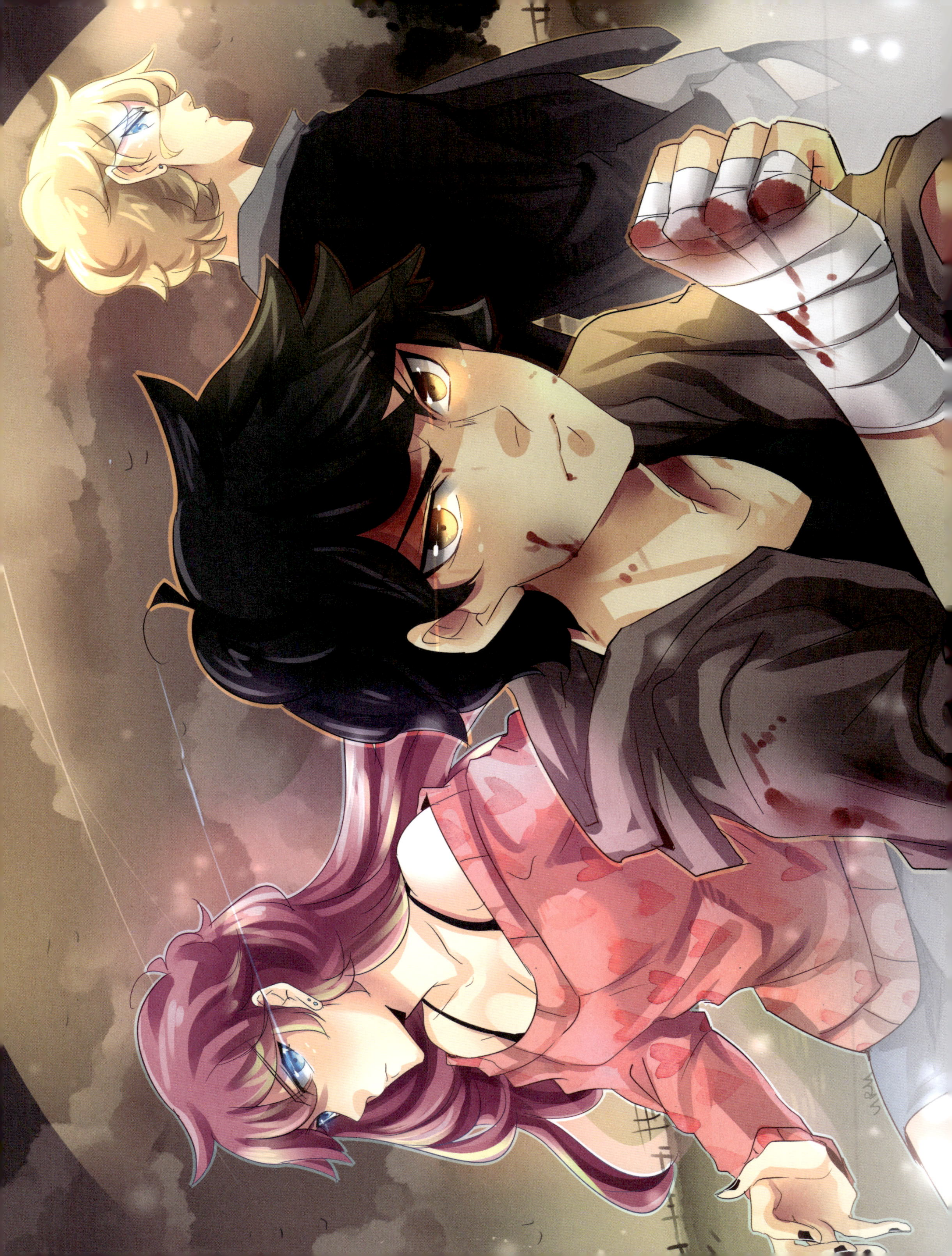

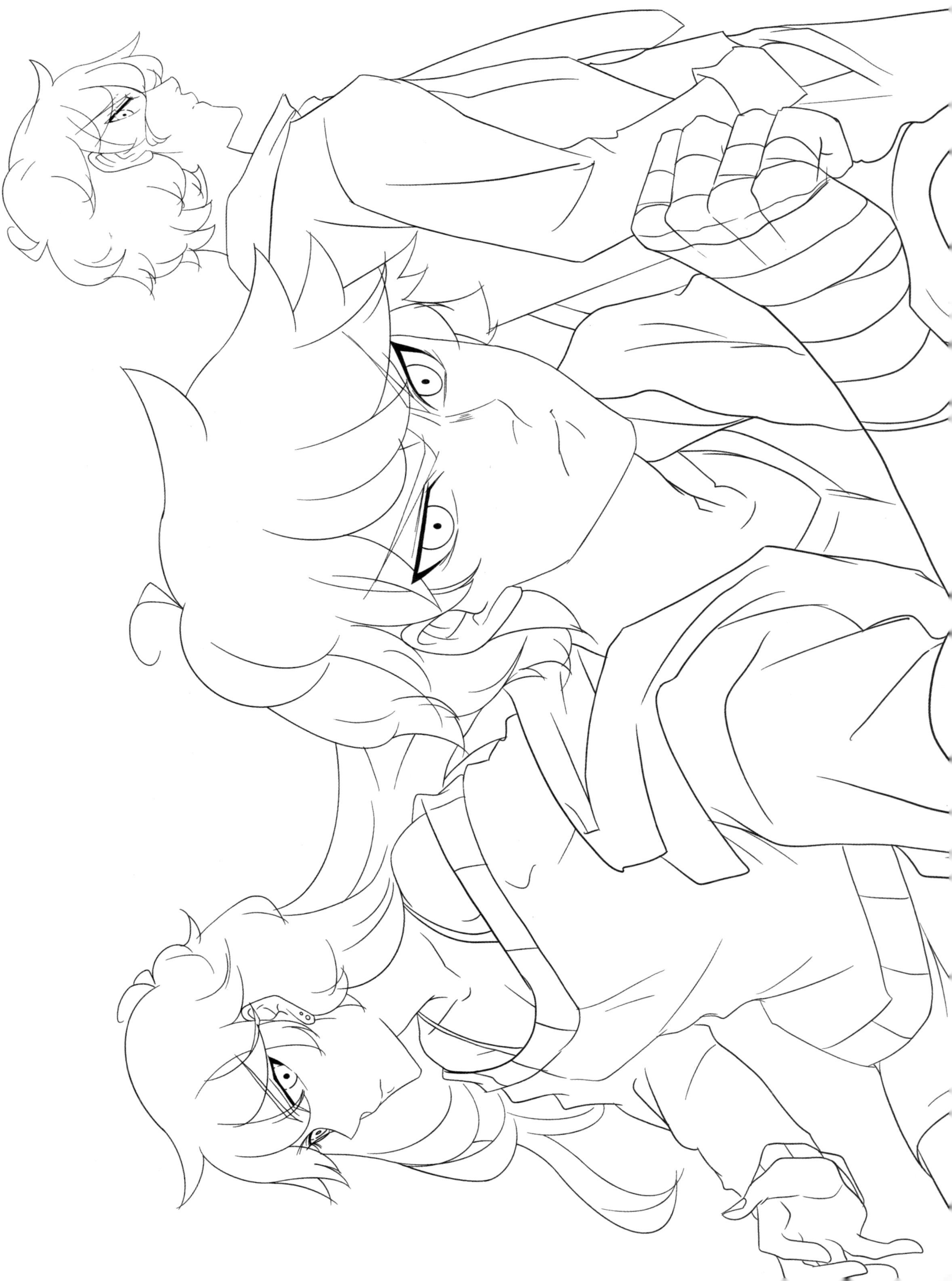

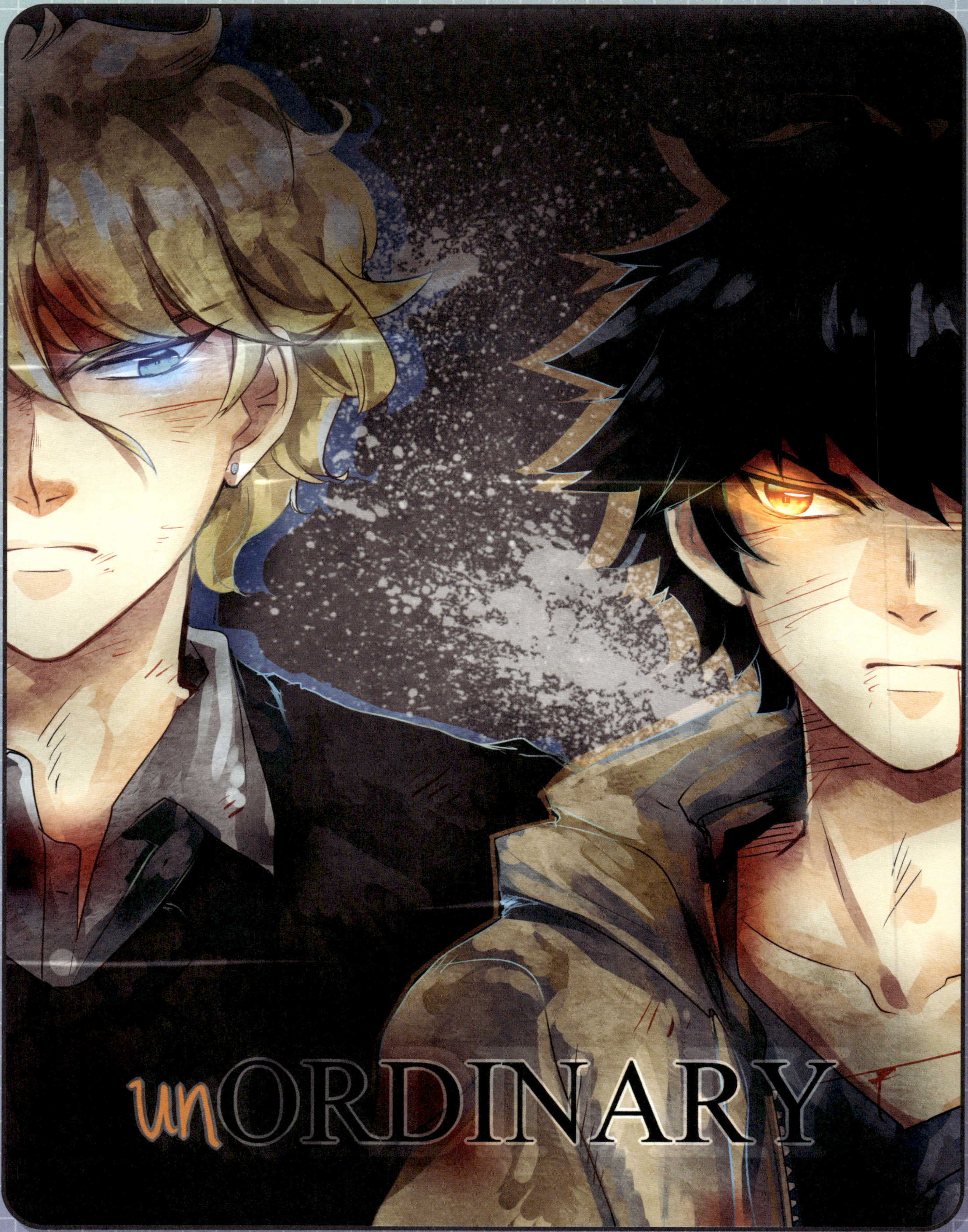
unORDINARY

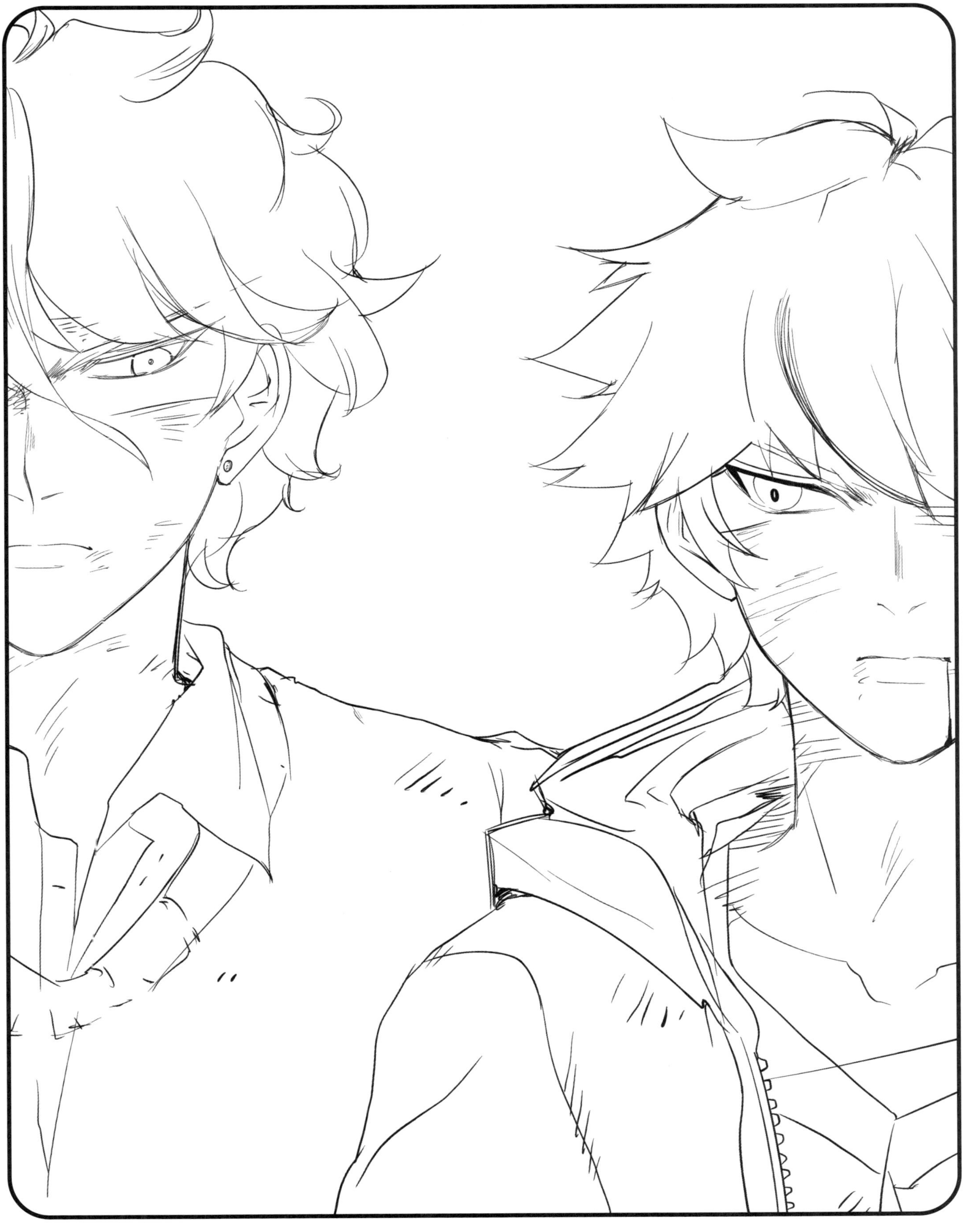

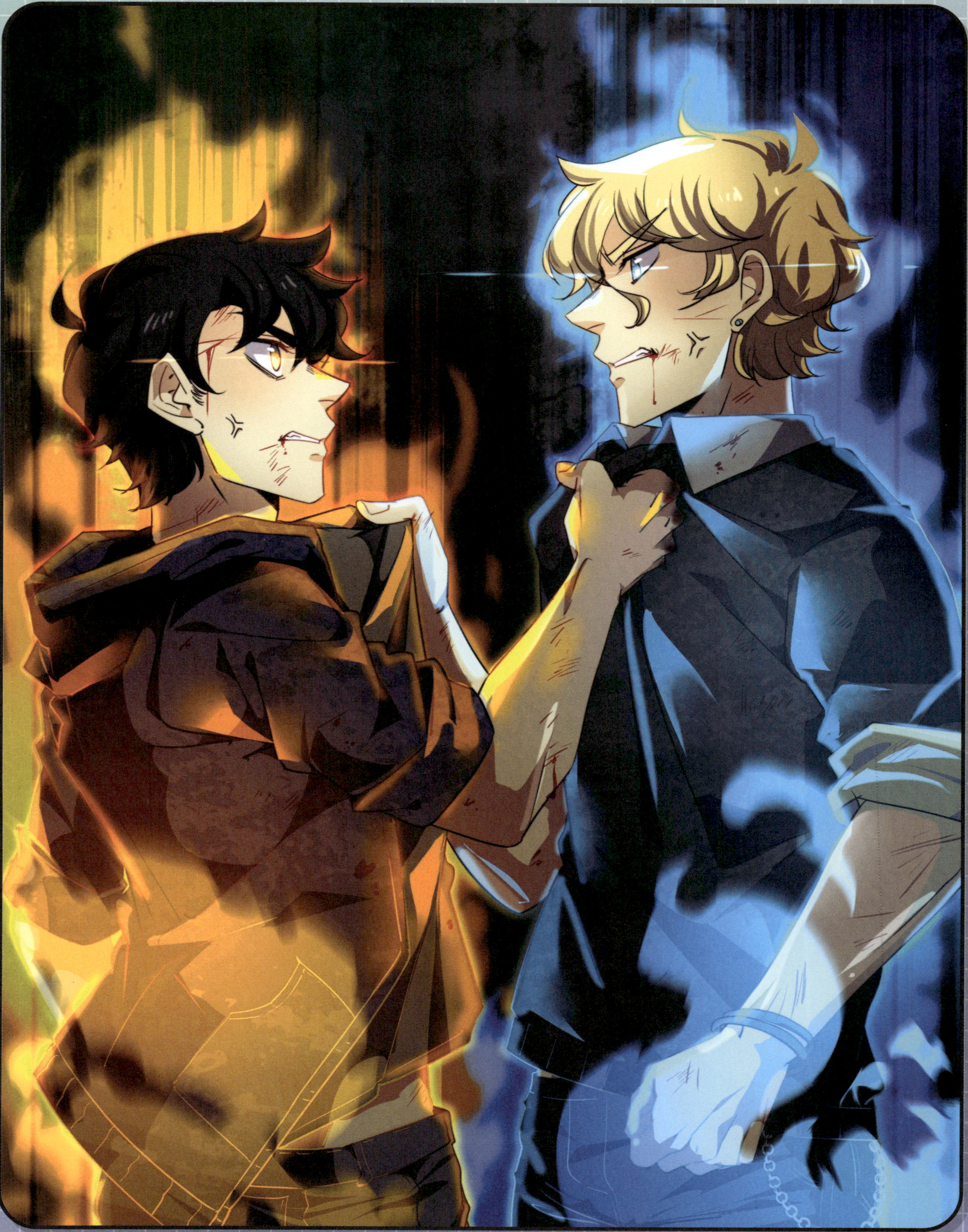

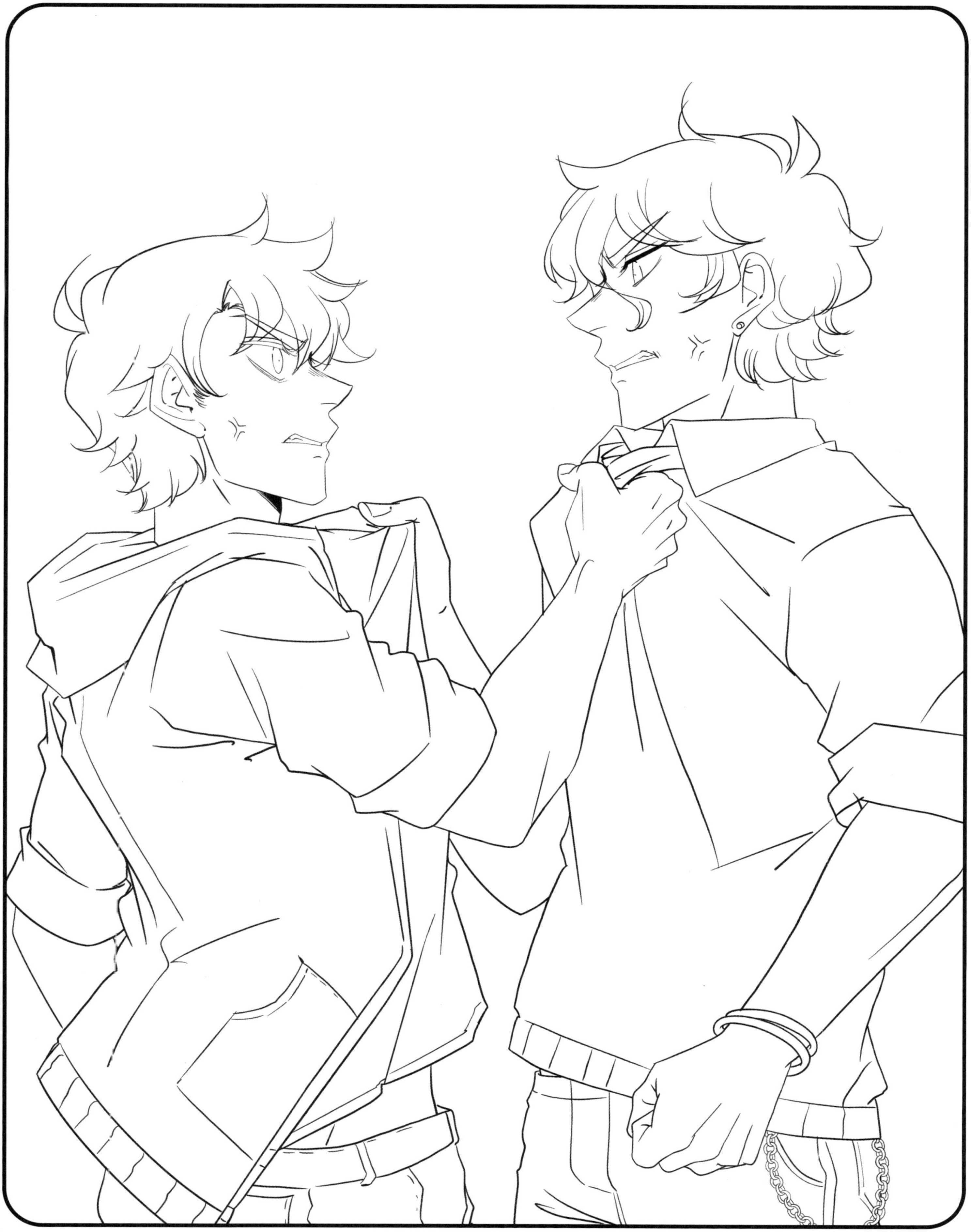

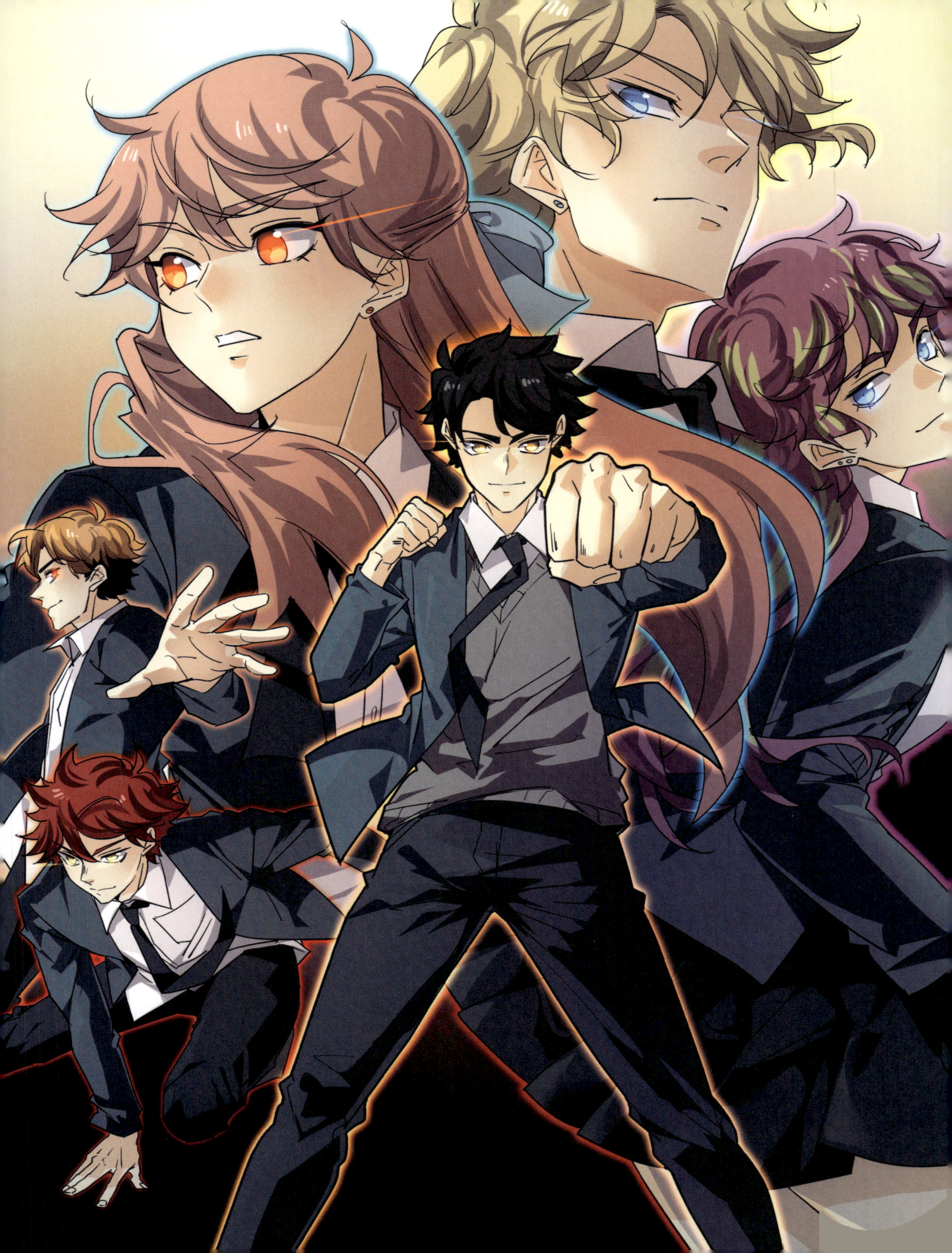

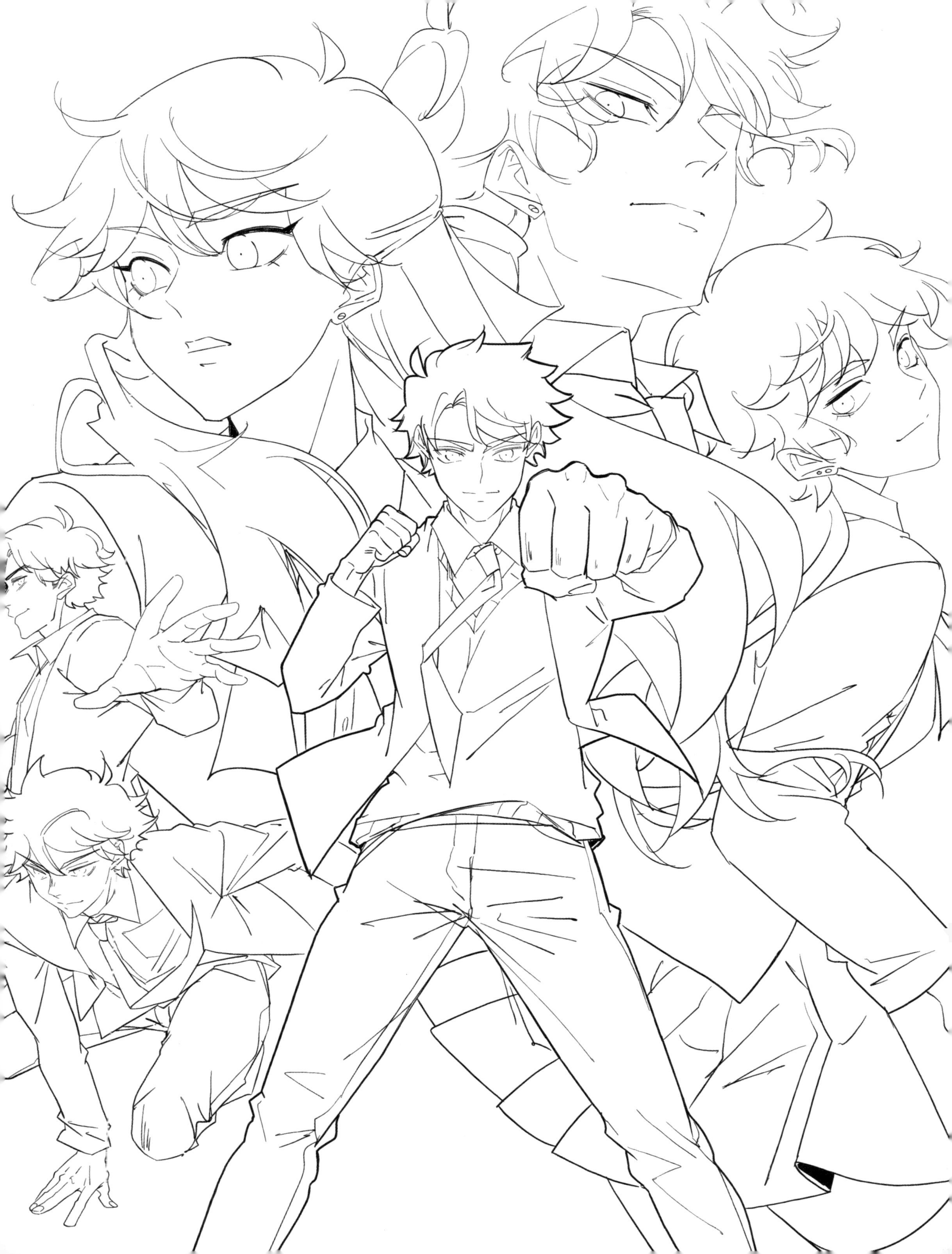

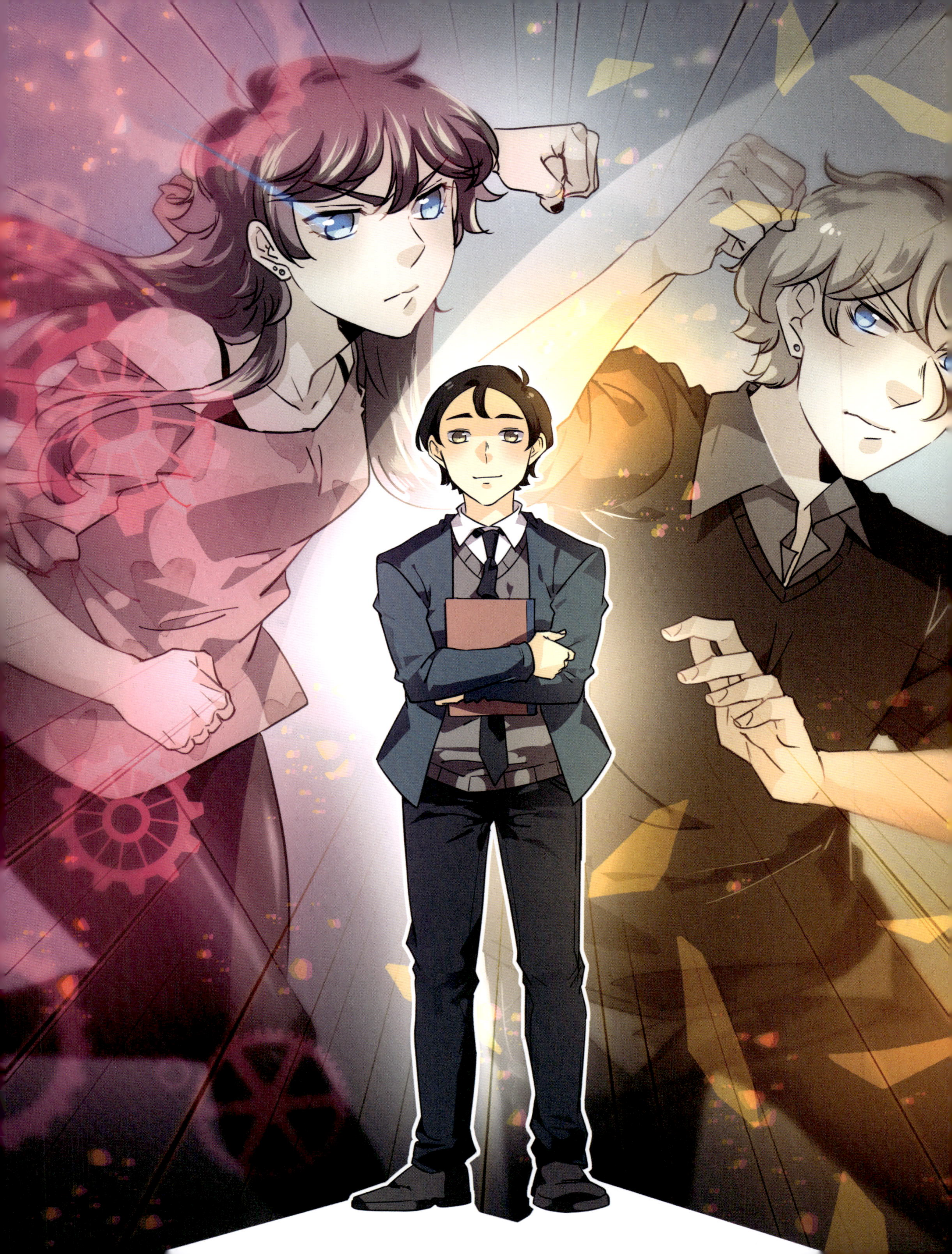

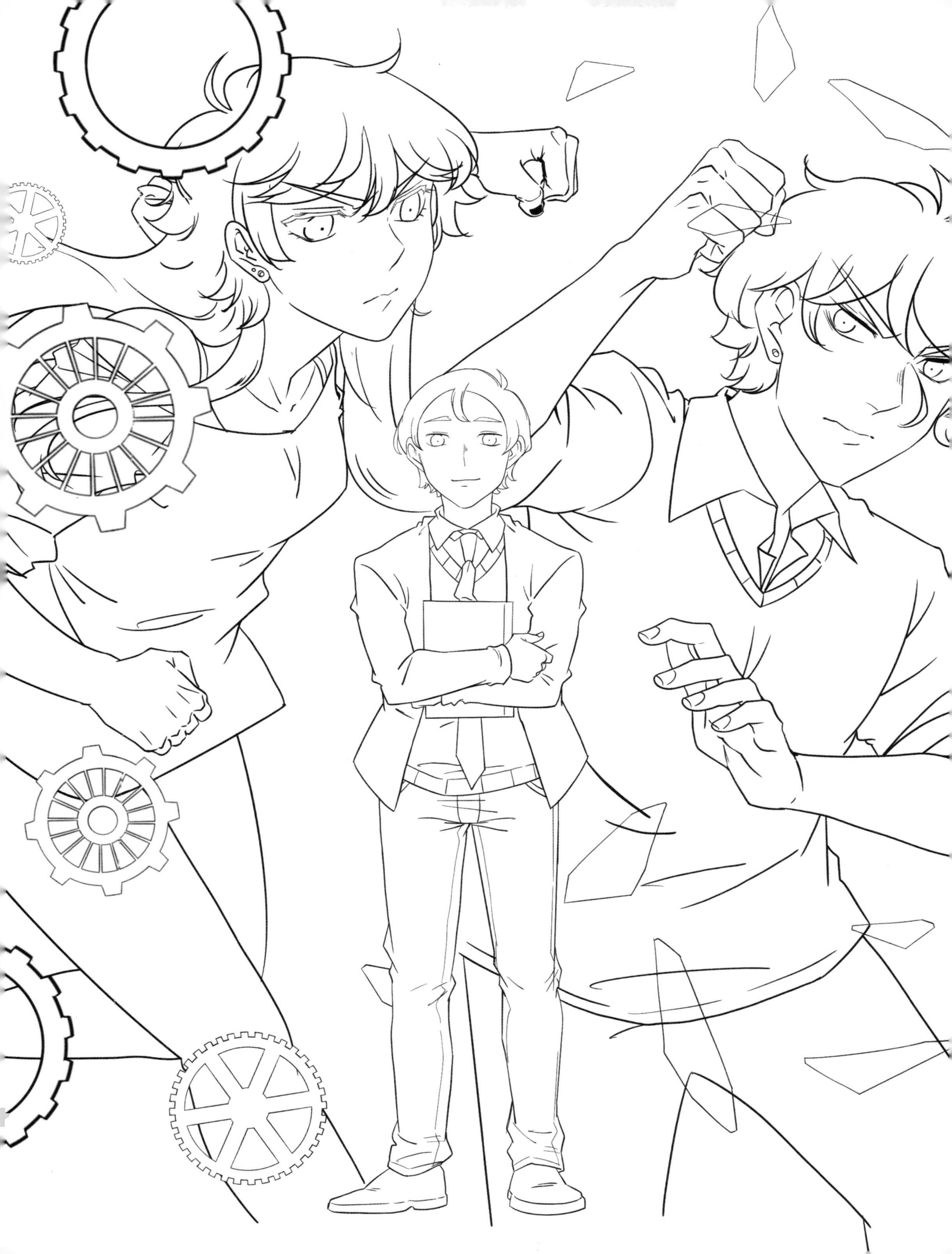

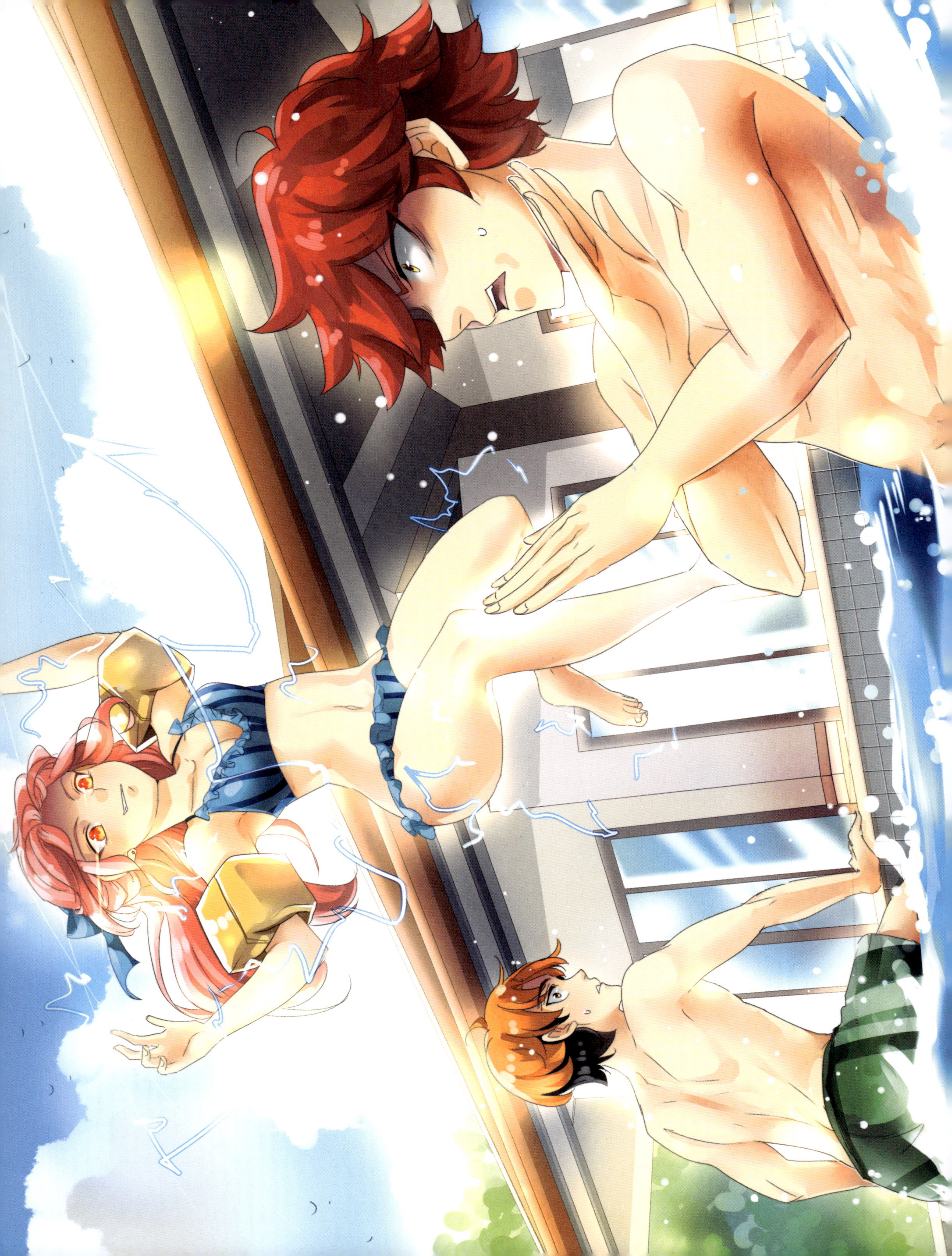

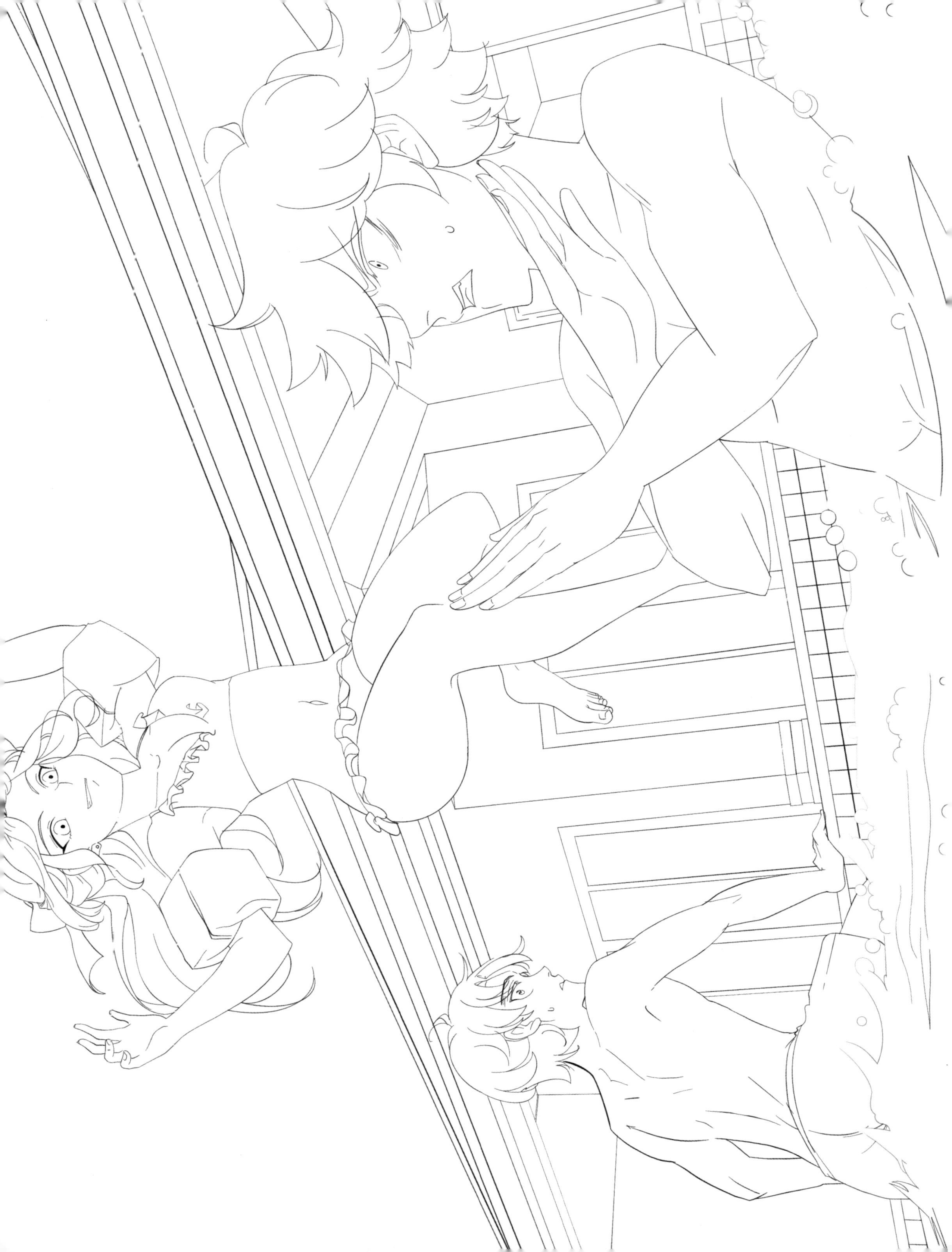

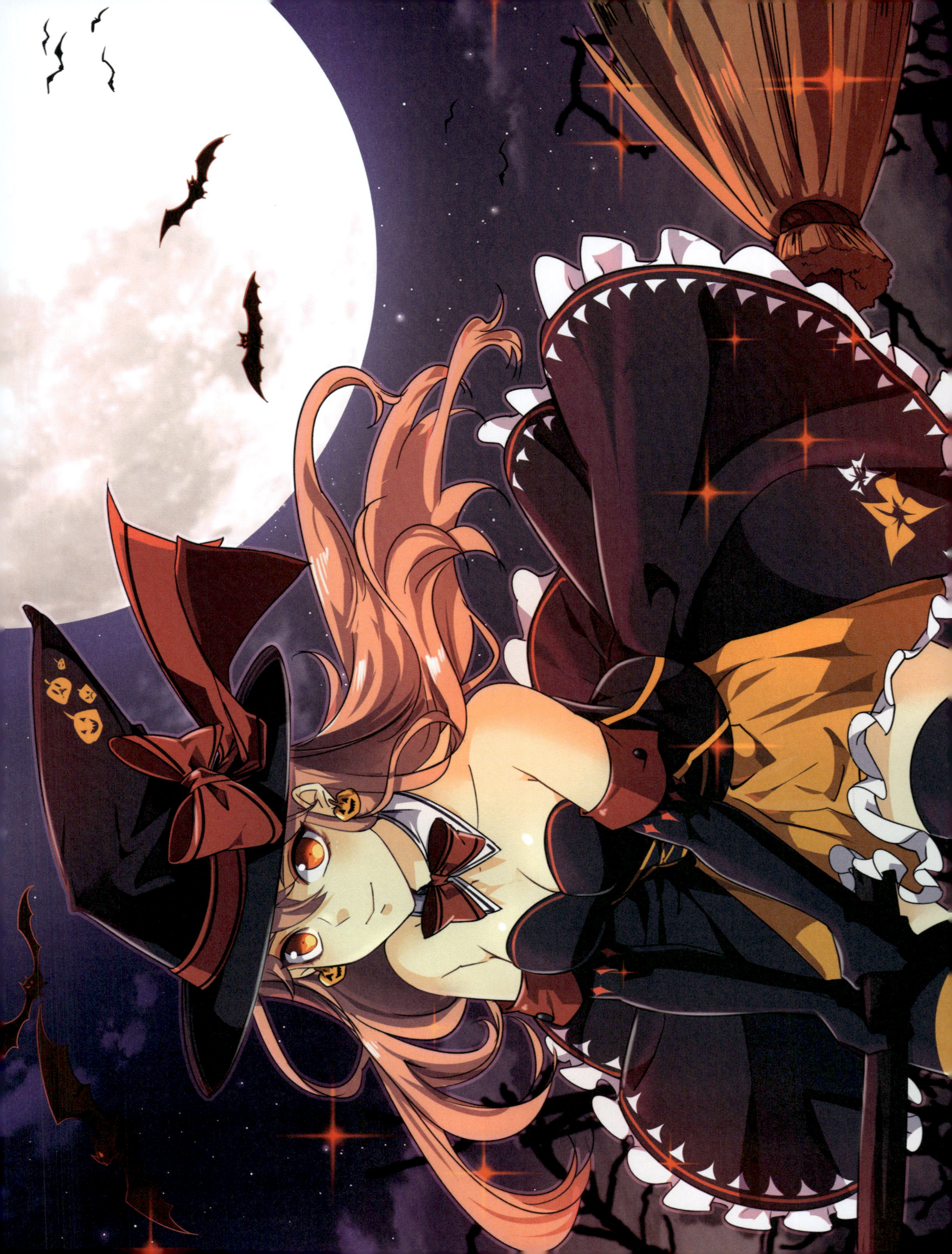

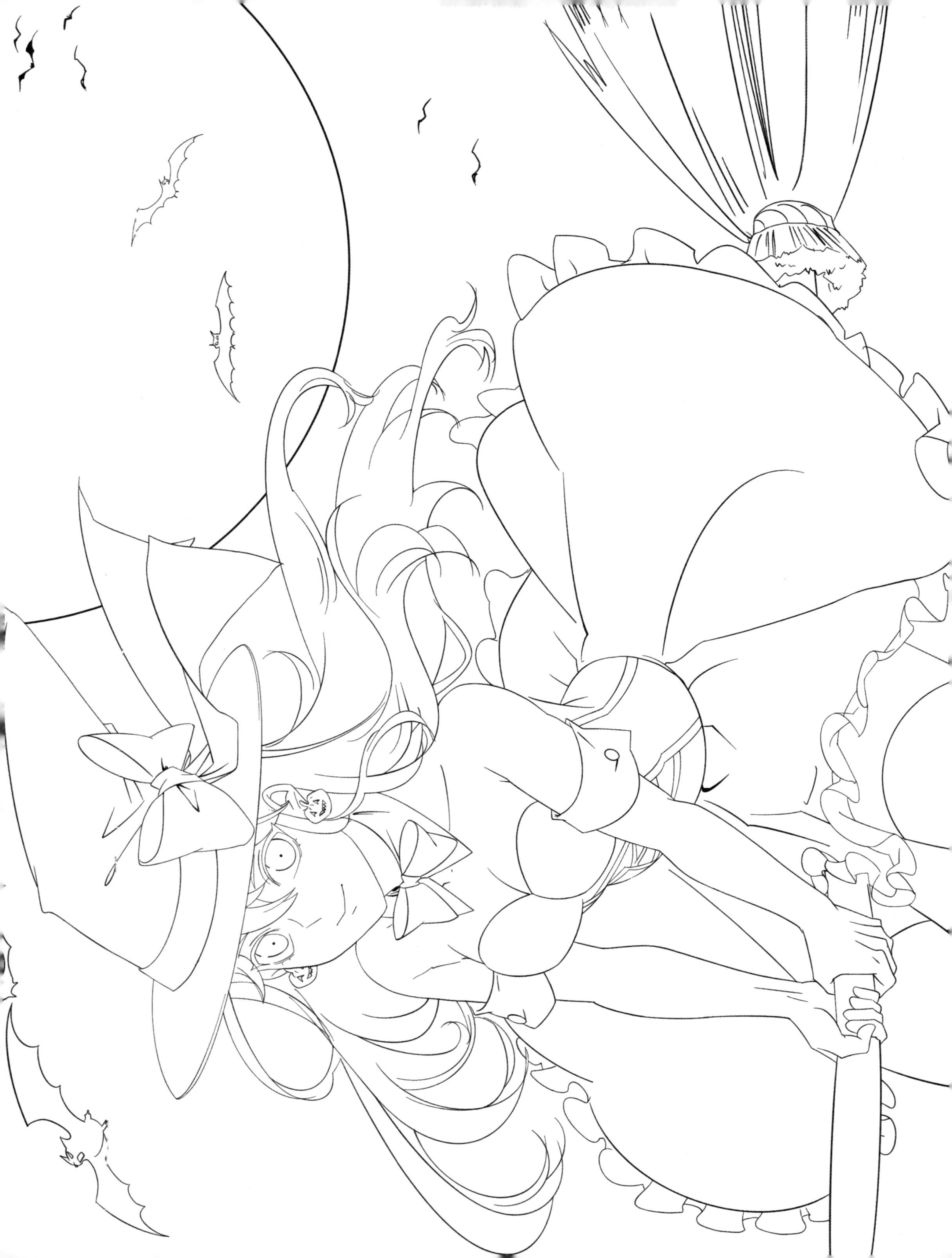

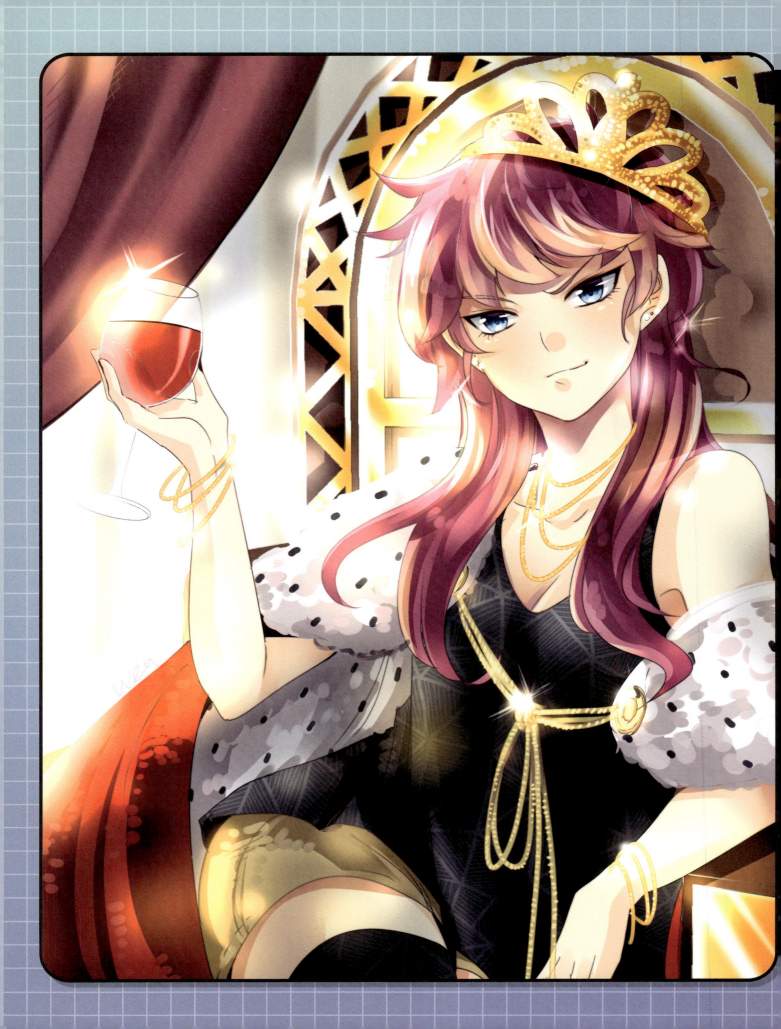

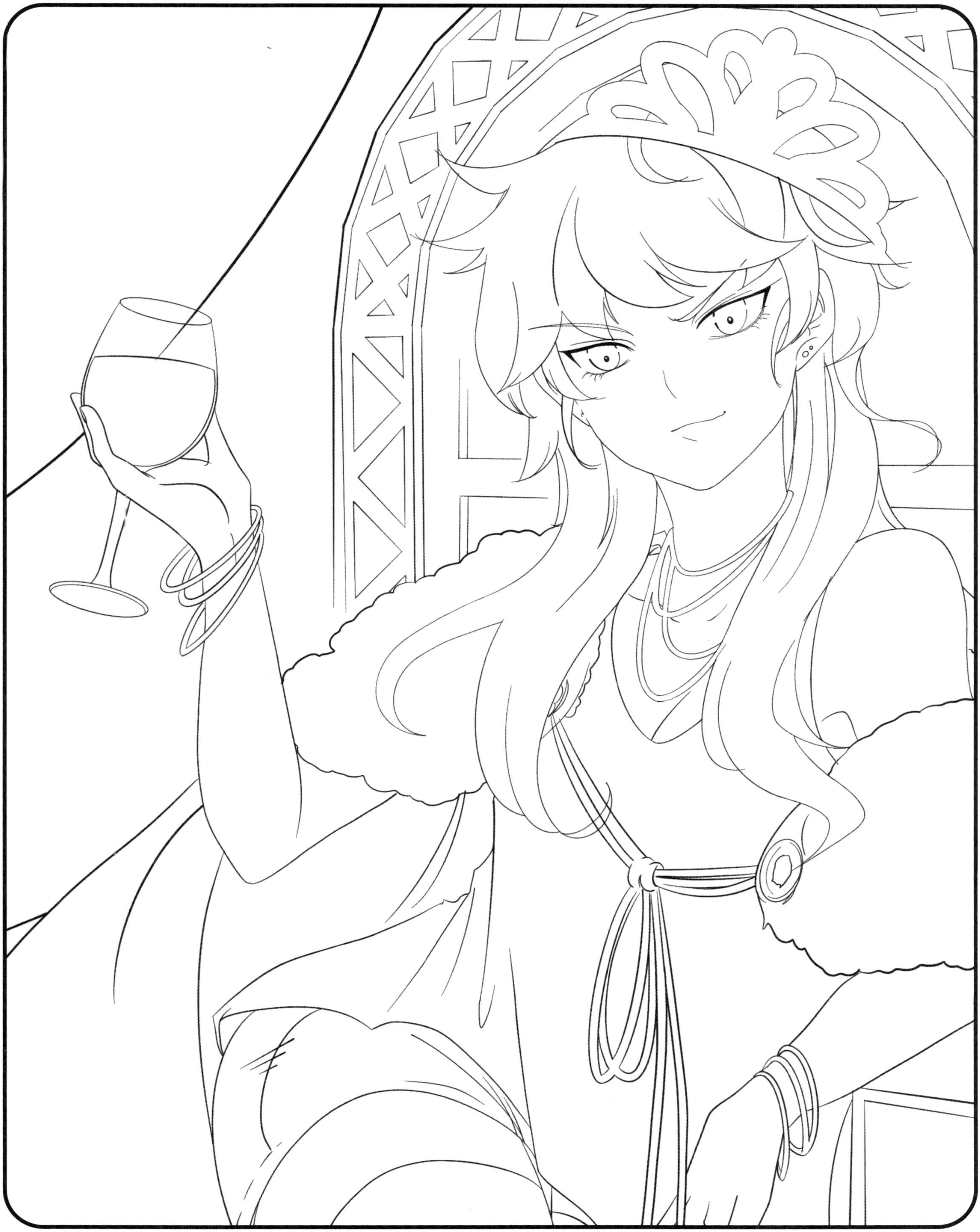

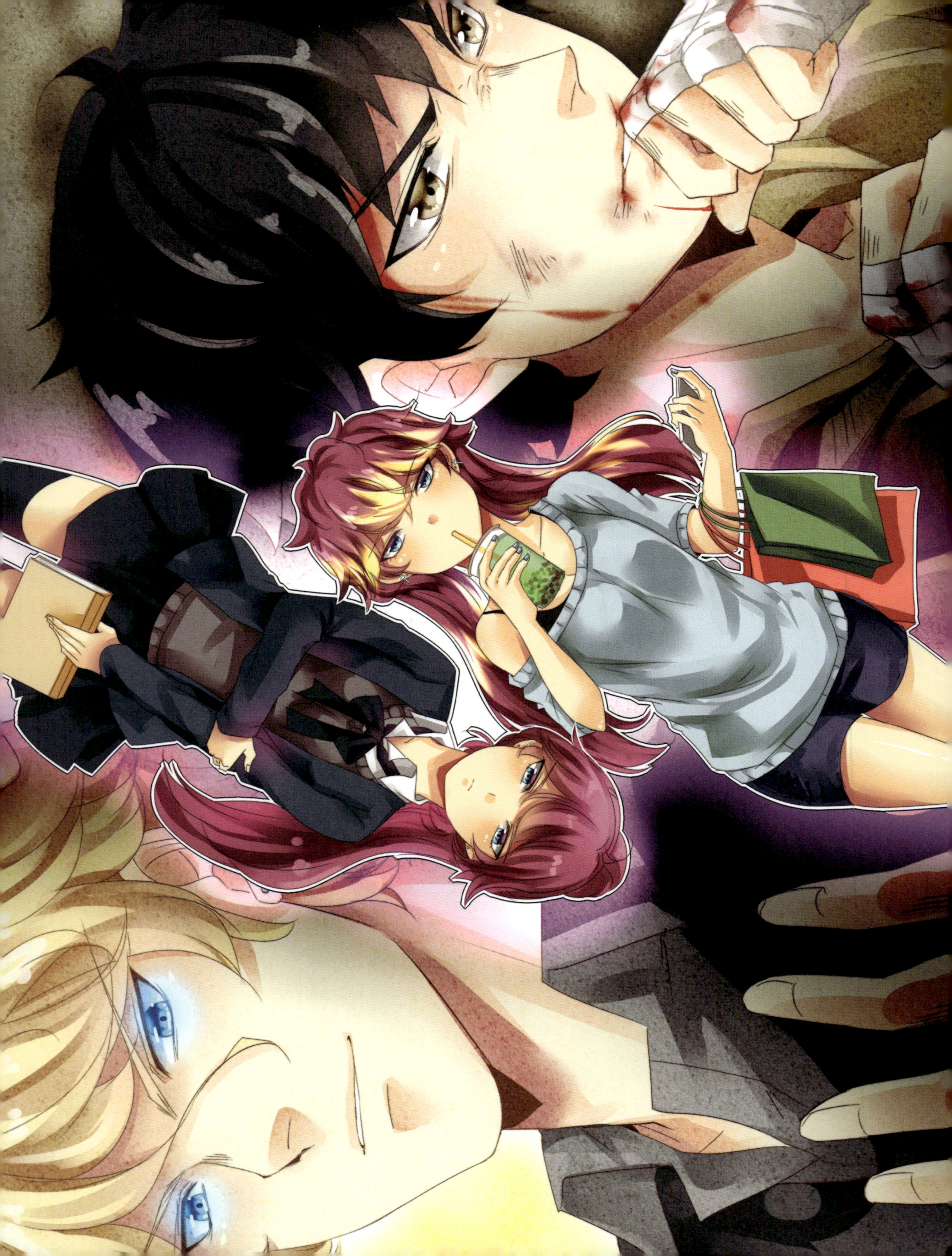

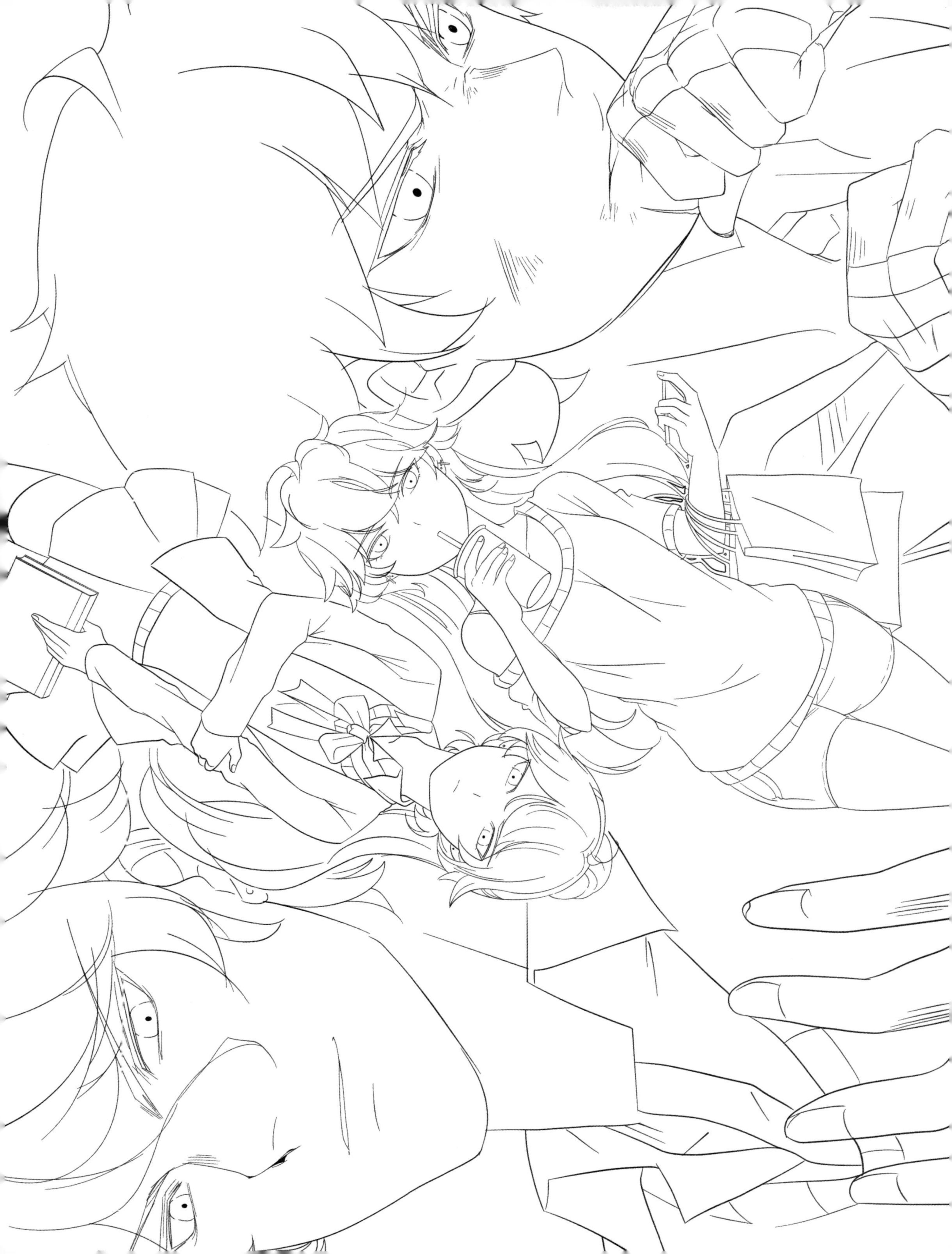

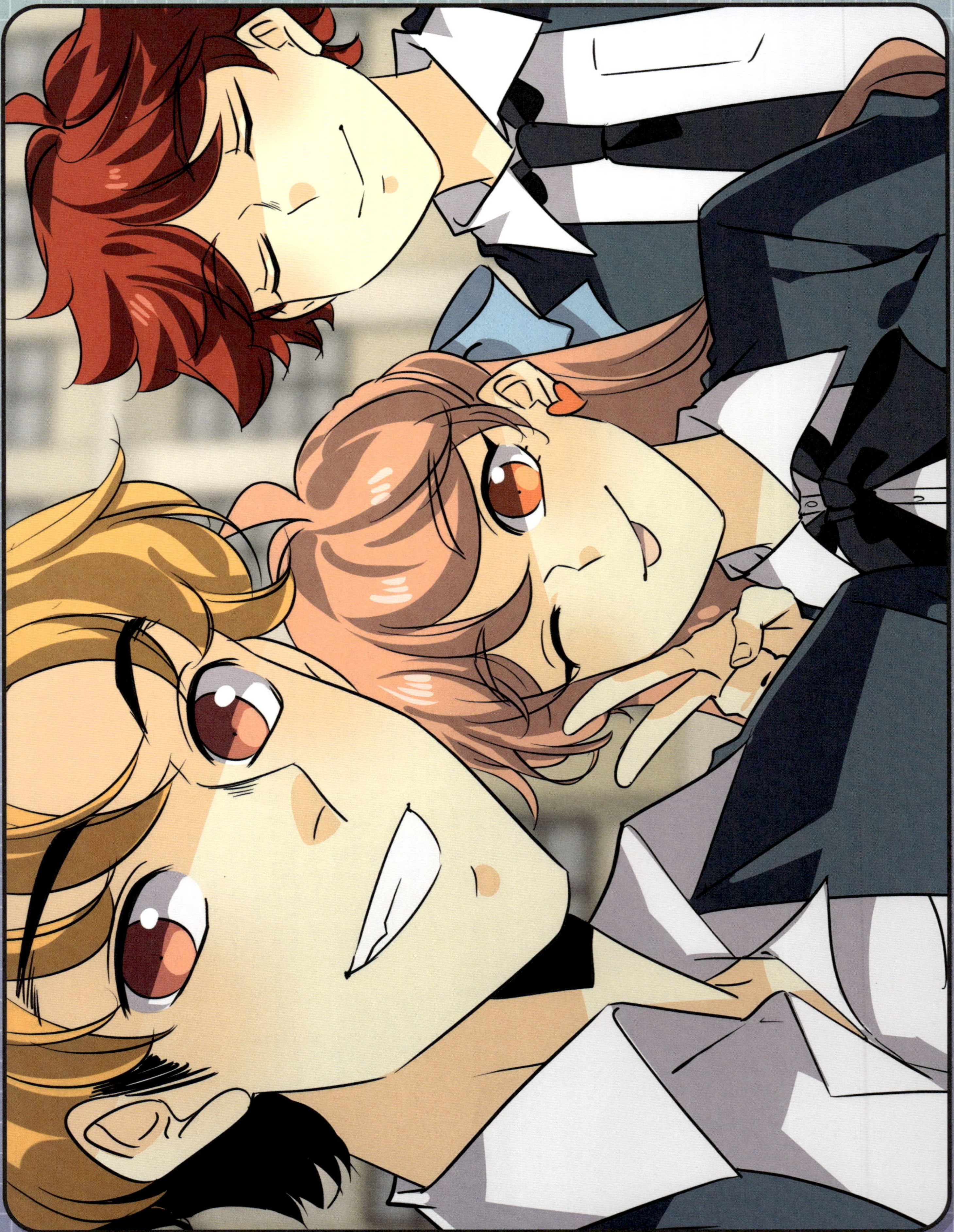

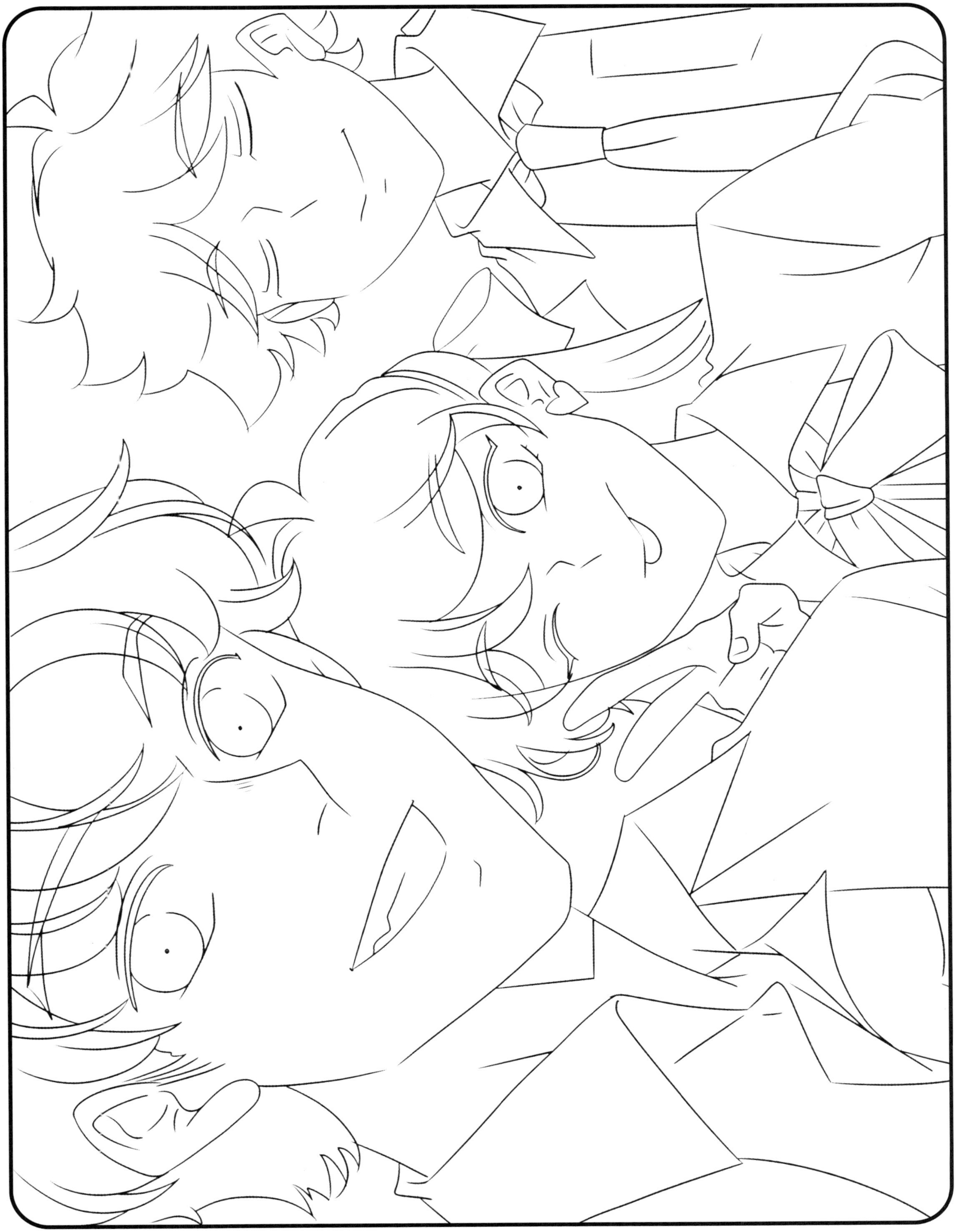

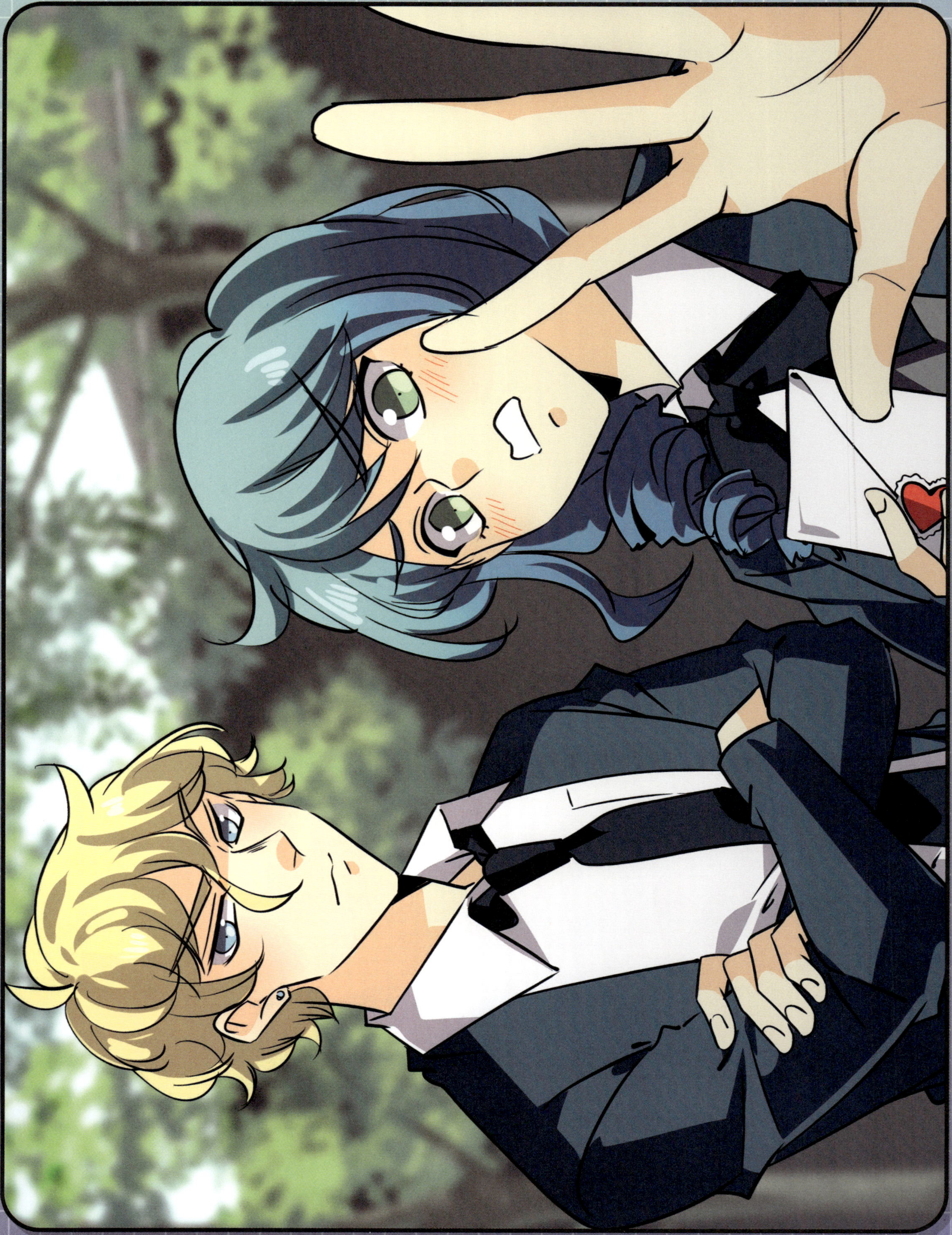

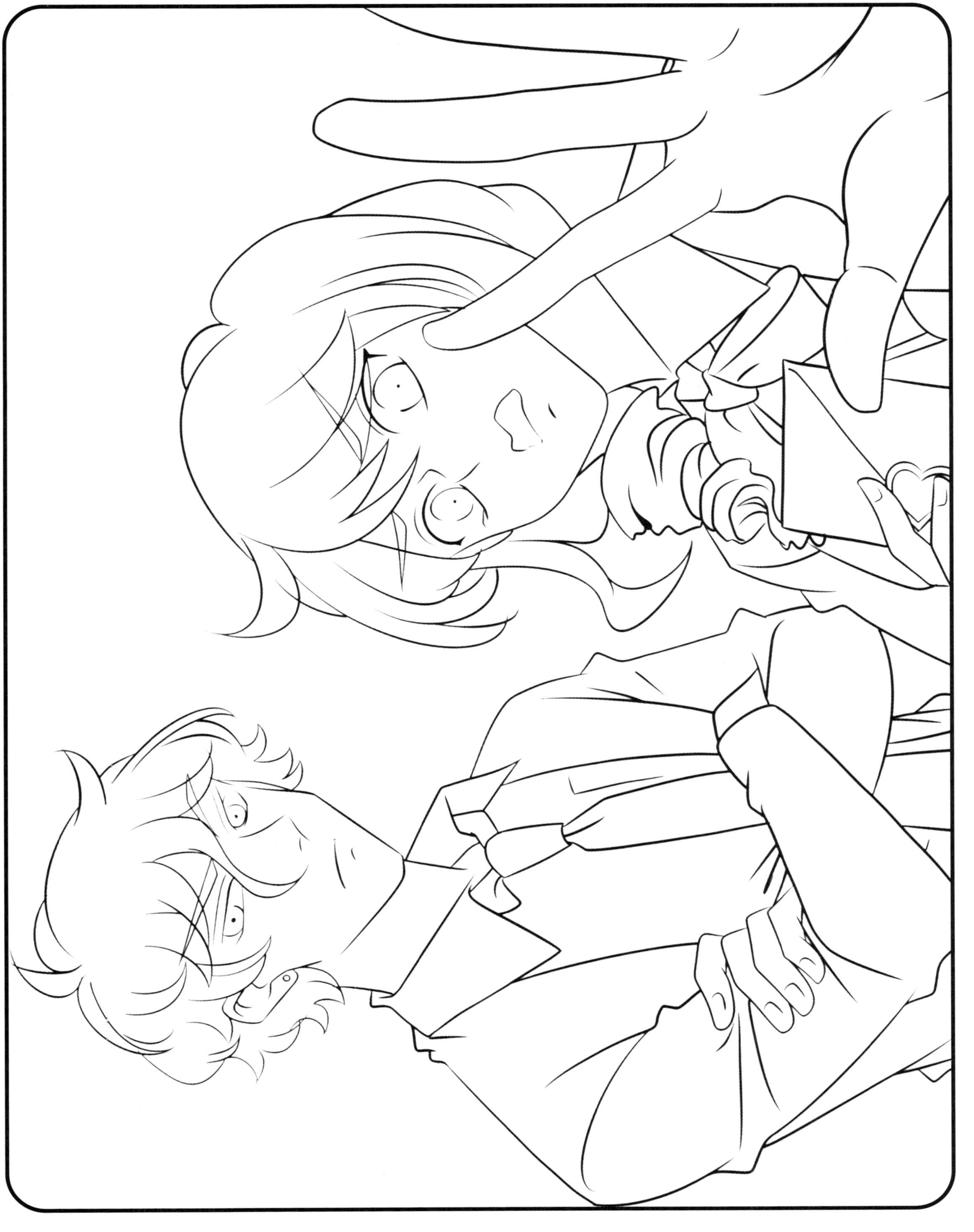

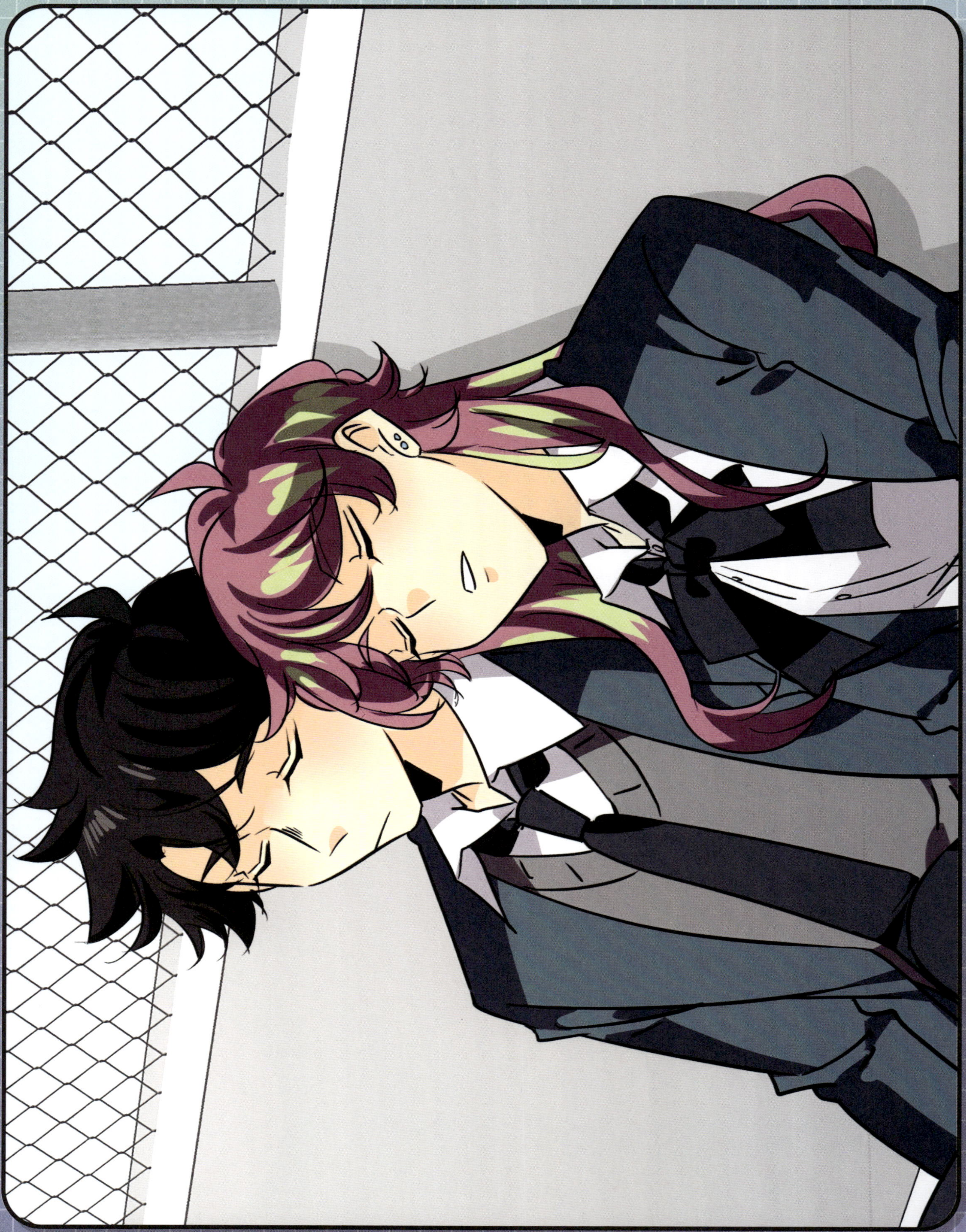

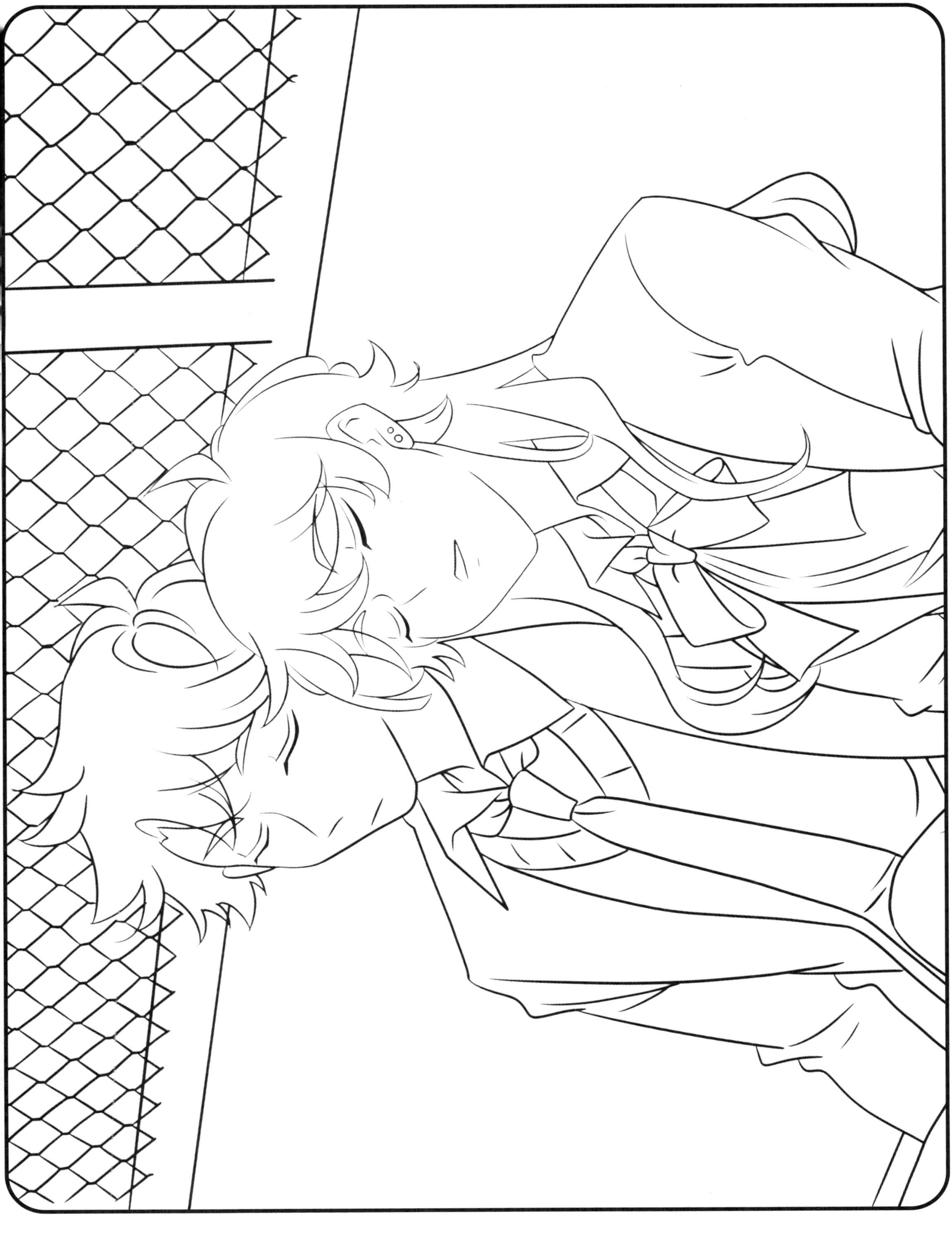

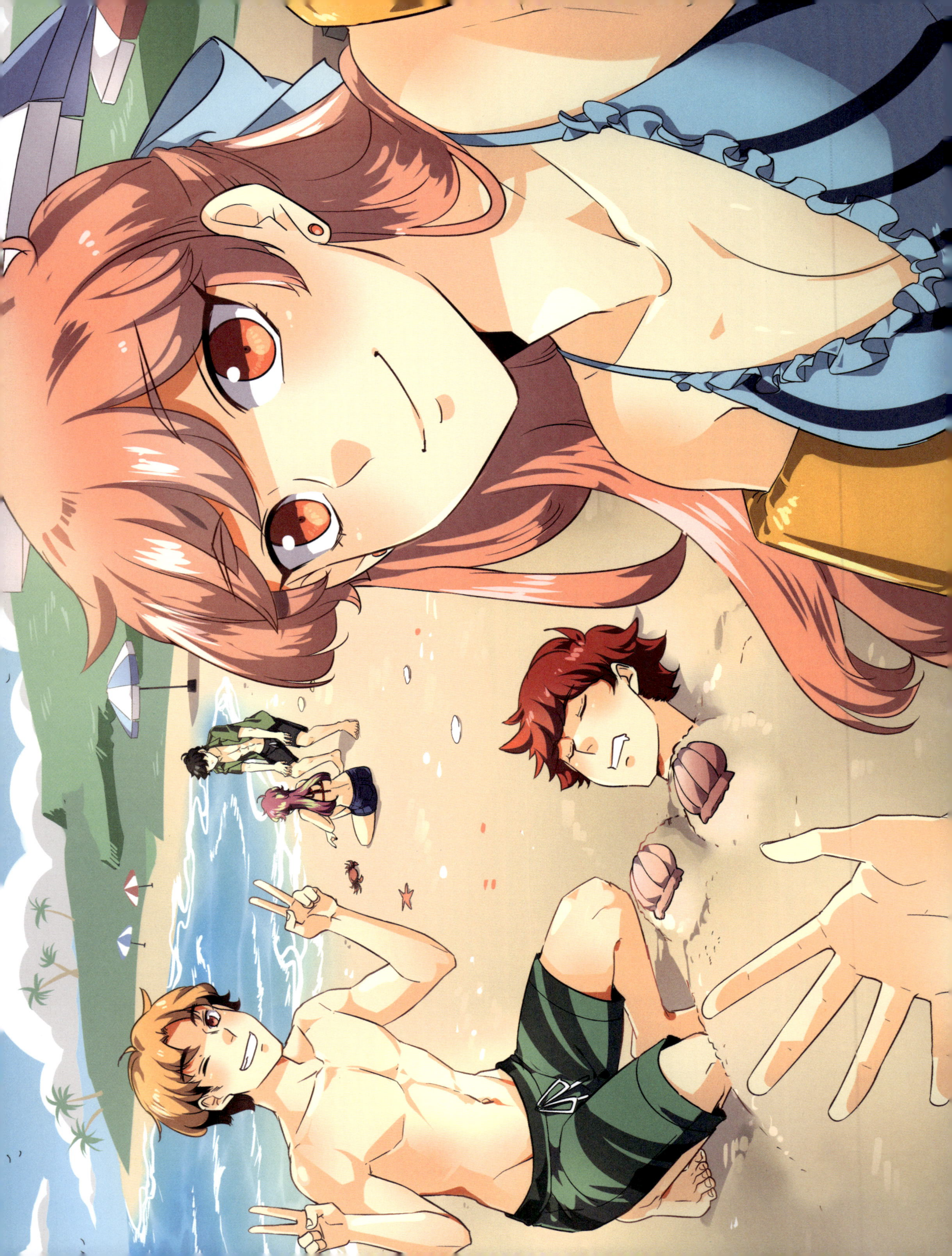

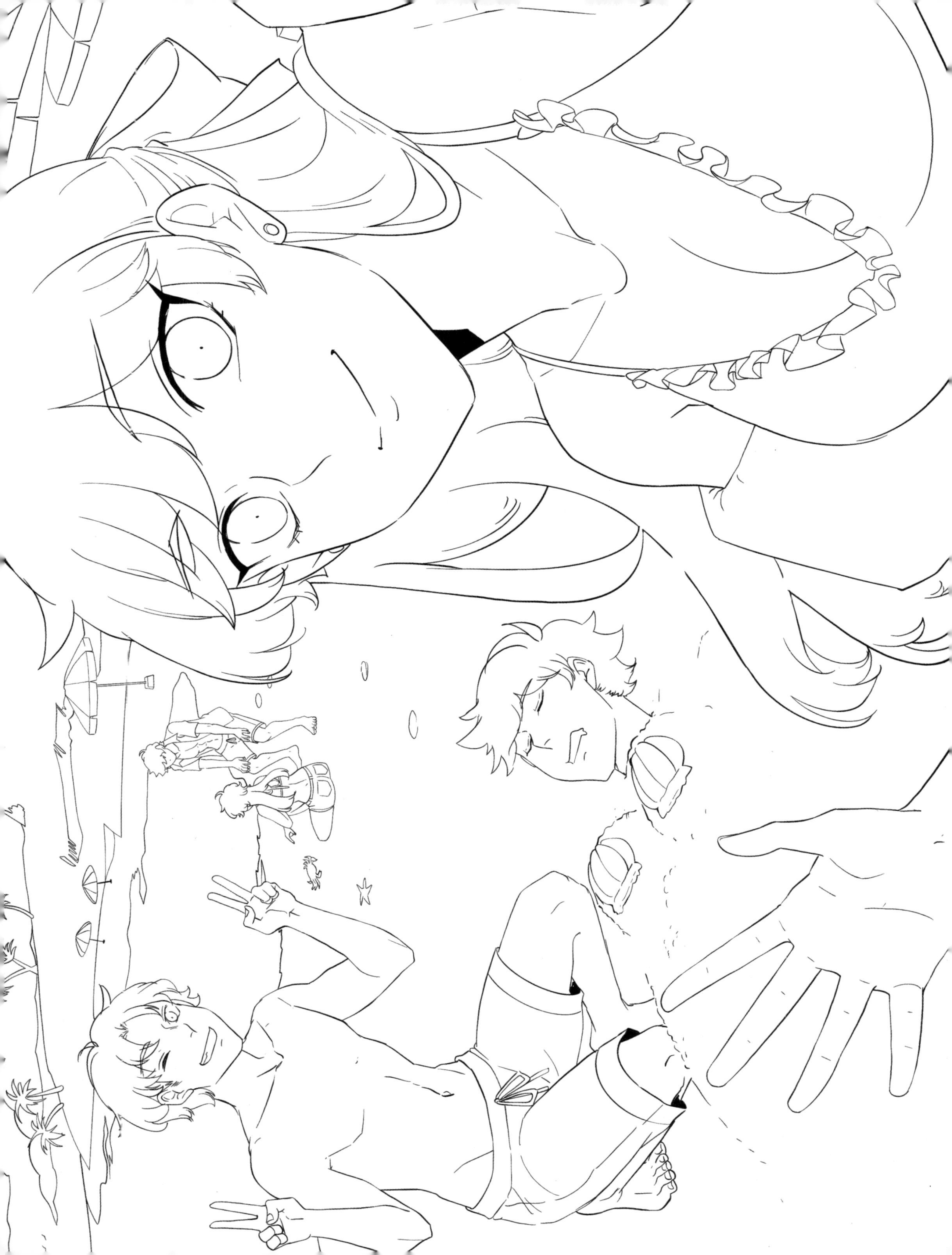

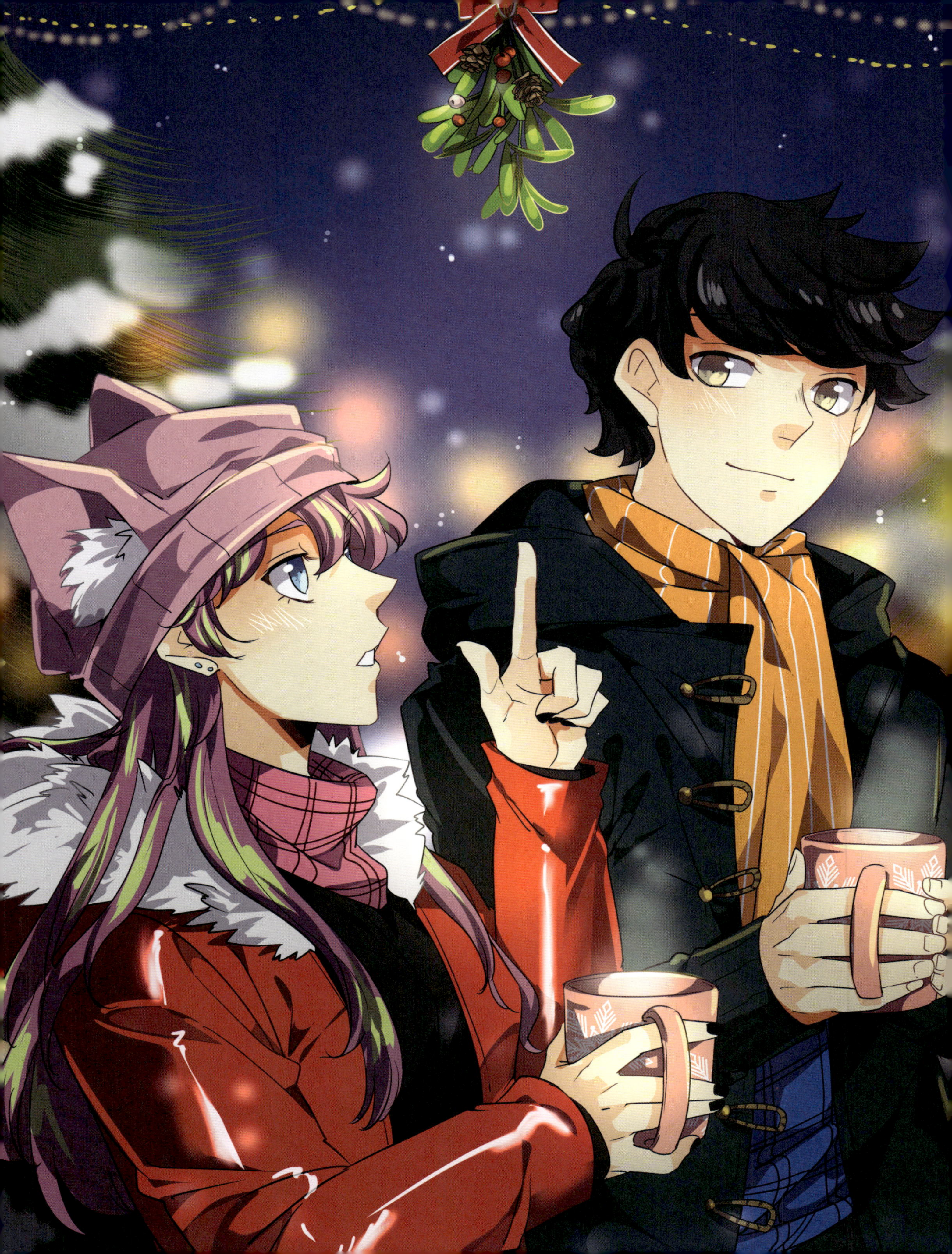

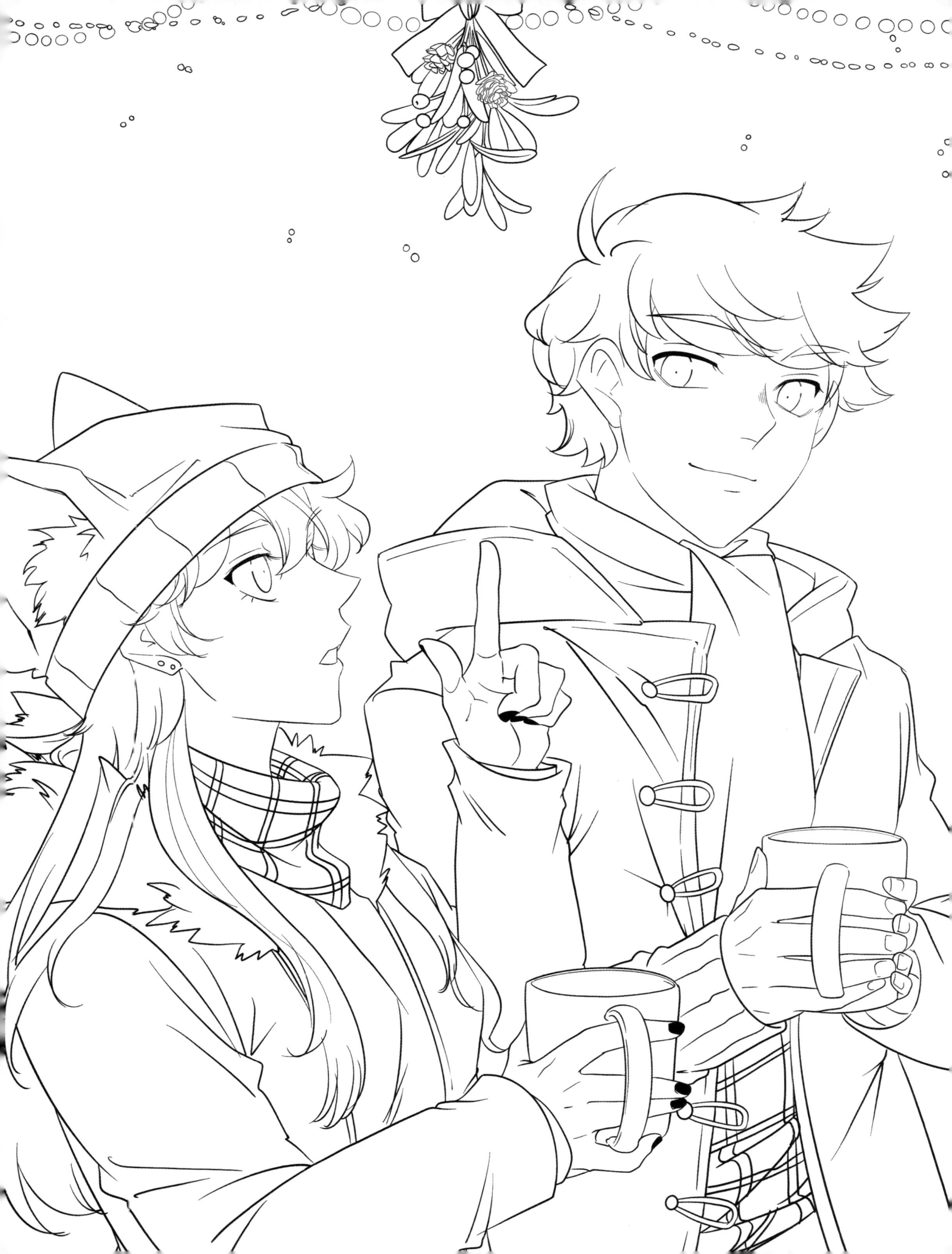

Quarto.com | WalterFoster.com

© 2024 Quarto Publishing Group USA Inc.
unOrdinary © uru-chan and WEBTOON Entertainment Inc. All rights reserved.
WEBTOON and all related trademarks are owned by WEBTOON Entertainment Inc. or its affiliates.

First Published in 2024 by Walter Foster Publishing, an imprint of The Quarto Group,
100 Cummings Center, Suite 265-D, Beverly, MA 01915, USA.
T (978) 282-9590 F (978) 283-2742

All rights reserved. No part of this book may be reproduced in any form without written permission of the copyright owners. All images in this book have been reproduced with the knowledge and prior consent of the artists concerned, and no responsibility is accepted by producer, publisher, or printer for any infringement of copyright or otherwise, arising from the contents of this publication. Every effort has been made to ensure that credits accurately comply with information supplied. We apologize for any inaccuracies that may have occurred and will resolve inaccurate or missing information in a subsequent reprinting of the book.

Walter Foster Publishing titles are also available at discount for retail, wholesale, promotional, and bulk purchase. For details, contact the Special Sales Manager by email at specialsales@quarto.com or by mail at The Quarto Group, Attn: Special Sales Manager, 100 Cummings Center, Suite 265-D, Beverly, MA 01915, USA.

10 9 8 7 6 5 4 3 2 1

ISBN: 978-0-7603-8983-6

Line art: Ryan Axxel
Design, editorial, and layout: Christopher Bohn and Coffee Cup Creative LLC
WEBTOON Rights and Licensing Manager: Amanda Chen

Printed in China

ABOUT THE CREATOR

uru-chan (Chelsey Han) is the storyteller and artist behind unOrdinary, the popular webcomic that made its WEBTOON Originals debut in May 2016. uru-chan grew up in Acton, Massachusetts. She always had a love for manga and anime and taught herself how to draw and write her own stories. As a teen, she enjoyed posting short comics online for others to read.

Follow uru-chan:
Instgram: @uru.chan
X (formerly Twitter): @uruchanOFR